Santa, Bring My Baby Back

By Cheryl Harper

Santa, Bring My Baby Back

CHERYL HARPER

AVONIMPULSE
An Imprint of HarperCollinsPublishers

Excerpt from *Stuck On You* copyright © 2013 by Cheryl Harper.

Excerpt from *Can't Help Falling in Love* copyright © 2013 by Cheryl Harper.

Excerpt from *Once Upon a Highland Summer* copyright © 2013 by Lecia Cotton Cornwall.

Excerpt from *Hard Target* copyright © 2013 by Kay Thomas.

Excerpt from *The Wedding Date* copyright © 2013 by Lisa Connelly.

Excerpt from *Torn* copyright © 2013 by Karen Erickson.

Excerpt from *The Cupcake Diaries: Spoonful of Christmas* copyright © 2013 by Darlene Panzera.

Excerpt from *Rodeo Queen* copyright © 2013 by Tina Klinesmith.

EPub Edition DECEMBER 2013 ISBN: 9780062276407

Print Edition ISBN: 9780062276414

JV 10 9 8 7 6 5 4 3 2 1

*To my aunts, who introduced me to
Memphis and Graceland*

Chapter One

CHARLIE MCMINN PUSHED back his gold lamé sleeve to check the time and cursed under his breath. The bride and groom were twenty minutes late.

Five more minutes. That's it.

He thumped his head against the high back of the leather chair and frowned as he stared up at the ceiling. This was not how he'd spend his Saturdays given a choice. Marrying happy couples at the Rock'n'Rolla Hotel was bad enough. He'd been guilted, cajoled, and generally coerced into agreeing to doing so for the first three December weekends by a woman with a sweet smile and iron will, the single person on the whole planet that could make him do something he didn't want to do: his mother, Willodean Jackson. But wasting time instead of actually performing the weddings was just too much.

Insult to injury. She gets me here, and then the bride and groom don't show.

He'd negotiated hard to make her agree to find a permanent solution by January. He kept reminding himself this was just temporary.

At least the stock exchanges were closed on Saturday, and he'd wrapped up his latest investment deal before he'd packed up the truck to head for Memphis. Otherwise, he'd be wasting money too. And that was where Charlie McMinn drew the line.

He shoved himself up out of the comfortable chair, yanked down the gold jacket that somehow fit like a second skin although he'd never been measured for it, and paced from one side of the small stage to the other. Red, pink, and white poinsettias lined the raised platform, the only shot of color in the hotel's new chapel except for the dancing dots of light through the stained glass crosses over the door. Dark gray carpet, light walls, elegantly simple wooden pews, and tall, clear windows along one side of the room created a nice, airy place where Charlie could catch his breath. It was nothing like the rest of the hotel. There was nothing outrageous here except the price tag, which was excessive, a little like Willodean.

Had she just run out of time, or had she intended to create a restful place?

After all, no one but his mother had been sure the chapel would be finished in time. He thought he could still smell fresh paint; she'd probably had crews in all night finishing up. And it wouldn't surprise him a bit. That was the way Willodean worked. She decided she wanted something, and then, come hell, high water—

or outrageously expensive overtime bills—she made it happen. Getting this building up and running for the weddings she'd booked in advance had taken about four months and twice as much money as he would have spent.

As Willodean's financial advisor, he knew to the penny how much this latest project had cost. And it was a very good thing she had a lot of pennies because his mother had taken the phrase "money is no object" and embraced it as lifestyle. Just keeping up with her inspired ideas could be exhausting.

Thank God he'd inherited her lucky streak and learned everything he knew about investing from his first stepfather. Otherwise, he'd still be working for a firm in Knoxville. And she and all of her Elvis memorabilia might be living with him.

Wherever Willodean went, "The King" was sure to follow. He'd spent his life surrounded by Elvis. He liked his restored farmhouse with its sparse furnishings much better. Quiet woods, open spaces, and not one single rhinestone to be found.

Maybe he missed the excitement that surrounded his mother sometimes, but he didn't miss the frustration or uncertainty that came with it.

Charlie took a deep breath and forced himself to exhale slowly in an effort to dispel some of the irritation that was threatening to boil over.

When he'd slipped out of his comfortable flannel and into the white dress shirt and gold lamé, he'd cursed his inability to tell his mother no. But the first couple and their small group of friends and family had made him forget for a minute how uncomfortable he was. They weren't what he'd expected, and being part of their celebration had been nice. The bride and groom were sports attorneys from Dallas who had been snowed in over Valentine's Day at the hotel and had gone from co-workers to a whole lot more. The bride and her maid of honor had worn red. The groom and his best man wore suits. And there was something about how happy Luke and Julie were when he pronounced them man and wife that made Charlie think they were going to last. It must've been the Christmas spirit in the air. Everything seemed possible at Christmas.

Including, possibly, a chance to figure out a way to smooth over his relationship with his mother. It seemed like he'd been irritated with her for a long time, but he loved her more. He had to let go of his guilt, forget his annoyance or whatever emotion was making this hotel feel like a prison, and accept Willodean the way she was. The rest of the world loved her. He felt like a total jackass sometimes because he wanted to complain about his life.

At some point, he was going to have to either get over it or accept that he might be, in fact, a total jackass.

Until then, they lived on opposite ends of the state. Maybe moving to the mountains of east Tennessee hadn't been his original plan, but he was satisfied there. Dropping out of the competitive investment broker game had given him plenty of free time. As county mayor for two consecutive terms, he'd used his business experience to serve, but now he had way too much free time on his hands. Choosing not to run for re-election was supposed to give him time to try something new. He wished he had some idea what that might be. Keeping Willodean's spending in line was his biggest time commitment. Otherwise, he dabbled, researched, and gambled small amounts on risky firms and larger amounts on solid businesses. And he had worked on restoring his old farmhouse, but that project was finished now. That was how he'd gotten ramrodded into performing weddings. He couldn't very well point to his busy schedule as an excuse.

He needed a new hobby. Or seven.

He'd been thinking lately it was probably time to find a wife, someone compatible who wanted a nice, stable home like he did. As usual, he'd made a plan and a timeline to do so. So far he was on schedule. When he told his mother he was going to be spending some time in Memphis to work on that project, she'd be over the moon. The dating pool in Newport was shallow. Memphis would broaden his selection. He had two dates lined up this week with women he'd met through an online service. One was a psychologist, the other a pharmacist. One could tell him what his problem was and the other the prescription that might fix it.

And if he just needed to grow the hell up . . . well, knowing was half the battle.

When his stomach growled, he checked his watch again. If he didn't hurry, he'd run out of time before the next wedding. He never, ever skipped a meal. And he'd been thinking about the meat loaf sandwich at Viva Las Vegas, the hotel restaurant, since he'd agreed to do this a month ago. If he didn't go now, he'd be late and the next bride and groom would have to wait on him.

Charlie rolled his head from one side to the other, straightened his shoulders, and then fought his way out of the shiny gold jacket. He slipped it on the hanger in the small dressing room behind the stage and then carefully closed the door. He stretched his arms and soaked in the bright winter sunlight streaming through the windows.

When his stomach growled again, he hit the door to the lobby with a stiff arm, set on getting back to his own schedule. After four determined steps, he stopped. He could see a line of light under the door to the bridal suite.

Charlie mentally cursed again. Something about that light told him this was going to be more trouble than a man who hadn't eaten in over four hours should attempt to deal with. He'd sent his assistant for the day out to check on the bride and groom earlier. When she'd come back to say the rooms were dark, he'd sent her on to lunch. He should have followed, obviously. If that light represented his late bride and groom, his schedule would be off for the rest of the day.

After two perfunctory knocks, Charlie turned the knob and shoved open the door.

He froze on the spot when he saw the bride seated in a froth of wedding dress. Like a priceless work of art, she was lit by a spotlight that highlighted the flawless creamy skin of her bare shoulders, the gleam in her dark hair, and her bright red lips. When his eyes met hers in the mirror's reflection, he couldn't remember just exactly what he thought he might say to the inconsiderate bride or groom if he ever found either of them. His schedule was forgotten. He was lucky to remember to breathe in and out.

"Aw, crap, he ain't comin', is he?"

A small frown wrinkled the pale skin of her brow and something about her east Tennessee twang set everything back in motion.

He reached up to run his hand through his hair but hit crunchy product and decided to rub his neck like that was what he'd intended all along. "I was hoping that you could tell me. What happened to your groom?"

"Well, I can't say I exactly expected this, but I ain't as shocked as I should be either." She gave him a wide smile that didn't quite look genuine, but he liked it a whole lot better than tears. "Tommy Joe told me he'd meet me over here, knock on the door when he was ready. Since he's always late, I expected to wait a bit but . . ."

She shrugged, and he had to bite his tongue to keep from being drawn back under her spell as light played across the pale skin of her shoulders and chest. She stood gracefully and smoothed the sides of her elegant wedding dress. Her hourglass figure was outlined faithfully by the dress and accented by dainty hands she propped on her hips. "He didn't sound like a man looking forward to his weddin'. Cold feet set in, I imagine. My hook wasn't set, and I guess he wriggled off."

Charlie frowned as he considered her answer. He fought back the urge to ask what kind of fool would wriggle off her hook. A man might not know he was caught until it was too late . . . but what a way to go.

Rubbing his hand down his face, he wondered what the hell had happened to his brain. Starvation. That was the only answer. Marriage was a necessity, sure, but he didn't know this woman at all. Like any other big decision, picking a bride should be about black-and-white benefits outweighing the risks, not how amazing she looked in a gown. Or possibly out of it.

"Yeah, well . . ." What should he say to a woman dumped at the altar? "It wasn't very considerate of him to keep us waiting."

She snorted and Charlie liked her better, if that was possible. A princess was one thing. A beautiful woman with an unladylike snort, that was real. "You said a mouthful there, Elvis."

If Charlie looked at the big picture, he could understand her sarcasm. Maybe she had a better reason to complain about inconvenience than he did.

When his stomach gave a pitiful rumble, Charlie told himself that he needed to step out of the room, get moving, get back on schedule. But she reached up and removed some sparkling clips from her hair and then stepped out of her shoes, two more changes that took her from fantasy to reality.

And suddenly he didn't want her calling him Elvis. He'd had a long and complicated history with the King of Rock and Roll, thanks to his mother's fandom. He wanted this woman to use his name.

"Charlie . . ." When he heard a ridiculous squeak on the end, he cleared his throat. "My name is Charlie, not Elvis."

She pursed her lips and then nodded. "Got it. Thanks for letting me know, Charlie. My name's Grace. Andersen. Should be Huffle by now, but it looks like I'll keep the original for a bit longer."

Charlie thought she'd gotten the better end of the name deal there, but he didn't say it. He pointed over his shoulder and said, "Sure. I'm going to go." He motioned vaguely around the room. "It won't take you long to pack all this up, right?" That was a good idea. She'd need to clear out pretty soon for the next bride. He didn't want to mess with the schedule any more.

The sooner this woman, with her crazy effect on his brain, moved along, the better. There was absolutely nothing about this situation that said he should be attracted to her. A bride? At her own cancelled wedding? She would be at the top of his list of people not to be drawn to. And she was definitely not in his plan.

She looked in the mirror and then braced an elbow on the top of the vanity. "Won't take me long at all, Charlie. I'll just make a new plan and get to it." She looked his way again, and he felt his pulse speed up. She glanced away and fiddled with something on the vanity as she muttered, "Find a job. How hard can that be?"

Charlie knew she wasn't really asking. But it could be pretty hard, actually. He spent a lot of time studying industries and employers and statistics—all things that mattered to the county mayor and to a savvy investor looking for underfunded companies on the verge of breaking out. He knew unemployment numbers, but he didn't figure she'd benefit from knowing them too. Besides, she'd landed in the one place she was practically guaranteed to find a job or a loan or a brand new family, if that's what she needed.

The Rock'n'Rolla Hotel.

He'd spent a lot of time being annoyed over that fact. His mother would take care of her, just like she did everyone she adopted. For the first time, he understood Willodean's impulses.

There was something about Grace Andersen that made him want to help, even after decades of trying to guard his mother and her money against people and stories like hers.

He wouldn't mind being Grace Andersen's hero.

To avoid doing something stupid, Charlie turned to go but stopped when she added, "Oh, Charlie, could you do me a favor?"

She shuffled toward him, the rustle of the wedding dress sweeping the floor loud in the silence. "Could you unzip me? I thought I was going to dislocate a shoulder getting it zipped in the first place." She turned and bent her head so that all Charlie could see was smooth, pale skin across her shoulders and the loose dark hairs that tickled her neck.

When he didn't move quickly enough, she turned her head to look at him over one perfect shoulder.

Remembering to breathe became a struggle again.

He forced himself to step closer. He grasped the zipper with one hand and slid the other under the fabric. The zipper made a quiet hiss as it slid down to the curve of her back, every centimeter showing more beautiful skin.

And out of the blue he wondered if unzipping Grace Andersen would ever get old. Finished, he took two steps away to keep from smoothing his hands over her shoulders like he wanted or tracing a finger down her spine just to see goose bumps.

She turned her head. "Thanks."

As he pulled the door closed behind him, Charlie tried to remember the last time he'd seen anyone as pretty as she was in real life. Never. But she wasn't his type. He preferred career women who wore glasses and looked like they could quote stock prices or legal precedents. He liked women with sharp minds and sturdy savings. He'd had enough excitement growing up with Willodean McMinn Holloway Luttrell Jackson. Now all he wanted was a comfortable home, an easy, companionable, stable relationship, and maybe a baby to keep things interesting. Maybe.

Grace Andersen looked like . . . magic.

He propped his hands on his hips and shook his head as he looked out at the guitar-shaped pool that was covered for the season.

Magic? He hadn't been in the hotel for a full twenty-four hours and already his mind was going. Something about being that close to her had melted it. But Grace Andersen was just a woman. She'd been left at the altar but didn't seem too broken up about it. He hoped her new plan, whatever it was, meant checking out of the hotel immediately. Beautiful Grace Andersen might have the ability to wreck his plans along with his logic if she stayed.

"WELL, GRACIE, HERE you are again." Grace said the words out loud, but in her mind, she could hear her mother's dry, pragmatic tone. She clutched the front of her dress and actually appreciated how the matter-of-factness snapped her back to reality. There for a minute with Charlie, she'd started to feel like she'd stepped out of this world and into a place where only the two of them existed. When her eyes met his in the mirror, everything else had faded in the face of an instant connection, one she'd never had with Tommy Joe Huffle.

For just a second, she'd had a flash of what a wedding day with a man who hooked her that easily might be like. A nice fantasy, but not very helpful for a woman stranded in a strange city with maxed-out credit cards.

Maybe she hadn't found her lucky break yet, even after years of auditions and chasing the next big idea. That didn't mean she wasn't a great actress. She was sure she'd convinced Charlie she knew exactly what to do next. But she had no idea.

She also wasn't sure why it had seemed important to convince him that everything was under control. Maybe that was just another thing she'd gotten really good at pretending.

She stared hard at her reflection and did her best to ignore the fine lines around her eyes. At least she could keep the gray at bay. Thank God for beauty in a box. As she tossed her inexpensive makeup and brushes, her hair spray, and everything she'd brought to transform herself into a princess for a day into the bright pink case she carried most places, she tried to tell herself this was just the latest adventure. Maybe being stranded in Memphis would turn out to be the best thing that ever happened to her.

Grace never lost faith that she was right where she needed to be. No matter how many times she had to make a new plan, she always believed in herself. This failure she could blame on her mother. Which never happened. She'd pursued Tommy Joe Huffle because of a conversation she'd had with her mother on her last birthday. Something about turning thirty-two had made her think about her long-term goals. That happened so infrequently she could count the times on one hand. Possibly two fingers. Apparently her mother had been on the same page:

"It's now or never, Gracie."

Grace pursed her lips as she looked at herself in the mirror and shook her head. Maybe her mother had a point, even if this wedding had been a bad idea. She didn't need a man or a wedding to try something new like a real, full-time, normal job. She'd been a rolling stone for so long that the idea of settling down still seemed to fit her like new dress shoes on Easter. She hadn't worn it enough to work out the pinch. For years, she'd done exactly what she wanted and enjoyed almost every minute. She'd left town two days after graduation with a no-good scam artist who said he was going to get her a record deal. But Ann Andersen, mother to seven children, six of them successful middle-class citizens, had raised no fools.

No matter how crazy her ideas got, Grace had always been a pretty good judge of character. When her new "agent" had turned out to be overly concerned with what she looked like naked, Grace made a quick exit. And Nashville was the first place she'd picked up an order pad, strapped on an apron, and delivered greasy burgers to bikers.

Was that the dream? No. Was that the end of the world? No. And the bikers had turned out to be excellent tippers so soon she was on her way to New York to try modeling. At twenty, she'd been about forty pounds lighter and certain her thoroughly average five-seven height could be overlooked because she had personality.

Now she knew so much better. Successful models weren't really known for having bubbling personalities. And that was fine. She wasn't on magazine covers, never had been, but she also knew the pleasure of a comforting French fry and that was worth a whole lot.

Just the thought of all the places she'd lived and the careers she'd tried made Grace's shoulders slump. And again she could hear her mother's voice: *"You'll end up right where you started. College isn't looking so bad now, is it?"* Her mother was the kind of woman who accepted how things were without much celebration or gnashing of teeth. One day became the next, and that was the way it was supposed to be. No sense in getting too emotional.

And her mother was always right. Even at eighteen, Grace had been pretty sure her mother was right, but she'd been just as determined that if she tried hard enough, she could change her fate. Grace had wanted more than safety. She'd wanted highs: the excitement of roller coaster ups without any of the downs.

And she'd had a few ups. She'd also gotten pretty good at recovering from the downs.

Grace stood and slipped off the wedding dress. She'd hoped this was the winning plan, so she'd pushed her credit card limits with the perfect, outrageously expensive gown, beautiful shoes, and faux diamonds for her hair. When she'd slipped on the glittering tiara, she'd understood completely how the real things might be a girl's best friend.

Tommy Joe's oversight of a whopping diamond engagement ring should probably have been a real good clue to the level of his commitment. He'd promised she could pick her own rings in Atlanta, and she'd broken her own rule. She'd trusted him instead of her instincts.

If she ever needed another reminder, she could look at her credit card bills. Eager to please Elvis fan Tommy Joe, she'd planned and charged this trip to Memphis. So now she had a beautiful dress, a hotel room she couldn't pay for, and an expensive lesson in going with her gut.

If she learned nothing else from this setback, she needed to remember that, while other people would let her down, she could always count on herself. Her mother loved her, but she would never understand Grace. And the rest of the world? Well, she'd learned to be careful.

Half an hour ago she'd been ready to make this marriage work. She'd never looked better. Maybe there had been the niggling doubt—the question about whether giving up on her dreams of performing on a stage to grab what she could was the right thing to do. But wearing the sparkly gown was one dream come true, and she'd made it happen for herself. Her groom hadn't inspired a lot of romance, and the idea of finally growing up, settling down, and giving in, becoming just like the rest of her family, made it hard to breathe, but she'd only had to see her own reflection to quiet the tiny alarm.

She could blame the shortness of breath on cramming herself into a dress a size too small. For her perfect wedding day, she'd wanted to be size twelve and she'd pulled that off. Barely.

Somehow, the dress on the hanger looked like just a dress. It wasn't a dream come true anymore. It was an expensive reminder that she should have been smarter.

Not about choosing her groom. On paper Tommy Joe had been perfect—twenty years older, rich, divorced from his first wife, and on the hunt for the second. About fifteen minutes after meeting him, she'd been ready to pack up her few belongings in the ratty apartment she shared with two other girls in Las Vegas to move to Atlanta with Tommy Joe.

Not because she loved him. She just thought she could handle him. He was loud, a little ridiculous, and easy to please. Plus, he had three car dealerships to keep him busy. And she wouldn't mind not worrying about money any more even if she'd never tell her mother that.

As she slipped into the tight jeans and low-cut hot pink sweater that were Tommy Joe's preference, not hers, she congratulated herself on not telling her parents about the wedding. At least she wouldn't have to tell them about this failure, either. She'd just get enough money to make her way back to Vegas.

Maybe the hotel was hiring. She had plenty of experience waiting tables. She'd start in the restaurant and work her way to the front desk, if necessary. If she was lucky, she could find somebody who needed a temporary roommate too.

"Grace, you are a rolling stone. This was just not the moss for you." She scrunched up her face, stuck out her tongue, and waved her hands, a silly ritual she'd done as long as she could remember to shove away the doubts and disappointments. Happy free spirit was her most common character. She'd learned people liked to help her when she acted happy.

She slipped on the sky-high heels and resolved right then and there that maybe she had to save money for a trip back to Vegas, but she was going to buy more comfortable shoes at her first chance. Tommy Joe liked a certain type of girl, the kind that was more comfortable in leopard print platforms than she was, but Grace had played the part.

Now it might be time to just be Grace. The real Grace wanted her yellow Converse sneakers, loose jeans, her favorite purple hoodie, and a free Starbucks macchiato. Free was the most important part of that. She had the clothes. The drink would have to wait until she had a job. And a ride.

She packed up her bags, slipped in the beautiful shoes that coordinated perfectly with her dream of a wedding gown on top, and slung them over her shoulders before she hooked the dress hanger over a finger.

Whether it was a new job, a new plan, or a new man

she was looking for, Grace had to go where the people were. She needed help. For that, she needed people. She checked her lipstick, fidgeted with the classy updo she refused to take down, and forced a happy smile. "Viva Las Vegas, here I come."

Chapter Two

ALL THE WAY around the pool area with its cheery inflatable snowmen and flashing candy canes and down the long hallway decorated with album covers and three different themed Christmas trees, Grace rehearsed her lines in her head. She was going to need a job, a place to stay, and some time to pay her hotel bills. Checking all three off the list might take some finesse.

Grace paused in the doorway of Viva Las Vegas to give her eyes a chance to adjust to the change from the bright lobby to the darker restaurant. Her first impressions were of lush plants—a theme at the hotel—and some rocking Elvis tune competing with the clinks of silverware on plates and low conversations. A very cute, very young hostess dressed as a showgirl in Santa's workshop pointed her toward the bar. When Grace dumped all her baggage in a seat and draped the dress over the top, she noticed Charlie, but he didn't look up from his plate.

Thanks to his concentration, Grace had a chance to observe him before she announced her presence. His crisp white dress shirt and black tie were covered by a large cloth napkin, which might also be a tablecloth in real life. She appreciated his broad shoulders and the flex of muscles in his back as he twisted on the seat. The edges of his sleeves were white flashes as he made steady progress of clearing his plate with quick bites, not like he was in a hurry, but took pride in efficient operation. And his long legs were propped up on the brass footrest that ran along the bottom of the bar. His slicked back black hair was probably the stillest part of his body. Charlie seemed capable. Strong. Solid. For some reason, she had the urge to wrap her hand around his arm and maybe rest her head on his shoulder.

Not exactly what she expected from a man with rock-star good looks and enough gunk in his hair to preserve his style in a tornado.

She patted her own, slightly crunchy updo and decided to give him props for that. It showed commitment.

When he'd opened her dressing room door, the first thing she saw were his dark brown eyes. For a minute, she'd been frozen by the connection. Then she'd noticed his Elvis-like hair and had to wonder what his story was.

"Hey, Charlie," she said as she slid onto the stool next to him. She leaned one elbow on the bar as the bartender slid a menu in front of her. She smiled over at Charlie as he nodded and chewed. She tried not to roll her eyes as she glanced over the menu choices. Lots of southern delicacies here. Then she saw the desserts and had to bite her lip to remind herself she was broke and stranded. Even if she had enough money to buy the banana pudding, it wouldn't taste nearly as good while she slept under a bridge somewhere. She tried not to whistle out loud at the prices and wondered if they'd let her order off the children's menu. After she waved the bartender off, Grace said, "Is that meat loaf? I didn't see it on the menu."

Charlie took a drink and then wiped his mouth with his napkin. "Best thing about this place, and it's not on the menu."

"I used to be a vegetarian, but I don't think I am anymore." Grace glanced around the restaurant and the light crowd. All the waitresses were dressed as showgirls or maybe the Disney version of showgirls anyway. She'd spent too much time in Vegas to miss that this was an homage to the 1964 Hollywood version. Today, real showgirls would be thirty pounds lighter and have plastic pieces to fill out anything that needed filling out. She ought to know. Girls like her could take orders, but they couldn't hit the stage. She ought to fit right in around here.

"You *think* you're not a vegetarian? You don't know?"

Grace laughed at Charlie's small frown. He looked like he was trying to work out in his head how that could be possible and was running up against math theorems and scientific laws that all said such a thing could not happen. He was cute when he was confused.

"So it's meat loaf just like Mom used to make?"

Charlie coughed and took a long drink while he

considered the answer to her question. He laughed and nodded. "Exactly like Mom used to make."

Now *she* was confused. But she could absolutely go with the flow. She didn't get the joke, but she liked what it did to his face. Sober Charlie was good-looking. There was no question about that. He had dark hair, dark eyes, and a full bottom lip. But when he was smiling like this, he was devastating. It was like they had their own private joke, and it was them against the world.

One of the challenges of following her dreams was moving around so much that it was hard to keep friends. Every new place was an opportunity to make more, but not before she spent a lot of time alone.

She'd always wanted a partner to go up against the world with as needed.

Now she just wished she understood the joke.

"You've changed," he said. Grace watched him lean back to take in her whole outfit and could almost read his mind. The outfit was cheap. And hot. She didn't like it either. She was dressed for attention, and this sweater always got very high marks from men so it surprised her when he added, "I think I like the wedding dress better."

Grace was shocked, and then she was amused. She squeezed her eyes shut and went with amused. "I know exactly what you mean. I like it better too."

Maybe Charlie was oblivious to start with, but he picked up on his error quickly. "And I'm an idiot. I shouldn't have brought up wedding-anything. Sorry."

Grace took a deep breath and was happy to see Charlie watching her closely before he glanced away. The sweater was facing early retirement, but at least it was still on the job. She had no idea why it mattered what Charlie thought, but suddenly it did. "I understand. I may not be used to plain-speakers, but that doesn't mean I don't appreciate it."

He nodded. "I'm just glad you didn't burst into tears. That's the kind of reaction I'd expect from a woman who's just been left at the altar." His lips tightened. "And I think I just did it again."

Grace shook her head. "No, that time you were fishing for information, like maybe why I don't seem that brokenhearted over being dumped in such a spectacular fashion."

Charlie's eyes narrowed as he considered her answer. "Maybe he didn't dump you. Maybe he's dead in a ditch somewhere."

There was an awkward beat of silence between them. Then Grace picked up his glass and took a long drink of his sweet tea. When the ice cubes rattled in the glass, she let out a happy sigh and thumped it back on the bar. Then she said, "Charlie, I think that might actually be the worst thing to say to a jilted bride. The idea of my one true love dead in a ditch would certainly bring on the waterworks."

He looked like he wanted to object to her hijacking his glass. Most people would. And Charlie gave off the vibe that he was very committed to a lot of personal space. But he didn't. "I see your point. And I should shut the hell up now. I'm sure your true love is just fine, maybe stuck in traffic somewhere or something."

Grace shook her head. "No, I imagine he's on a plane

headed to Atlanta by now." She sighed. "And there's no way he was my one true love."

She could see a million questions on Charlie's face, but he bit his tongue. Somebody had taught him some manners, even if he forgot them now and then.

Charlie wadded up his napkin and bent his head down to look through the window into the kitchen. When the chef did the same and waved, Charlie said, "Great job as usual, Sal. Thanks for making it for me."

Sal waved a spatula. "My pleasure, Mr. Charlie. Anytime."

Grace watched Charlie open his mouth to respond, but whatever he was going to say he thought better of. He turned to face her, and she had to will herself not to retreat. There was something about him. He was big, for one thing, but being this close to him it was like he was also ... supercharged ... or something. The air between them sparked.

Charlie seemed to feel it too. He straightened slowly and studied her face. Finally he rubbed his hands on his black dress pants. "If you're checking out today, you should hurry. You're past check-out time, but I'm sure Laura will waive the extra charge if you go now." He glanced at his heavy stainless steel watch. "And it's almost time for my next wedding."

Grace watched a flush cover his cheeks.

"Wedding, bride, groom, husband, fiancée, ring, wife, altar, dumped, deserted, marriage, chapel." Charlie stopped and squeezed his eyes shut. When he opened them again, he nodded. "That should be all of them.

Maybe it's out of my system now, and I can stop saying things to remind you."

Grace appreciated the effort. "You forgot love."

Their eyes locked, and there was nothing she could do to look away. The music changed, but she had no idea from what to what. The bartender filled an order on the other side of the bar. And the clinks of silverware on plates faded. Until Charlie looked away, she was lost.

Hours or seconds later he blinked and that small smile, the one that she wished said he knew her and liked her and wanted to share a secret with her, was back. He slid off the stool, his legs brushing her thigh with a wave of heat. He yanked off the impromptu bib and pulled his wallet out of his back pocket.

"Now, Mister—Charlie, you know you don't pay," Grace heard the bartender say, but she was immobilized this time by the width of his shoulders and the heat of his body.

He dropped two bills on the bar. "Sure, Cat, but I do tip. Be sure Sal gets a big chunk."

The bartender shook her head as she scooped up the cash and dropped it in the tip jar. Then she asked Grace, "If you aren't going to order lunch, how about something to drink?"

When Charlie turned to look at her, Grace wanted to say something light and airy, something that made it seem like a valid choice to skip lunch instead of a budgetary necessity. Instead she licked her lips nervously and leaned closer to the bar. "Actually, Cat," Grace said breezily as if this wasn't the whole goal of her visit to Viva

Las Vegas, "I was hoping you could point me toward the manager. I have lots of experience waiting tables and—" She glanced over her shoulder at Charlie who hadn't moved, no matter what he said about his schedule. Darn it. "—I really need a job. And a place to stay if you know of anyone with an extra room." She smiled, crossed her fingers, and tried the power of positive thinking.

Cat wiped the bar. "Well, we're fully staffed as far as I know, but Laura's the manager. You could talk to her at the front desk." With a glance at Grace's pile of wedding dress, she added, "Leave your stuff. I'll watch it while you go talk to her." She looked over Grace's shoulder at Charlie and gave a little shrug. In the reflection of the mirror behind the bar, Grace saw him shaking his head.

So Charlie didn't want her hanging around, did he? She straightened her shoulders and brightened her smile. "Thanks, Cat. I appreciate your help."

Just because she could, Grace pivoted and stepped up to Charlie, the toes of her shoes against his plain black lace-ups. Apparently, Charlie hadn't fallen under the spell of her happy-and-charming act. That never happened. She wrapped one hand around his arm and squeezed. "Why don't you introduce me to the manager before you go?"

He glanced down at her hand until she got the message and slowly stepped back. Then his gaze met hers for a long minute. This close she could see long eyelashes and a sharp intelligence that worried her just a little. Then he inclined his head and let her go, turning his head to nod at Cat. Grace caught her breath as she watched him pick up her wedding dress and the bags she'd dropped at the bar. "Fine. Let's make this quick then. And I'll save you from having to pick these up on your way to the airport."

Grace thought he might have said "airport" through gritted teeth. "You bet, Mr. Charlie." He started to say something again but instead turned and walked out of the cozy shadows of Viva Las Vegas into the brighter lobby. She was curious about the respect he'd gotten from the restaurant staff. He had to be more than an Elvis impersonator. He *was* performing weddings. Maybe he was a judge or justice of the peace. She glanced up at his perfectly frozen hair. Maybe not.

As they walked across the amazing lobby that she'd read online was a nod to Graceland's Jungle Room, Grace was sidetracked by an unhealthy interest in the way Charlie's muscles flexed in his dress pants. He ducked under a few aggressively full palm fronds outlined in white Christmas lights and then set one of her bags on the cool, natural stone floor. They waited for the woman behind the desk to end her call, and Grace was enchanted when a droopy bloodhound wearing green bows at the ears and red velvet collar covered in small bells meandered over to sit right on top of Charlie's feet.

"Hey, sis." Charlie reached down and ruffled the dog's ears, and the dog stared up at him with sleepy devotion.

"Her name is Sis?" Grace walked over to run a hand down the dog's silky back. She loved dogs. Growing up, her family had always had dogs. One of the worst parts of being a rolling stone was having to travel light. Being free to go wherever she wanted meant no strings, no obligations, and no one to miss her when she was gone. But sometimes having someone to welcome her home at the end of the day would be nice. And she'd missed the warm weight of a dog at her feet.

"Her name is Misty." This time when he smiled she knew he was thinking of another inside joke. She'd spent a lot of time on the outside trying to get in, so she ought to be used to it, but she really didn't like it here. She wanted to share a laugh with Charlie. Considering he was only doing his best to hasten her exit, that could be a real problem. And the fact that she'd never really experienced such an immediate connection to anyone made her think he might have the right idea. If she hung around for too long, things could get complicated. She jerked when Misty swiped a lick from her fingers to her wrist.

Grace was laughing when the woman behind the front desk hung up and said, "Yeah, her name is Misty, and it should be Licksy. She's Willodean's bloodhound." Then she turned to look at Charlie. "What can I do for you today, Mr. . . . I mean, Charlie?"

Charlie's lips tightened, and he smiled even if it didn't reach his eyes. "Is Willodean in her office, Laura? Grace is looking for a job so I thought I'd introduce her."

Laura studied her for two seconds. Since Laura had also checked her in the day before and sent her over to the chapel that morning, Grace had no idea what the woman might think of this setup. Something in her eyes seemed to say she knew exactly why Grace needed a job, like maybe Tommy Joe had made an impression on his way out just like he had on their arrival. At check-in, Tommy

Joe had done his best to appear to be both a big fish and a stud. He always tried and never succeeded. As a successful car salesman, Tommy Joe was used to working a room, shaking hands, and generally making people uncomfortable with his wider-than-normal blinding white smile. He also liked to wink.

When Tommy Joe and Grace finally made it to the front desk, Tommy Joe stretched his arm out across the front desk to offer his hand to Laura and introduced himself with a wink. When he said, "Pleased to meet ya, Laura, darlin'," Laura had placed her hand in his and then had to brace herself against the desk as it was vigorously shaken. Tommy Joe believed that bigger was always better. Then he and Grace had had an argument because she insisted on two rooms instead of one. Grace had wanted her last night of freedom badly enough to stand her ground. Now, Grace was pretty sure that was the beginning of the end of her wedding plans. If somehow Laura had forgotten all that, she would surely remember the size of his lightning bolt belt buckle. Plus, there was the wedding dress clearly visible through the bag over Charlie's shoulder.

"Let me check to see if she's in her office." Laura picked up the phone and pushed a button. "Willodean, Mr. . . . I mean, Charlie's here and would like to introduce you to someone. I'm going to send them back, okay?"

Grace could hear the exclamation through the phone but couldn't make out the words. Laura shook her head and then hung up the phone. "I think she's happy to see you."

Charlie leaned down to pick up the bags. "Let's do this then."

He walked around behind the desk but paused at a doorway when she didn't follow. At his pointed look and flash of wristwatch reminding her of his schedule, Grace lurched into motion and noticed Misty followed. They walked down a short hallway. At the end of the hall, she could see a man with short, dark hair, dark eyes, and a faint frown on his forehead. He was sitting behind a very neat desk, all the papers lined up in precise rows. He glanced up and did not appear to be friendly to either of them in any way. Charlie stopped before reaching that office, thank goodness, and motioned her through a different door.

As soon as she cleared the doorway, a smallish woman with a cloud of black hair piled on top of her head, bright red lips, and the loudest green Christmas sweatshirt Grace had ever seen rounded the desk piled with folders and launched herself at Charlie. "Why, Charlie McMinn, I've missed you!"

Grace tried not to laugh as she watched Charlie juggle her bags, her dress, and an armful of woman. He hugged her the best he could and dropped both of Grace's bags on the floor. As the cosmetics bag made a loud *thunk*, he shot her an apologetic glance. "Really? It's been . . . what, four or five hours tops since you did this to my hair." He pointed at his pompadour.

"I know. Isn't it grand? Stuck like a charm."

Grace almost laughed at Charlie's longsuffering expression, but she had to wipe the amusement off her face as the woman spun around and held out her hand. "But I'm guessing you're the reason he's here. Willodean Jackson, hon. And you are?"

Grace shook her hand and had to fight the urge to step back. Willodean Jackson was high energy. And it was a small room. "Grace. Andersen."

Willodean clapped her hands together. "Well, it's quite a pleasure to meet you. It ain't every day that Charlie here takes time out of his busy schedule to pop in." She smiled sweetly at him and then went back to her chair behind the desk. "I'm guessing you must be something special."

Grace had no idea what to say to that. She glanced at Charlie, but he didn't look any more certain than she was. Finally he cleared his throat. "Grace here was supposed to be"—he glanced at her and shrugged— "married today, but her groom didn't show. Now she wants a job. Since the hotel's fully staffed, I thought I'd help her get a cab so she can go . . ." He trailed off like he had no idea where she'd go. Grace could understand that because she didn't know either. He ran a finger under his collar and waved his wrist around a bit. "But I've got to get back to the chapel so if you'll just tell Grace we're fully staffed, I'll pay for her cab to the airport." Grace watched him try to communicate with Willodean how serious he was with his eyes. He didn't want her here. That part was clear. She just wasn't sure exactly why. Did he have a problem with the poor and unemployed? Surely he wasn't that kind of jerk, but his warning was pretty clear.

Willodean narrowed her eyes at him and gave a little toss of her head. "Well, you go on then. Don't let us keep you. Hiring and firing is my business, after all." When he didn't move from his spot, she raised her eyebrows and waved her bare wrist at him to remind him of the time.

"Fine. I had to try." With a clearly resigned expression, Charlie glanced at Grace and then draped the bag with her dress in it over the chair, took two large steps back out into the hall, pivoted, and disappeared. Grace stared at the spot she'd seen him last and then shook her head.

When she turned back to face Willodean, Grace noticed she was doing the same thing. "Sometimes that boy's a trial, Grace. Bossy. Way too careful. Certain he always knows best. I'm just warning you now."

Grace had no idea what to say to that either so she sat, laced her fingers together, crossed one leg over the other, and leaned back in her chair.

"On the bright side, though, this is the first time he's brought me a prospective employee, even if he only did it to tell me not to hire you. He knows being fully staffed wouldn't stop me from giving you a job if I want to, but if you knew Charlie better, you'd understand what a big deal this is. Maybe he's learning. Before this he'd have run you off, shoved you in a cab, and pretended he had no idea what I was talking about when I asked. I do wonder why he thought I needed a warning. Of course, if I knew why you're carrying around a wedding dress, I might understand better." Willodean propped one elbow on the desk and rested her chin in her hand. "What's your story, Grace Andersen?"

This was it, her time to sell her story, her chance to

get help. Grace forced the nerves away and made the all-important eye contact as she said, "Well, I checked in yesterday with my fiancée, Tommy Joe Huffle. We had a little argument last night about what he expected and I was willing to give, but I woke up this morning ready to have the wedding of my dreams. I slipped into that dress and felt like a princess until Charlie knocked on my door a half hour after my wedding was supposed to start, and together we decided my groom wasn't coming." It wasn't hard to put on a sad face. When she thought about what she'd have to do to get back to Vegas, she was a little dispirited. But it wouldn't last. Grace patted the dress. "Now I've got a nice dress when what I need is a job and maybe a room to rent for a month or so, just until I can get back home."

Willodean's interest showed in her bright green eyes. "How come you went for a job instead of a loan? I understand tight circumstances. Got a little extra money now that I didn't use to have. Maybe I could just buy you a ticket." Willodean leaned back. "I'm guessing that was what Charlie expected too."

Suddenly angry that either of them would have expected her to beg for money, Grace thought about storming out. Then she remembered her plan to marry a rich husband and decided maybe she didn't have a real strong position on the high road. Besides that, they didn't know her. And they sure didn't know her mother.

"I wish I could take you up on that, Willodean, I really do. But I can't take handouts. Never have, even in more than a dozen years of scraping by. My mother'd roll over in her grave, and she ain't even dead yet." Grace was happy Willodean laughed at her answer. She didn't want to blow an easy shot at employment.

"So Mama's alive and kicking then." Willodean studied her and tapped one finger on the desk. "East Tennessee somewhere, I think."

"'Bout as far east as you can go, twenty minutes outside Sevierville."

"I used to know that part of Tennessee like the back of my hand." Willodean patted the desk like she'd just come up with the perfect solution. "If that's where you're headed back to, I happen to know someone headed that direction. He'll give you a ride, and Mama can pick you up." Her eyes had a wicked glint as she waved her hand. "Not much of a handout, is it? That's just being neighborly. And just the right sort of justice, if you ask me."

For a minute, Grace wondered if the "he" Willodean was talking about was Charlie. It would be a nice irony if he had to drive her six hours away because she couldn't get a job. Grace shook her head. "No, ma'am. I need to get back to Vegas. And I'd rather have a job."

Willodean considered her. "Don't get along too well with Mama?" She seemed sad as she asked it.

"Well, it's not that we don't get along. I can just handle her 'I told you so' over the phone better. That helps us keep the peace." And that was the truth.

"So Mama didn't approve of the groom?"

"Mama didn't even know I was getting married," Grace said impatiently. "And if she had, she might have approved, but she would not be at all surprised by this turn of events."

Willodean said, "Well, now, I don't know what you paid for that dress, but we could find some place to sell it. You're a . . . what, size ten?"

Grace threw one protective hand over the dress and shook her head. "No, ma'am, I'm not sellin' the dress. Not yet." And she also wasn't correcting Willodean's guess about the size.

For some reason, she wasn't ready to let the dress go yet, flat broke or not.

Willodean's smile was slow, and it reminded Grace of someone, but she couldn't put her finger on who. She said, "Well, now, here's the thing. I like a girl who don't give up, you know? So let's just find you a job."

The tension she hadn't even been aware of building across her shoulders lifted, and Grace took a deep breath. There was something about making a decision, moving forward, no matter how good or bad the situation might be, that made her feel better, more confident. "What about Charlie? Should you ask him?" He'd seemed pretty certain she needed to move along. If she had the chance to find out, she would like to know why.

"My hotel, my rules, Grace. Plenty of people around here worry a little about that, Charlie being on the top of the list, but the Rock'n'Rolla Hotel is still all mine." Willodean cupped her hands around her mouth and shouted, "Hey, Tony! Can you come in here?"

Grace did her best not to cringe at the noise level or clap her hands over her ears, but the unfriendly guy from the next office whipped around the corner before she could catch her breath again.

"Willodean, that's what we have the phone system for." He crossed his arms over his chest and leaned a shoulder against the door.

"Sure, but I don't need it." Willodean looked so pleased with herself as she said it that Grace chuckled. "Here's our new employee, Grace."

Tony looked at her, and she realized that he might be serious but he wasn't mean. He was as amused as she was by Willodean but didn't reward her with laughter. That was probably a sound policy.

"I wasn't aware that we're hiring. Hotel's fully staffed right now, Willodean." He looked apologetic but un-worried.

Willodean pointed at the stack of files on her desk leaning precariously near the edge. "You got to be kid-ding me. I've got more papers stacked up here than I know what to do with, thanks to the new addition, and there aren't enough hours in the day to get it up and roll-ing. When the gift shop opens, we'll need help. And if none of that suits, she can help out in Viva Las Vegas."

Tony considered that answer. "What's your work ex-perience, Grace?"

This could be tricky. Employers generally frowned on hiring people who had lots of short-term jobs. On the other hand, she had a lot of different experience. If it could be done, she'd probably already been there, done that, and collected the pink slip. "I've acted, modeled, and sung in absolutely nothing you would have seen. I've waited tables, walked dogs, and served as a raw foods chef for a very eccentric actress. I've run a cash register at a gas station, a grocery store, and a pawnshop where I'm pretty sure the owner was doing a nice side business in marijuana sales. I answered some very strange calls as a receptionist for a private investigator. For a short time, I owned part of a doggie spa."

"What happened?" Willodean looked fascinated.

"I lost a poodle." When neither Willodean nor Tony said anything, Grace added, "In my defense, he was a biter. And he ran all the way home so the story has a happy ending for the poodle."

She looked from Willodean to Tony and then watched them communicate silently with each other. Finally Willodean blinked slowly and said, "So what you're saying is you ain't afraid to work."

"No, ma'am, I'm not." Ann Andersen had made sure all seven of her children had solid work ethics. Six of them had regular paychecks and paid time off to show for it. And Grace . . . well, she was never unemployed for long. Her mother's voice in her head made it impossible to rest without a job.

"How come you've tried so many different things? I mean, seems like if you want to act, you go, you stay in one place, you work a part-time job until it works." Willodean tilted her head. "What keeps you going?"

Grace blinked, surprised at the question. Most of the time, employers just assumed she couldn't keep a job, not that *she'd* decided to move on. "Well . . ." The fact that she couldn't really answer it worried her.

Willodean nodded. "Maybe you're just trying the jobs on for size, looking for the one that fits." She shrugged.

"Or the place. And if Vegas is it, you gotta get back." She didn't look convinced.

Relieved Willodean had provided an answer she could live with, Grace smiled. "I really appreciate your help."

Willodean's sunny smile was back. "I appreciate a girl who doesn't give up. Reminds me of myself on a good day."

Tony held out his hand. As Grace shook it, he said, "Sounds like we've got plenty of options around here to put you to work. We'll make up a schedule, maybe start you in Viva Las Vegas while we figure out the rest. How's that sound?"

"Waiting tables?" Grace nodded. "Sure, although I should mention why I was fired from my last waitressing job . . ."

Tony's eyebrows rose. She took that as a sign to proceed.

"I don't like handsy patrons. I was waiting tables at this bar and one guy, Grunt was his name, put his hand on my . . ." Maybe that was too much information. "Anyway, I yanked it off, twisted his arm, and would've broken his finger except his squeals brought the bouncer running."

When silence filled the room to overflowing again, Grace thought maybe she should have just kept her mouth shut. She looked down at her crossed legs. "I don't put up with that sort of stuff."

Willodean tried to keep a straight face, but her lips trembled first and then the floodgates opened. Her giggles were contagious and the release of tension had Grace gasping for breath and laughing. Her chuckles died when she looked at Tony.

He wasn't amused. He looked dangerous. "That doesn't happen at the Rock'n'Rolla Hotel. Not if I know about it. Anyone touches you, you let me know." She believed the poor misguided soul would be sorry he ever heard of Tennessee if Tony got a hold of him. And she wanted to tear up a bit. It had been a long time since she'd had anyone but herself to depend on. She sniffed and watched Tony's whole body tighten up. He pointed over his shoulder. "I'll just, uh, grab the key to Randa's studio. Since it's empty, I'm sure you'll ..." And he disappeared. First Charlie. Then Tony. Maybe it was a magic doorway.

She looked back at Willodean. "Did I do something wrong?"

Willodean pulled out a folder and slid a stack of papers across the desk. "Marine. He can't handle the tears. You ever get in trouble, try waterworks, but I'll deny it if you ever tell him I said so." She tapped a finger on top of the file. "Tony's the hotel manager. Laura is his assistant. They'll get you set up with a schedule, uniforms—stuff like that. Here's the paperwork we'll need in the morning. You can give it to either of 'em. Tony's going to show you to the staff apartments. Happily, he just convinced his girlfriend, Randa, to move in with him so we've got a space open."

"Staff apartment? For me?" Grace had been afraid finding a place to stay would be the hardest part, but maybe ... She tried to tamp down the flutter of relief and excitement building in her abdomen. A space of her own here at the hotel. Her life had just gotten so much easier.

"Only if you want it, Grace." Willodean waited for her to answer, warmth, concern, and a hint of curiosity in her eyes.

Grace had to clear her throat. It was suddenly clogged with relief and gratitude. "Yes, ma'am, I would love to have a spot here. Thank you."

Grace took the stack of papers and started gathering up all of her baggage. "I guess I need to check out too, get my stuff out of my hotel room." The bill. She'd completely forgotten it. "Willodean, would it be possible for me to make payments on the bill for the hotel rooms and the wedding too? I mean, I might have room on my credit card but . . ." She *so* did not have any credit left. She'd been spending like she was about to have a rich husband.

Willodean shook her head. "That no-good jerk left you holding the bills too?"

"I made the arrangements. I used my cards to book everything. I sincerely doubt he decided to do the right thing as he went out the door."

Willodean came around the desk and wrapped her arms around Grace's shoulder. "Now then, here's something I see. Kindness makes you tear up but problems don't. You'll fit right in around here, mark my words. And don't you worry about that bill—"

"No handouts, remember? I'll take care of it. Eventually." Grace raised her chin in the same stubborn gesture that used to send her father to the refrigerator in search of a beer.

Willodean raised her hands in surrender. "All right, now. I can go along with that. You check out. I'll just let

Laura know to print you out a folio and set something up for your checks to pay it back. Deal?"

Grace nodded, satisfied that she wasn't a charity case. At least she had that much going for her. "Deal."

When Willodean cupped her hands around her mouth again, Grace squeezed her eyes shut like that would keep her eardrums intact.

Tony stopped in the doorway. "Don't yell. I'm right here." His longsuffering expression made her want to laugh again, but she was so relieved she couldn't work up the energy. "I'll show you to your new place, if you're ready."

Grace reached over to pick up the rest of her stuff, but he brushed her hand away. "I've got it." Then he moved efficiently to the door and paused to wait.

"You go on now, Grace. Get settled. And when you see Charlie, you give him the prettiest smile you can, all right?"

Something in Willodean's eyes spelled cagey interest in Grace's reaction so she smiled. "Definitely, Willodean, I will. I owe him a big thank you for introducing us, even if he had another goal in mind. He doesn't seem to like me, but I'll work on him."

Willodean's small chuckle worried Grace. "You do that, hon. Get some rest tonight. Weatherman's saying we might see some snow and that makes even the most levelheaded people lose their minds around here."

Grace waved a hand and followed Tony's precise march back out into the lobby. "Laura, this is our new employee, Grace Andersen."

Laura smiled. "Nice to meet you again, Grace. For the third or fourth time."

Grace nodded. And Tony was on the move. He called back over his shoulder, "She's staying in Randa's studio and starting work in the morning. She'll meet you here at nine." As he disappeared around the corner, Laura shook her head. "You better catch up. He gets that close to Randa, and he's ready to take a nice long break."

Grace waved and trotted after him. He'd paused in front of a small gym. "You can use the gym and the pool in the summer on your own time if you like." The Elvis album covers lining the walls blurred as she raced to keep up. The decorated trees they passed—one with all green decorations, another all red, and one in a rainbow color scheme near the gym—were bright flashes in the corner of her eye. She stumbled to a stop in front of a hot pink tree decorated in Santa Claus flamingo ornaments. He opened the glass door to the pool area and held it open just long enough for her to step through.

"On that side's the new addition. Chapel, spa, and meeting rooms." Grace was out of breath by the time he held open a small gate. "And these are the staff apartments. To get back into the hotel, you'll need this key." He slipped it into a lock and then opened the door. "I'm right next door if you need anything, but I think you'll find it stocked. Randa just moved out a week ago."

"I thought I heard your voice." Grace and Tony both turned to see a long-legged blonde in the doorway. And then Grace noticed the goofy grin on Tony's face and decided this must be Randa.

Tony dropped her bags on the floor and absentmind-edly spread her dress bag over the couch while Randa held out her hand. "I'm Randa, the spa manager."

"Grace. Waiting at Viva Las Vegas and maybe helping with weddings in the chapel and whatever else needs to be done." Unsure what to do with herself as Randa and Tony made eyes at each other, she looked around the small apartment. In this one room, she had a couch, a chair, a bed, and a small kitchen. Two doors must lead to a closet and a bathroom. And it was nicer than the apartment she'd been sharing with two other girls in Las Vegas. She had to sit down to take it all in.

Tony pointed. "We'll be next door. If you need any-thing, like a ride somewhere, we'll help out, okay?" Then he pushed Randa out the door and shut it behind him. Grace could hear Randa's outraged voice and his quiet answer before their door shut behind them.

And then the silence in the tiny apartment was loud. For the first time since Grace made up her mind to follow her mother's practical advice to find a man and settle down, the anxious flutter in her stomach was gone. Grace smiled as she kicked off her heels and tried to figure out what was next.

Chapter Three

CHARLIE LEANED ONE hip against the front desk while he waited for his mother. Sunday mornings were usually busy in the lobby with travelers leaving for home, but the weather forecast had spooked many into leaving early. Natives would know the chances of snow that early in December were the same as finding a front-door parking spot at the mall the day after Thanksgiving. It could happen, but it would take a miracle or perfect timing.

He could see his mother in the doorway to the restaurant talking with Marcy, who was flashing an engagement ring. Since weddings were nearly his mother's favorite thing in the world to talk about, there was no telling how long it would take. While he waited, he tried to make small talk with Laura and Randa while Tony glared from behind the front desk.

"Are you headed back home today, Charlie?" Randa said his name slowly like she was testing it out. He appreciated the effort. More often than not, staff had to stop midstream so that instead of Mr. McMinn, he was Mr. Charlie.

He smiled at her to show his appreciation and noticed she had a pretty good grip on Tony's shoulder. "Actually, I decided to stay this week to do some work on the budgets for next year. Maybe get something set up for the conference area. Spend some time with my mom."

"Oh, Charlie, that's wonderful." His mother's smile was huge as she skidded to a stop in front of the desk. "It's so nice to have you around." She nodded as she glanced around the small group, and everyone but Tony nodded their agreement.

Charlie glanced down at his scuffed black boots as he thought about the surprise he had for her. He should definitely wait for a better time, but there was something about Tony's disapproving glare that made him say, "Actually, I've got two dates set up this week, so this is the perfect time for a longer visit."

He didn't have to say anything more. His mother hooted. Then she said, "Christmas miracles do happen!"

Charlie's shoulders twitched and he said, "Calm down. It's just a date." He glanced at Tony. From the minute his mother introduced him to Tony, he'd known exactly what the Marine thought of him and it wasn't much. Charlie had stayed away for too long, and now, even after he and his mother had smoothed things over and he'd started helping out at the hotel a bit, Tony thought he should do more. Every time he ran into Tony at the hotel it was like this: Tony frowning, judging, and Charlie doing his best to hold on to his temper. Since he knew he deserved a little disapproval, he bit his tongue, but the longer he stayed, the harder it was to get along with Tony Ortega. Maybe Charlie disappointed his mother regularly. Even if Tony had been adopted into the family and seemed like the son he should have been sometimes, Charlie could still make his mother beam like she'd just won the lottery.

If he felt a twinge of guilt over how easy it really was to please her, he would never show Tony.

"Two! Two dates! I've been worried about you becoming some mountain man hermit out there all on your own. A little time with a pretty girl will do you good." Her green sequined sneakers flashed in the bright lights of the lobby as she danced where she stood.

"I was actually going more for successful, stable, and mature than pretty, but—"

Waving her hands to make him stop, Willodean heaved a disgusted sigh, spun in a circle, and they all noticed Grace standing behind her. Willodean towed her forward into the group. "And, if that ain't wonderful enough, I had an inspiration last night while I was making a to-do list for this week. A true epiphany. Grace is going to be the answer to one of our problems."

When everyone turned to look at Grace, she tugged at the bottom of the large, old purple sweatshirt she was wearing and then plastered on a bright, sunny smile. "Good morning, Willodean. I'm ready to get to work." She waved the bent file folder. "I brought my paperwork back. I thought Laura could point me in the right direction and I could pick up a uniform."

Grace met Charlie's stare directly and raised her chin. Charlie had to acknowledge her challenge. He tipped his head and fought a smile. He was not surprised at all that his mother had ignored his unspoken warning. She'd been ignoring his warnings for years. If he could have, he would have bet his fortune, hers, and any change he could find in the parking lot that Grace would be working at the hotel today. He might have been a little surprised that she faced him head-on even after he'd tried to hurry her on her way. What he really hadn't expected was that he'd been happy to see her standing there, looking absolutely nothing like either of the Grace Andersens he'd met the day before. This morning she looked soft, natural, and young with her hair falling down around her shoulders and clothes a size too big.

Willodean patted her hand. "Sure you are, hon. I know you like to work. First, let's talk about my epiphany, why don't we?" Willodean motioned over her shoulder and headed off for the offices behind the front desk. "Come with me. Charlie, you too. And Tony." She paused. "Well, I guess this could affect all of us. Laura, can you call someone to keep an eye on the front desk and join us? We've got some business to discuss." She grabbed Randa's hand and pulled her along as she disappeared.

When Randa stuck her head around the corner and said, "Tony," Charlie watched his eyes narrow. Then Tony turned and followed the group. As soon as the newest front desk employee skidded to a stop behind the desk, Laura turned to Charlie and said, "Are you coming?" Then she paused in the doorway.

Charlie took a deep breath and rolled his shoulders before he glanced at Grace. He shook his head. "Another day at the Rock'n'Rolla Hotel, another brainstorm." He motioned at the doorway. "You better go on. I think you're the key ingredient."

Grace nodded. "Okay, but I just wanted to say . . . I know you don't want me here. I'm not exactly sure why, but it's okay. I don't want to do anything more than work long enough to pay my bills and head back to Vegas. That's it." She smoothed her hair behind her ear. "I don't need a handout." She tilted her head and then followed the group, her yellow sneakers squeaking as she went. He ran his hand down Misty's back while he considered her words. He almost believed her. The hotel bill and a plane ticket were well within the money he budgeted for his mother's causes so whether she worked to make her own way or Willodean handed her the ticket, he was prepared. He tried to ignore the memory of how she'd made him think about magic instead of compatibility the day before as he took a deep breath and followed Grace to his mother's office.

By the time he squeezed in, Charlie had managed to regain a bit of his patience. That was a very good thing. One more pissing contest with Tony this morning, and he'd lose it completely. He wouldn't bet a lot of money on his chances of taking Tony down, but he could guarantee he wouldn't be the only one in the ambulance on the way to the emergency room. Of course, a throw-down between her real son and her adopted son would break his mother's heart and he'd promised himself he wouldn't ever do that on purpose again. Causing her divorce from her third husband, Travis Luttrell, had been enough heartbreak to last a lifetime. For both of them. So he bit his tongue and tried to hold on to his temper.

Instead he focused on Grace. So far he'd seen her dressed as a princess bride, a woman on the prowl, and this morning as a . . . what? She looked ten years younger and so much more delicate than she had the day before. Her face was pale, and he thought he could see evidence of a sleepless night.

Since he'd spent entirely too much time last night lecturing himself *not* to think about her—where she would go, how she got to the hotel, what she'd do next, or how amazing she'd been in that wedding dress—he knew what that was like.

"There she is." Willodean was sitting on top of her cluttered desk because her office was over capacity. They'd passed standing room only. "Got all the decision makers here. And the job candidate. I'm thinking we have us a job interview and fill our event planner opening this fine Sunday morning."

"We're hiring an event planner." Tony didn't phrase it in the form of a question, but Charlie had a feeling it was news to him. He'd intended to ask his mother about new staffing needs before he finalized the next year's budget but hadn't gotten around to it.

About the end of January every year, Charlie asked himself why he even bothered with setting up a budget for the hotel. His mother treated it like her horoscope, a bit of fun nonsense that had no real effect on her plans.

She ran the hotel like she ran her life. She never once expected anything less than the best.

Willodean scooted on top of the desk and folded her legs. Every movement set small bells sewn to the bottom of her green sweater jingling. She waved her hands in the air, the office light hitting the massive emerald ring she'd worn forever, as she said, "It came to me in a flash. We're going to be having business meetings and small conferences and weddings and fan club events. Unless we hire a planner, somebody"—she glanced meaningfully around to indicate that it was someone in that room—"is going to be swamped."

Willodean turned to Laura. "Now, I know we talked about it being part of what you do, but I can't imagine how you'll fit it in, what with the restaurant and the new gift shop and keeping KT in line in general." She motioned at Grace. "We've got a real jack of all trades here. She knows entertainment, planning, food. And we have plenty of housekeepers and waitstaff right at the moment. What we don't have is someone to make sure that addition over there is booked to capacity, somebody who's good with the big ideas." She folded her hands in her lap. "What do y'all think?"

Charlie was sure they didn't need another person with new big ideas. His mother was a one-woman idea generator and all of them cost big bucks.

Everyone swiveled to look at Grace. She licked her lips nervously. "Well, as far as what I think . . ." She looked like she had no idea what to say. "Can I do it? Definitely. Would I enjoy it? I already have a few ideas. But I guess

I should just . . . warn you. I don't stick in one place for long, or at least, I haven't." She shrugged. "And my plan is to head back to Vegas as soon as I have enough saved up, so I'll be leaving pretty soon."

There was silence in the tiny office for a second or two before Willodean, Laura, and Randa started to laugh. Even Tony's lips were twitching like the amusement was just bubbling up.

Grace glanced at Charlie and when he looked into her eyes, he felt the strange connection again, like out of all the people in the room, she actually understood him. He'd never experienced it before. Under the influence of that rush, he wanted her to say yes, so he dipped his head in a subtle nod. Then he had to ask himself what he was doing. "No" was the right answer. Getting her on a plane back to Vegas immediately was the best solution for Grace and his own plan, obviously. But there was something about her. When she looked at him, he wanted to say yes. He was afraid it didn't matter what the question was. But since he'd spent his whole life saying yes to his mother even when he should say no, he had to be stronger here.

Willodean patted Grace's hand. "Hon, if you only knew how many people have come here with no plans to stay. Tony's been here the longest, but the day we met, he had the look of a man on the verge of falling off the edge of the earth. Now look at him, running the place. Laura came for a temporary job to make ends meet. Her husband-to-be came for a week to shoot a television show. Randa wanted to tear the place down. But once they move in, I can't get 'em out. There's something special about my Rock'n'Rolla Hotel. Even if you go, it draws you back. I'm willing to make a considerable bet that you won't find it easy to leave."

Willodean shook her finger. "How about this? You give me two weeks' notice when you're ready to leave, and we'll call it even. We'll work together so I'm ready when you go. There's plenty to do, and a job like this won't be too hard for someone to step in if needed. You can start . . . today, I guess, if you want to."

Grace frowned like she was hardly convinced but straightened her shoulders like she would try to tackle anything. "All right, Willodean. You won't be sorry."

"Oh, honey, I know that. I got the magic touch, just you wait and see." Everyone in the room laughed, even Charlie, and he was happy to see some of the color return to Grace's face. Then Willodean slid off the desk, pointed to the computer, and said to Charlie, "I know you're chomping at the bit. Go on, check your futures or prices or stocks or options or whatever."

She grabbed Grace's hand. "Charlie, I'll expect you for dinner tonight. Seven o'clock. Don't be late. The rest of you, go . . . do something fun. Not work. I'm gonna give our newest employee the grand tour."

He watched his mother tow Grace toward the door, reluctant to let either of them leave. Protecting his mother had been his number one goal for a long time, but she made it hard. And Grace . . . maybe she wasn't someone looking to take advantage of his mother, but he thought about following them out, just to keep an eye on things.

Then he realized Randa, Laura, and Tony were watching him. So he moved behind his mother's desk as ordered. Just before he sat, he looked up and Grace paused in the doorway. Her bright smile was accompanied by a wink, and he had to keep from smiling. She'd gotten exactly what she wanted. She'd won this round. And he didn't even mind for some reason.

Then she was gone and the others were filing out. As he pulled up his e-mail program, he wondered how long he'd be able to resist checking up on the hotel's newest employee.

GRACE FOLLOWED WILLODEAN and did her best to keep up as they went through all three floors of the hotel, the restaurant, the lobby, the small gym, and new space for the coming gift shop. Every inch of the hotel was dedicated to Elvis. Album artwork lined the hall of the first floor. The second floor was all about Memphis, and the third Hawaii. Gold carpet with black music notes, black-and-white photos, and an Elvis soundtrack spilling out of Viva Las Vegas made it clear the King of Rock and Roll was always number one at the Rock'n'Rolla Hotel.

She didn't know much about Elvis, except that Tommy Joe could recite the names of all thirty-one of his movies and the concert specials in both alphabetical and year-of-release orders. But there was something about this hotel that felt like it was stuck in a time warp of the good old days but also that it was timeless, eternal.

Added on top of the hotel's normal bright, fun décor

was Christmas, Christmas, Christmas. Every corner had a Christmas tree and an animatronic Santa spent his days riding the elevator. Even the mess of renovation taking place to convert a meeting room into the new gift shop had a touch of holiday spirit. The display window was outlined in blinking multicolored lights, and the *Coming Soon* sign featured a red-nosed reindeer.

As Willodean bumped open the glass door to the pool area with one hip, Grace noticed a sprig of mistletoe above. Willodean was clearly excited by the idea of her own gift shop as she said, "Gonna have the finest Elvis memorabilia you can find anywhere as well as your standard refrigerator magnets and key chains in the new shop once it's ready. Everybody tells me the end of February, but I got my heart set on the middle of January, so I guess we'll have to see who's right." She winked at Grace. "I've been having the best time shopping for those, but I'm afraid once Charlie sees the bill for all my *inventory*, he'll cut up my credit cards and close my checking account. Soul of an accountant, that boy, not an entrepreneur. And from such good genes, I just can't understand it."

A million questions popped up, but Grace wasn't quite sure how to ask "Who is he?" without coming right out and saying it and that seemed rude. The very last thing she wanted to do was to offend the woman who'd given her a place to stay and a job, so Grace trailed Willodean around the pool and waited for her to unlock the door to the new building. "Apartment okay?"

When Grace nodded, Willodean did too. "Expect

the neighbors with all their cooing might grate on your nerves."

Grace smiled. "I've had much bigger worries. Plus, it's nice to see them together."

Willodean shook her head. "Just wait until KT gets here. Then it's like Noah's ark around here, and those of us who ain't paired up gotta stick together so they don't shove us out of the boat." Willodean paused to think. "'Course, that makes me Noah, and I'm the one driving the boat. That ain't too bad, I guess." She wrinkled her nose. "Still might rather be paired off, though, don't you know?"

Before this whole "settling down" plan, Grace hadn't really thought much about it. She'd been happy on her own more often than she'd been happy in a relationship. But now, after the planning and the thinking and maybe even after her weird, instant connection to Charlie, she thought she knew what Willodean meant. Watching Randa and Tony had made her both uncomfortable and little envious.

Willodean flipped on lights as they entered the large open lobby. "Wedding chapel this way, but I expect you know that." She pointed across the lobby to large glass doors. "New spa's going there. 'Taking Care of Business' . . . it's a good name, right?" Willodean looked over her shoulder, so Grace nodded dutifully but her reaction must have been disappointing. Then Willodean placed her hands on both hips. "I can't believe it. TCB? Taking care of business? It was kinda Elvis's motto." She waited for a reaction, her eyebrows raised in question, so Grace shrugged.

Willodean threw her hands up. "Somehow I've picked up another person to feed who doesn't know a thing about Elvis."

Grace shifted one loose strand of hair behind her ear. "I know 'Blue Suede Shoes' and 'Jailhouse Rock' and a little of *Viva Las Vegas* . . ."

Willodean huffed in disgust. "You'll have to do better than that. It's like I need to start a remedial Elvis course, make it part of the employee training." She jabbed the elevator button and then stepped on. "You got some making up to do, but I bet you'll get it done. If you need some movies, Laura's daughter, Holly, has 'em all. I'll introduce you. You have one of those iPod things, right? Download some music. It'll help with planning Elvis events, and I've got a long list of entertainers who can help with big parties."

"Yes, ma'am." Grace followed her off the elevator and stepped out into a business-class version of the hotel. As they walked through six smaller meeting rooms, Grace read plaques that accompanied beautiful black-and-white prints of Tupelo, Sun Studio, Las Vegas, and Hawaii. The larger, multipurpose space that could seat 150 or be broken down into two rooms was done in tasteful grays with lots of photos of Elvis and Memphis landmarks. It was perfect for business meetings or receptions.

"What do you think?" Willodean looked anxious for her opinion. "I didn't do this one myself. Hired a decorator instead, and Mike likes all this sophisticated stuff." She held up her hands and made air quotes as she said,

"'Southern traditional' he calls it. Thought it worked for conference rooms."

Graced nodded. "I can see how this would work for all kinds of functions. Business meetings, family reunions, wedding receptions. With the right decorations, you can go serious or fun. I like it."

Willodean motioned for her to follow. "Well, now, I'm glad you brought that up." She shoved open another door at the end of the long hall, and a cavernous room with haphazard stacks of chairs and tables and very little else was lit by harsh overhead lights. "This ain't much to work with, so we're going to have to do some buying. We'll need some standard decorations to help jazz up the place for our run-of-the-mill events and then you'll work up budgets for the special, high-dollar events. You can do that, right?"

Grace had to be honest, even if the idea of shopping for parties filled her with the urge to laugh and clap her hands in excitement. "You know I'm not a decorator, right, Willodean? I've never done something like that, although I've lived on a budget for a long time. That part's no problem."

Willodean winked. "Well, now, the decorating ain't too hard either. I've done that hotel more times'n I can count on one hand, and I haven't read one decorating book in my life. It's all Elvis. You remember that. I think it's like working with neutrals. You just buy Elvis and it all goes together."

Grace considered her philosophy as they walked back through the building. She thought she might even be able to work with it. And she couldn't help it. She started to laugh.

Willodean's eyebrows shot up, and she stopped next to a door nestled to the side of the elevator. "Too much stress?"

Grace threw her arms around Willodean's neck and squeezed her tight. When Willodean returned the hug, Grace had to sniff back tears. "This is so much better than waiting tables or making beds. And I don't mean to sound ungrateful because I appreciate a good job, no matter what kind, but I can't even begin to say how happy this chance makes me. I've never done anything like this and I'm looking forward to learning something new." She squeezed Willodean again and then stepped back to rub at her nose.

Willodean shook her head sadly. "Already you're a goner, and I haven't gotten you paired up. You're the easiest one yet, Grace."

Grace's laugh was a little gurgly, and she waved her hands. "The job's enough. I don't need a spot on the ark."

Willodean opened the door and said, "I had intended this to be an office someday. It's all wired up and everything, got a computer and phone. It's small, but I don't expect you'll spend a lot of time behind a desk."

Grace sat in the cushy desk chair and gave it a whirl. "Me. With a desk, a phone, and a laptop. And all of them in Tennessee. My mother's going to think it's the apocalypse."

Willodean crossed her arms and leaned against the doorjamb. "Been telling you for years to settle down and get a real job?"

Grace pulled open an empty drawer to avoid meeting Willodean's gaze. "More like come home and then they'd find me a real job. I could pick. Secretary, clerk, bookkeeper, customer service . . . anything with a regular paycheck that would afford a mortgage in a nice-enough neighborhood."

Willodean sighed. "I've known you less than two days, and I can see all over you that that won't work."

Grace managed to meet her stare that time. "Sure, but that might be because you want to." She shrugged a shoulder. "They love me but . . . they don't see me, you know?" She rolled her eyes. "How silly. I was the youngest of seven. I felt like they had a hard time remembering my name most days. Leave home, work twice as hard for half as much, just because you don't fit in quite as well as you should. College and kids and bills and Christmas at home. I could have had that."

Willodean pursed her lips. "Sure, sure. Lots of people do. And it makes them happy. Maybe that doesn't make you happy, Grace, and honestly there's nothing wrong with that."

Grace nodded.

"What would you have given up? What's the best story you can tell at dinner parties?"

Grace didn't even have to think. "I once served drinks at this big shot agent's holiday party and dumped a tray of shrimp cocktail on Mariah Carey."

Willodean snorted. "Do not pass go, do not collect two hundred dollars, am I right?"

"I'm lucky they didn't call the cops. But every now and

then, I think about that, and no matter how things are going, I'm happy because I know if I ever run into Mariah again, she'll remember me."

She and Willodean looked at each other and then the guffaws started.

When they laughed themselves quiet again, Grace ran her hand over the desk. "This is going to be great, Willodean. I can do this. You won't regret giving me the chance."

Then Grace shook her head. "Why? Why are you giving me this chance? Waiting tables is one thing. This is a shot at something big. You don't know much about me except that I've managed to leave or get fired from a really impressive list of places." Grace told herself to shut up. Telling the boss to reconsider her employment was a terrible idea. But the honest, hard-working Andersen part of her couldn't let it go. "On paper, Charlie was right to warn you away from me."

Willodean studied her face and Grace fought the urge to squirm. "Well, now. Two things. I need help. I want this expansion to be a success, partly to prove Charlie wrong. If you can help there, you're worth your weight in gold to me." Her lips twitched. "But as far as choosing you goes, I have a lot of experience winning gambles on good people. I believe you'll do the best you can, and honestly that's all I can ask. You go when you're ready. Otherwise, you do the best you can here." She shrugged. "Simple as that. And if my Rock'n'Rolla Hotel gets a hold of you the way it has so many others, you'll stay, have a career of your own. And either way, I'm right so I can't hardly lose, can I?"

Grace had never felt this way before. Always, when she was presented with a new opportunity or a once-in-a-life chance to try something or even having to make the best choice between two bad options, she'd done it fearlessly because she knew it was only temporary. She could move right along if it didn't work out, and if she let anybody down, they wouldn't suffer long. Willodean seemed so certain that now that she was here, she'd never leave. But sometimes Grace felt like staying in one place for too long meant the end of something. She wasn't sure what.

Even scary as it was to make a change like this, to decide to accept what might be a permanent place with responsibility, she needed a job. And she couldn't deny the thrill of anticipation she felt, so she was just going to do the best she could while she was here. Just like Willodean said. Grace nodded. "I can do this."

"Of course you can." Willodean flipped off the light, and they stepped back outside to ride the elevator down. Willodean shivered as she locked the door. "Might be the weatherman got it right this time. Think the temperature's dropping. We may get snow before Christmas." She wrapped an arm around Grace's shoulder. "Hope you brought a coat."

As they walked back into the hotel, Grace said, "Guess I'll need to catch a ride somewhere so I can get one. My coat's with all my other stuff, boxed up in Las Vegas, ready to be shipped to Atlanta. I didn't come prepared to stay."

"You just take my car over to the Wal-Mart. Get what you need today, then tomorrow you can start with an inventory." Willodean paused. "Grace, I'm about to get in your business so bad that even I can't believe I'm going to ask. You just tell me to shove off if you don't want to answer."

Grace took a deep breath. That wasn't a setup she heard every day.

"Your groom . . . you don't seem too brokenhearted. How long am I going to have to wait for you to be ready for my matches?"

Grace's eyebrows rose. "Your matches? Like, dates?"

Willodean shrugged. "I got two hobbies. This hotel and matchmaking." She patted Grace on the shoulder. "I think you're my next project."

Grace opened her mouth and closed it again, uncertain of what she'd meant to say or how in the world she might answer this. Finally, she said, "Well, I'm not brokenhearted. It was a match made out of practicality, I guess. He was rich. I wanted to be, and in exchange I was ready to work hard at being the wife he wanted. But I'm not great at picking the right man. Obviously." She didn't really care for the excited gleam in Willodean's eyes. "Don't you think that makes me a horrible person that I was ready to marry a man for his money?"

"Girl, I've been there, done that, and have the hotel to prove it." Willodean winked. "Just 'cause you were set to marry a man for his money, that doesn't make you a bad person. My second husband was the same, and I loved him *and* his money and thank God every day I met him when I walk these halls. I think as long as you were prepared to give as much as you were going to take, you got nothing to feel bad about." They both watched Charlie stoop to pet Misty in front of the door to Viva Las Vegas. "Must be noon. That boy's like clockwork with his lunch. Whatever you do, don't mess up his schedule, okay? He gets really testy about his schedule."

Grace nodded. "That's it? That's all you have to say?"

Willodean looked up at the ceiling while she considered the question. "I've had four husbands, Grace. The first one and the last one, they were love matches, and thanks to both of them for different reasons, I have my son. The second one became love and I have my hotel because of him, but I'll promise you that he never once regretted picking me."

Grace waited but she didn't say anything else. "And the third one?"

Willodean sighed. "Well, if you want to talk about selfish motives, he might be the one we need to talk about. Some people thought he was a gold digger too, a man looking for a rich wife. And I didn't give one bit of care over that. He was young, and fun, and handsome, and perfect." She looked older when the smile slid off her face. "But I didn't consider what he'd do to my son, the one who'd lost his father at such a young age and his stepfather too soon. Making a decision to please myself . . . well, let's just say I can see now the dangers of doing that. Sometimes you break things you can't fix."

Grace wanted to hug her and promise her there was nothing that couldn't be fixed. But they would both know that was a lie.

"But your son, you said you got him back."

Willodean looked toward the lobby again. "Yeah, sort of. My last husband, Howard, was magic like that, a negotiator that could have you signing on the bottom line before you even knew you had the pen in your hand. Things were bad before that, but Howard, he patched 'em up."

"What happened to Howard, Willodean?"

She blinked. "Oh, well, when I met him, he was going through cancer treatment. We knew going in the clock was ticking. Guess you could say my men don't stick either, Grace. All but one, though, only death could take away. That's the kind of sticking a woman can appreciate, you know? Depending on which side of the coin I choose to look at, I either have bad luck with husbands or the very, very best."

Grace crossed her arms over her chest and stared at the gold carpet until Willodean patted her on the shoulder. "Never mind about all that. What I shoulda said is I've got good references on my matchmaking abilities. I'll take good care of you."

Grace rubbed her forehead. "Willodean, if you think you can do it, I say go for it." Then she clamped a hand over the tight knot in her stomach. Just because Willodean set her up, that didn't mean love and marriage and forever. She could still go whenever she wanted. Grace had to repeat that to herself until she could breathe normally.

Willodean pumped her fist in the air. "Well, now if that ain't something! I don't usually have much cooperation. This is going to be fun." She narrowed her eyes. "Gimme your list. What kind of man am I looking for?"

For some reason, Charlie's face popped up in her mind. "Tall. Athletic. Likes the outdoors." Why she said that, she had no idea. Ever since she'd lived in Vegas, she'd done her best to avoid any contact with Mother Nature. Charlie just seemed like a guy who could find his way around in the woods. Maybe something like that could come in handy. She shook her head. "Flexible."

Willodean frowned. "Flexible . . . you mean he can go with the flow, right? Not stretchy enough to pat himself on the back."

"I mean, I mentioned I might not stay here long. It's not because I don't like it here. I just . . . something in me makes it hard to sit still for too long."

Willodean nodded. "I think I can understand that, but did you ever consider that maybe you just have to land in the right spot to stick?"

Grace shook her head. She didn't know what to say to that either. She'd started to think maybe there wasn't a right place. Maybe there was a problem with her, something that made it hard to put down roots. Almost any man would have trouble with that.

"Anything else?" Willodean was watching her closely. "Want another rich man?"

Grace thought about Charlie and then told herself to stop being stupid. Maybe there was some connection between them, but he was a man who liked schedules. Here in the hotel, people treated him with a lot of respect, like he had some important title. Maybe that explained why he was so bossy. Instead of lamé, today he'd dressed all in black, probably because it was easy, efficient. She'd call it boring. They'd mix like oil and water.

Grace pursed her lips. "Well, I wouldn't say *no* to a rich man."

Willodean's chuckle was contagious. "Smart girl. I could tell that about you, you know."

"Have anybody in mind, Willodean?"

She took Grace's hand and started pulling her toward Viva Las Vegas. "Sure, I have one prospect." As Willodean led her into the restaurant, Grace looked around. The crowd was very small, and there were only two men in the place. Tony sat at the end of the bar closest to the door and Charlie was as far away as he could get on a stool near the order window. Both men stared straight ahead at the mirror behind the bar. Being this close to the conversation about setting her up made connecting the dots way too easy. Grace tried to dig her heels in, but Willodean was suddenly unstoppable.

"There he is, my favorite person in the whole world." Willodean hugged Charlie's broad back and Grace tried to become invisible, certain she knew what was coming.

Charlie glanced over Willodean's head and managed to catch Grace's eye before he set down his sandwich and wrapped his arm around Willodean's shoulder. "What is it now, Mom? You know it's lunch time, right?"

Mom? Grace jerked and glanced around quickly, hoping she could find someone to confirm what she thought she'd heard. Charlie was Willodean's son? The one she'd lost and found?

And, if she was reading the conversation correctly

and she was frantically replaying it in her head to be sure she had followed all the trails, Charlie was also Willodean's first matchmaking attempt. For her, a confessed gold digger who couldn't stick in a place more than twelve months. A mother setting her son up with a fortune hunter. *Ex*-fortune hunter maybe, but still. Had Willodean lost her mind?

Chapter Four

As Charlie steeled himself for whatever the next request from his mother might be, he glanced over her head to watch Grace. She looked like she'd just been goosed with an electric prod for some reason. Maybe she hadn't guessed Willodean was his mother. He had always been more exasperated than embarrassed by his mother and her ability to collect new friends and family like rusty pennies, but the distance between them made it easier to treat her more like a client sometimes than family. Hotel employees never let him forget he was the boss's son, but Grace wouldn't have any clue.

And he didn't know why it would matter. She'd been perfectly polite to him—with the exception of invading his space now and then and making him think words like "magic" unexpectedly—just like every other hotel employee. Well, every employee except Tony, who didn't think he did enough for his mother, didn't like him, and didn't hide it.

And wasn't that just one more reason to spend as little time as he could here? If his own guilty conscience didn't beat him up, Tony would be happy to do it. When he remembered how his mother's heart had broken over her divorce and his own part in it, he wondered if maybe he shouldn't just let Tony throw the first punch. He'd tried staying away, but that hadn't made anything easier. And being back . . . between his mother's determined happiness and Tony's killing stare, he had too many reminders of his mistakes. All he could do was make amends the best way he knew how: making his mother happy today.

"I'm in a good mood, Mom. I just had the best meat loaf sandwich in the history of sandwiches. Hit me with whatever it is." Charlie watched Grace gather her composure and straighten her shoulders. She'd learned somewhere never to let others see her sweat.

"Grace is going to need some help with inventorying what furniture we've got for the conference area. Since you'll be punching the numbers and crunching the calculator to come up with a budget, I thought maybe you could help her out in the morning." His mother's face was perfectly innocent as she waited for his answer. That alone was enough to raise an alarm. "That way you'll have a very good picture of *exactly* what Grace needs."

A day of moving furniture. The idea filled him with only low-level irritation. And it would please his mother. He didn't want to take too close a look at why his pulse sped up at the idea of spending the day with Grace. He also didn't want to point out how many other hotel employees could help her as well as he could. And that reminded him of why he'd wanted to put her in a cab the day before. She was dangerous.

"Well, when you put it like that, perfectly tailored to get my cooperation, how can I say no?" Obviously his mother was up to something. Instead of the small crease of worry on her forehead and a smile that didn't quite reach her eyes, she wore a guileless look complete with fluttering eyelashes. Somehow she'd forgotten he wasn't one of her usual marks. That didn't mean he didn't find it cute. And he felt a little of his stuck-in-Memphis blues ease. His mother had always been good at that, lightening things up. It was no wonder everyone loved her.

Willodean waggled her eyebrows. "Years of experience, my boy. Someday, you too will be able to work magic like mine."

"Only if I'm lucky, Mom." For the first time in a long time, Charlie felt easy around his mother, like they used to be before . . . well, before he'd had to be proven right above all else. Then instead of apologizing for a too-blunt assessment of his second stepfather, Travis Luttrell, he'd stormed off, headed as far away as he could get from Memphis, the hotel, and his mother. That had led him home, even if it was six hours away.

Staying at the hotel instead of going home would probably never be his first choice, but if he could repair things with his mother and get rid of some of his guilt, it would be worth a little inconvenience and the low-level stress city life caused him now. He'd gotten used to his renovated farmhouse on his grandfather's land. He'd rebuilt it. And it was as different from the Rock'n'Rolla Hotel as night was from day. He didn't even allow an Elvis song on the radio. The clutter and noise and chatter that followed Willodean Jackson made him a little homesick for peace and quiet.

"Hon, did you need to grab some lunch before you head out?" Charlie glanced from his mother to her newest project. Somehow, the idea that Grace had been adopted into the family as easily as she had been wasn't causing him the heartburn it had with others, especially Tony.

Grace shook her head. "Nope. I like to keep to a tight schedule." Crickets would never be heard inside Viva Las Vegas. The music was too loud, but the three of them were quiet for a long minute. Willodean tried to look innocent again and failed. Charlie shot them both suspicious looks but didn't say anything. Nothing about Grace had struck him as rigidly punctual. In fact, that sounded more like something his mother would say about him. Had they discussed him and his schedule? "Where are you headed to? Got a hot date?" As soon as the words left his mouth, he regretted it. His mother's eyes lit up like the she'd just hit the jackpot.

And the light bulb went off. He was being set up with the newest hotel employee. Maybe she wasn't his type, but it looked like he was going to have a chance to verify his opinion one on one. Why didn't he hate the idea? He had a plan already, and he'd never plan for someone like Grace. His mother was wasting her time. And Grace's. He was willing to give up a little of his own time, though. He tilted his head back to study the dark ceiling of the restaurant while "Hound Dog" played in the background.

"I'm headed out to pick up a few groceries. Save money, you know?" Grace cleared her throat and added, "Are you sure you don't mind me borrowing your car?"

Reminded again in a flash of how his mother trusted too easily, Charlie's head snapped up. His immediate response was an angry "no" headshake but he stopped when his mother stepped on his foot. "Borrow the car? What a stupid idea. Round-trip cab fare would cost less than a new car, Mom. What if she decides this is a shot to get back to Vegas now instead of in a month?" He glanced down at his mother's green sequined tennis shoe, planted firmly on top of his boot. He bit back the offer to take Grace to the airport and buy her a ticket himself.

His mother patted his arm. "Grace didn't come prepared to stay, so she needs things." She raised an eyebrow. "If you're so worried, I guess you could take her if you'd rather. That would be very neighborly."

Charlie felt the offer to take her wherever she needed to go poised on the tip of his tongue. One look at his mother's face said she expected him to react as he always did, with suspicion and a hard no. And Grace seemed to be waiting for his answer too, her arms crossed over her chest and a brow raised in curiosity. Charlie decided he wanted to surprise them both but not enough to go to Wal-Mart on a Saturday three weeks before Christmas when the weatherman was making a very unlikely snow forecast. That had hell written all over it. So he shrugged his shoulders.

"Guess that's what we have insurance for." He slid back on the stool and watched the two women glance at each other like they couldn't believe he'd given in that easily. He picked up his tea glass and took a satisfying drink. It was nice to do something different than what was expected of him.

His mother waved her hand. "Are you sure you don't need to go? Maybe you forgot something?" She looked meaningfully into his eyes and pointed her chin toward Grace.

Now was the time to be strong. "Not my kind of fun, Mom. Why aren't you going?"

His mother huffed a sigh. "Arlene and I already made plans with Holly for this afternoon. We're going over to the movie theater to see something Laura won't take her to see. I think there are vampires." She shrugged her shoulders. "At least there'll be popcorn."

Charlie chanced a direct glance at Grace to see that she'd crossed her arms tightly over her chest. And her chin was raised in challenge. He didn't apologize, but he thought about it. Seemed like a good idea to wait and see if she actually brought the car back first.

"All right, kid, I guess you're on your own. Meet me at the front desk to pick up the keys. Got a nice long Caddy, perfect for hauling groceries. Plus, without someone along, you can take your time." Willodean shook her head at Charlie like he was a real disappointment, but it didn't reach her eyes.

For a long time, all he'd seen when she looked at him was worry. So what if it took a very obvious attempt at matchmaking to make her light up again? He smiled over his mother's head at Grace. "Good luck."

Grace said, "Give me fifteen minutes." She held up her bare wrist. "Shall we synchronize our watches?" She winked at him as his mother chortled. Then Grace left the restaurant at a near run, her hair swishing back and forth and the squeak of her sneakers keeping time.

"I guess tomorrow I'll be moving furniture, although I would think you'd have plenty of staff on hand who could help. Or we could hire temps. Or if there's so little of it, maybe Grace could actually do it on her own." He watched his mother's face closely. "Loaning her your car, Mom? You'll be lucky if she isn't back in Las Vegas by this time tomorrow and we're headed to the dealership to buy another fully loaded top-of-the-line luxury sedan in your signature color." He slid off the stool. "And we don't even know her, but you're trying to set me up with a girl who's just been left at the altar. I guess I understand helping her, even if I wish you'd be more careful. But throwing us together? Want to tell me why?"

"Well, I think . . ." Willodean fluffed her hair. "Just trust me. I have a nose for these things. Last time we talked about how you need to get married, you told me you were thinking along those lines so—"

"You mean the last time you told me I *should be* and I didn't disagree, right? That time?"

One corner of his mother's mouth tilted up. "Maybe it was that time, yes. But I think . . . no, I *know* you were impressed with her. Against your judgment and normal safety rules, you introduced us. And I like her, Charlie. She reminds me a little of myself."

The crashing realization that she was absolutely right,

that Grace did seem a little like his mother, hit him. He ought to pack up his stuff and leave, no matter what his mother thought of it. The very last thing he needed was to fall for a girl that he was bound to upset and disappoint like his mother.

"That might be the best warning you could give me, Mom." As he watched her face fall, he knew she'd misunderstood him again. She thought he meant there was something wrong with her or Grace, but what he really thought was that he couldn't spend his life with not one but two women who he'd never fully understand and fail over and over again to please. But before he could figure out what to say, she hugged his neck and stepped back before stretching up to kiss his cheek.

"I'm glad you'll be here this week. This place feels absolutely perfect when you're here." She patted his arm and left the restaurant. Charlie propped his hands on his hips for a minute to think. Then he waved through the order window at the chef and followed his mother out.

At the door, Tony stopped him with a hand planted in his chest. Charlie glanced down at the hand and then at Tony's grim face while he calculated the odds of making it out of there with all his teeth if he shoved the hand away. Before he could decide whether the price was too high or just right, Tony stepped back. "McMinn, I just wanted to say . . . I'm glad you're here this week. Willodean misses you. I know she's thrilled."

Charlie tilted his head, uncertain if he'd been insulted or Tony was sincere. Maybe both.

Control. He had to hold on to it. He took two deep breaths. "Believe it or not, Tony, I want to please her."

Tony snorted. "Right. Well, you have a funny way of showing it."

"You mean, by investing her money, making sure she has enough to do anything she wants with this place she loves so much, giving up my time to perform weddings wearing a ridiculous gold lamé jacket and enough goop in my hair to stop traffic? Those *are* funny ways."

Charlie was ready to take his chances with the ex-Marine when Tony held up a hand. His lips were twitching like he wanted to laugh. And Charlie could understand why. It wasn't every day a man had to say a sentence like that.

"Listen . . . I know we don't get along but"—Tony scrubbed a hand over his military cut—"your mom . . . well, she changed my life. I only want the best for her. And I know she misses you, so this holiday time is nice. That's all I wanted to say." His face was sincere, and Charlie remembered all the times he'd been thankful Tony was here protecting the hotel and his mother. Maybe he hated how easily she picked up strays, but he had to admit he hadn't worried about her safety anymore after he met Tony. He was guard-dog protective.

Charlie rubbed his forehead. "Well, hell. I guess we're going to have to get in touch with our feelings." Tony crossed his arms over his chest. "My mom and I . . . well, we have some things to work out, mainly stupid things I did, and you have every right to think I'm a jerk. I want to change it, but I'm not sure I know how. And . . . I don't know. Growing up with this"—he waved his hands around the restaurant—"wasn't all it's cracked up to be. Making a choice to live here's one thing. I didn't have one and now I do. I choose something else. That doesn't mean I don't love my mother or want her to be happy." Tony considered him closely, and Charlie did his best not to fidget. Then Tony nodded once. "That's all true. There's more to it, though."

Maybe there was but Charlie wasn't going to examine his feelings any more.

"Think about treating her like a woman who knows what she's doing instead of trying to protect her from threats that might not even exist. That's my advice. It's not easy, but it's worth learning." Tony rubbed his forehead like he was as uncomfortable with giving advice as Charlie was at hearing it from him.

Just then Grace raced past the doorway. Tony glanced out at the lobby and then back at Charlie. "Here's the thing, McMinn. Willodean's easy. If you want to fix whatever it is, just do it." He shrugged. "I'll help if I can. I owe her my whole life and my future. Whatever I can do, I will." He held out his hand.

Charlie shook Tony's hand and did his best not to get into a death-grip showdown. "I might take you up on that, Tony."

Tony nodded once and then turned on a precise right angle and left the restaurant. Charlie followed him to the front desk. Grace smiled at Tony as he passed her and then looked back at Charlie with the familiar challenge in the tilt of her chin. He didn't like the smile. He didn't like the idea that Grace might prefer Tony to him. He didn't like the jealous burn he got thinking that, along with his mother, the rest of the world preferred Tony Ortega. Why wouldn't they? He was a hero after all. Charlie just signed the checks.

So he acted like a jerk. "He's taken, okay? And she's nobody you want to mess with."

When she saluted wordlessly, it was easy to see he'd overreacted. He had a feeling jealousy might be a common problem with Grace around. Another good reason to stay away from her, but he didn't want another Rock'n'Rolla Hotel employee treating him like the boss from hell either. Charlie rolled his head on his shoulders. "I didn't mean to snap at you for being friendly. I apologize."

Grace pursed her lips and nodded. "Well, all right."

"Just like that?"

Grace shrugged. "Just like that. You overreacted. You apologized. I accept. We go on. What else is there to do?"

"Storm off in a huff. Throw things. Yell. Cry. Yell and cry. Seems like there are a lot of options."

"Know a lot of drama queens, do you? They hold a lot of grudges?"

Charlie laughed and realized with a bolt of revelation followed by a wave of disgust that he might be the drama queen. He was definitely the one who held grudges. "No, not too many."

When she smiled at him, he couldn't see any wariness or disappointment or anger. Just like that, she'd really let it go. Amazing. First he'd received potentially good advice from Tony and a very small peace offering. And now maybe he should take a lesson from Grace.

"Well now, here you go, Grace." Willodean held out the key ring. "It's the nice green Caddy in the front spot there by the door. Matches my ring. Just leave the keys with whoever's here at the desk when you get back and have Sam help you with your bags, okay?"

Grace took the keys and nodded. "Thank you, Willodean. I'll be very careful with her and make sure I get her back without a single—"

"Sure you will! I'm not worried in the least. Better get a move on."

"See you in the morning, Charlie. Come ready to work." Looking very satisfied with her parting shot, Grace spun on one squeaky shoe and sailed through the lobby doors.

Charlie watched her until she turned the corner and then looked down to see his mother very interested in his reaction. "She forgot her coat," Charlie said.

Willodean shook her head. "Nah, she doesn't have one."

The insane urge to chase her down and give her his flashed across his mind before he told himself she was driving the finest Detroit had to offer. If she got cold, she could turn on the seat warmers. "Guess I better answer some e-mail if I'm going to spend all day tomorrow on inventory."

As he settled behind his mother's desk and pulled up his e-mail, he had to convince himself he was just bored, not dissatisfied at being stuck in the hotel instead of grocery shopping in a big box pre-Christmas madhouse.

With Grace. Just another odd feeling he could blame on the Rock'n'Rolla Hotel.

GRACE SIGHED WITH relief as she pulled into a front-door spot in the crowded parking lot. The whole way there she'd been praying under her breath for a safe, accident-free journey while she tried to follow her phone's map. More than once she'd been honked at for spending too much time at the traffic light, and she'd had to circle back a couple of times when she missed a turn. She'd seen parts of Memphis that she'd never expected to see, and this city under the threat of both Christmas and snow was not a friendly driving place. While she was praying and navigating a car that cost more than the three cars she'd owned in her life combined and had more buttons than anything other than mission control should, she tried to figure out just what she was going to do when she made it to the store.

The answer depended on her making just one decision. Was she headed back to Vegas as soon as possible? If so, she only needed basics: groceries, jeans, a jacket, maybe a cheap T-shirt. But if she wanted to stay a bit, try to make this work . . . she needed to add to the list, spend what she had. Go for broke. Again.

Taking another, even bigger risk on Memphis was scary.

But she'd never been one to look back. Going back to Vegas seemed like a step in the wrong direction. If she really trusted the journey, she needed to face forward. Right?

Giving up her tiny, clean, safe apartment and the opportunity to do a job that would challenge her for sleeping on someone's couch and serving drinks to strung-out gamblers made no sense. Not anymore. Maybe it was actually knowing someone who'd lend her a *car* if she needed it that was the tipping point. Willodean Jackson was a good person to call friend. Or employer. Or whatever.

As Grace pulled a buggy from the short line near the door, she was nearly run over by a harried store employee pushing a load of precious supplies down the wide, crowded aisle. Grace stopped to catch her breath and run through the mental shopping list she'd made while she considered her budget. She'd never been all that great at saving for rainy days, mainly because she needed everything she had to make it through the day she was in, no matter what the weather was.

"Well, I guess we all know how this is going to go." When the greeter shot her a suspicious look, Grace smiled at him, straightened her shoulders, and swept a meandering path through the destroyed store. She'd forgotten how the chance of snow made most people rush grocery stores. This one looked like it had barely escaped a zombie apocalypse. There was one mangled loaf of bread on the shelf and the only milk left was buttermilk. No matter how hungry she was, she didn't do buttermilk.

"Guess I'll put milk on the list for next week then."

Because she had the afternoon and nothing else to fill her time, she tried on several outfits, thumbed through a whole stack of magazines she couldn't afford to buy, and filled up on the samples offered in the frozen foods section. And each step she took behind the buggy with the wonky wheel felt better. She was surer that going forward, taking a chance on Memphis and Willodean Jackson and the Rock'n'Rolla Hotel was the right thing to do.

She'd just have to work hard while she was here and prove to Charlie that unemployed and broke didn't really mean untrustworthy.

Why it mattered what Charlie thought was something she didn't spend much time thinking about.

When she'd filled the buggy with a few clothes, most of them clearance finds, and some basic groceries to get her through the week, she waited in the endless line and then watched fearfully as the total on the register grew. Her mother's lifetime of frugal spending, coupon cutting, and searching for the very best deals served her well. She ran her card through and held her breath until the transaction was approved. Apparently she'd guessed how much credit she had left correctly.

"Y'all be careful out there in the snow, now."

Grace smiled at the woman behind the cash register and took her receipt. "Think we'll actually see any?"

The woman pursed her lips and fluffed her hair. "Doubt it. Too early even if it has been cold this year. But—" she shrugged, "I wouldn't mind a flake or two. It's nice to change things up a little."

Grace smiled at her and gave the buggy a shove to get it moving. Cans of beans and instant noodles seemed heavy all of a sudden. When she stepped out on the sidewalk and the automatic doors slid shut behind her, Grace looked left and right at the snarl of the parking lot. After dodging two drivers determined to park on the sidewalk, she pushed the buggy next to the Cadillac's trunk and unloaded her bags.

She rummaged in the bags and pulled out the huge, overstuffed men's jacket she'd found on clearance. Clearance coats in December. That was something to be thankful for. She'd figured it would be all swimsuits. And if it was blaze orange and looked like it should come with a rifle and binoculars as accessories, she wasn't going to complain. Cheap warmth had been her goal. And she'd met it.

Before she had the last bag out of the buggy, a man had one hand on its handle.

"Through with this?"

Grace nodded and managed to leap out of the way before he ran over her toes. Shaking her head, she hopped back in the driver's seat, flipped on the seat warmer, and turned on the radio. She'd driven over in complete silence, certain any music would ruin her concentration. But after the retail therapy and her decision to move forward instead of going back to Vegas, she was in the mood to sing. The streets were empty now that the sun was setting. She made it safely back to Willodean's parking spot, popped the trunk, wrapped both hands in the plastic bag handles, and heaved the bags out.

She was contemplating how to get the trunk shut again when Charlie reached out to take all the bags in her right hand. "Let me help."

She stifled the frightened squeak and had to catch her

breath before she could say, "You scared me. Don't sneak up on a person like that, Charlie."

He reached up and slammed the trunk shut. "You might have heard me if you hadn't been humming 'Jingle Bells' like a good little elf." While she was distracted by how her pulse raced when he was this close, he took all the bags in her left hand. She didn't know how long she stood there, just looking at Charlie, but eventually he shook the bags and raised an impatient eyebrow.

"Uh, I can get those." She reached out to take at least some of them back, but Charlie shook his head and started for the lobby door. "Were you watching for me? Well, I guess watching for the car. Have you called the police to report it stolen yet?" It burned. She wanted to let him know how much.

Charlie didn't answer her as they walked through the lobby. Grace waved at Tony at the front desk and was very interested to see that Charlie didn't even acknowledge his presence. When they made it outside to the Christmas wonderland built around the pool area, Charlie finally said, "I was a little worried. It's getting dark. You don't know Memphis. You've been gone a long time."

"You mean the car's been gone a long time." Grace held open the gate to the staff apartments. After Charlie walked through, she closed the gate with a clang and said, "I enjoyed the trip, Charlie. You might try it sometime. Got a little lost, but then I did exactly as I pleased. I bet you march in, grab the single item on your list, and stride out like a conqueror, don't you?"

Charlie's lips quirked up but he didn't confirm or deny her guess.

She was determined to make conversation. Maybe not about what his problem with her really was, but about something. "Think it'll snow? Most everybody in Memphis had already been down the bread aisle before me." He just shook his head. "That's too bad. I wouldn't mind seeing some flakes while I'm here. Snow was hard to come by in Las Vegas, Los Angeles, and Miami, and it was summer when I was in New York." She could keep talking indefinitely. He'd buckle soon enough.

She opened her door and smiled a little at Charlie's gusty sigh.

"Listen, about the car, it's just . . . my mother has a long history of taking crazy gambles on people. When I was in high school, she loaned her car keys to one of the waitresses and we never saw that car again. Most of the time, they pay off, but I feel like . . . it's part of my job to keep her safe. To do that, it seems like I expect the worst of people. And . . . I shouldn't. I'm sorry." He dumped all the bags on the counter and propped his hands on his hips. "Can we just start over?" He rolled his eyes. "Start over again?"

Grace crammed both hands in the deep pockets of her new coat. "Sure. I understand that. It's smart, Charlie. She's lucky to have someone to look out for her."

Their eyes met in the quiet, and Grace could feel that tug again, like there was something invisible that tied them together. He looked so serious dressed all in black, but there was something in his dark eyes that shifted then. And they both smiled.

"Couldn't you find a brighter coat?" His lip quirked.

Grace tilted her head. "This one met both important criteria. It was warm and cheap."

He nodded. "And you'll also never outgrow it. You can rent out room if the snowstorm comes."

Grace rolled up the sleeves so that she could use both hands. "Just think how cozy that would be . . . the two of us and my puffy orange coat." After the words left her mouth, she actually thought about being pressed tightly against Charlie's broad chest, his arms wrapped around her. And then she wished she'd taken off the coat. Suddenly, she was overheated, a little afraid there was sweat on her forehead. She fiddled with the zipper.

This time the silence was tense, charged, and it was all Grace could do not to look at the bed. Neither of them moved until Charlie cleared his throat. "Well, I guess I should let you . . . do whatever." He inched around her and paused at the door. "See you in the morning, Grace."

After the door closed behind him, Grace shrugged out of her coat and flopped across the bed. She should really get up, put away the groceries, and figure out just what she needed to do to prepare for her first day on the all-important new job. But for just a minute she wanted to think about how much she'd enjoyed her afternoon. And she wanted to consider the problem of Charlie.

She'd never felt this instant connection. If he were just a normal guy, she'd be ecstatic and scared to death at the same time. Her whole life had been spent looking for something, the chance to be someone special. With a connection like that, she'd be someone special to at least one person and that just might be enough. But not Charlie. He was rigid, suspicious, and had a right to be. He was also the boss's son. Even if the boss seemed to be just fine with shoving them together, Grace couldn't ignore the worry about what would happen when it fell apart. Would she lose her job? Her place here at the Rock'n'Rolla Hotel? That seemed like too much to risk, even on an instant connection.

Worrying about such a thing was a sign that things were different about this place and this job. She'd never worried much about the future, expecting it to take care of itself.

She rubbed her forehead and tried to tell herself they only had to work together for a little while on Monday. She'd get there early, come up with a plan, and get him on his way as quickly as possible. Besides, Charlie would never pursue any attraction he might have for her, if he *was* attracted. He was smart. He'd know better than to get caught up with a girl like her. Then she remembered he didn't know the whole story yet. When he found out she'd been there to catch a rich husband, he'd make tracks faster than a runaway train.

And that was a good thing. Grace slid off the bed to put away her groceries and did her best to ignore both the anxious dread and the sizzle of anticipation in her stomach. She'd spend some time with Charlie, enjoy it without getting too caught up, and then tell Willodean to hit her with her next match.

Chapter Five

WHEN CHARLIE WALKED off the elevator on the second floor Monday morning and paused outside of Grace's new office, he was surprised to realize that he had both pep in his step and a swarm of butterflies in his stomach. He couldn't pretend even to himself that they had any other cause but Grace. That could turn out to be a problem. No matter how often he told himself he ought to be looking for a way to get her out of the hotel, he couldn't convince himself to do it. Maybe he felt this instant connection to Grace, but that didn't make her the right kind of woman for him. She was too . . . bright. Unpredictable. It didn't surprise him that his mother liked her. He'd help out, make his mother happy, and then escape to refocus his attention on his work, his plan, and the two perfectly suitable women he was having dinner with this week.

He was disappointed to find Grace's office empty, but he didn't give up. He followed the faint singing he could hear down the hallway. He had to smile at how happy she sounded, her voice smooth and warm, just husky enough to make him think of holding her close while she whispered in his ear. Maybe her singing wasn't perfect, but he had a feeling he'd never get bored hearing it.

He paused in the doorway to a large, nearly empty storage room and watched Grace's hips as she danced to what had to be an Elvis song. Her sneakers squeaked on the concrete floor as she did a more exciting version of the Twist than he'd ever seen.

Of course she was an Elvis fan. Perfect.

Finally he had to get her attention, no matter how much liked watching her shake her . . .

" 'Jailhouse Rock'?"

She spun around at his question, one hand covering her heart like he'd startled her and the other yanking out one ear bud.

He wrinkled his nose at her. "Is that what you're singing?"

Her blush was pretty cute. "How long have you been standing there?" She smoothed her hair back. "Never mind. Long enough, right?"

She rolled her eyes. "I guess I didn't die of embarrassment so it's fine. Besides, it's good music, Charlie. You can't help but move."

He snorted.

"Oh, you can't dance?" She pouted and blinked. "So sad. And you had everything you needed to make it as an impersonator—mainly very good hair."

"I can dance. I can even sing. But I've spent too many

Halloweens dressed as the King already. I was nine before I could convince Willodean to let me skip the jumpsuit."

Grace groaned. "Oh, man. It's no surprise you don't love him as much as she does."

Charlie watched her foot tap. "I didn't know you were a fan."

She waved an iPod. "Willodean suggested I study the music and movies. Laura's daughter was nice enough to loan me both." She snapped her fingers with the song only she could hear. "I've enjoyed it this morning." She sniffed. "But in light of your recent confession, I can turn it off, wait until I'm alone to dance around."

He thought about telling her he wouldn't mind watching her dance around as long as she wanted. She was good, especially when she thought she was alone. Fearless. Free. Happy. And so sexy.

He'd never be able to keep up. Why did he want to? This was the thinking that was going to get him in trouble so he just said, "Thanks."

Grace had dressed for the season in a neon green sweatshirt with a red-nosed reindeer on front. "My mother would love your sweatshirt."

Grace looked down. "Well, I got it on clearance, but it seemed fitting." She tugged at the hem. "You don't think Willodean would mind that I'm so casual today, do you? I thought with moving furniture and . . ." She looked uncertain. He realized he hadn't ever seen her look less than sure of herself.

He shook his head. "Of course not. Besides, green is her signature color. She wears it every day. She'd be a fan."

"Green? Every day?" Grace tilted her head like she'd never considered such a thing. He could understand that. It was one of his mother's more eccentric choices. "And I guess yours is black?"

Charlie looked down at his black boots, black jeans, and black and grey flannel shirt and had to laugh. Maybe he made a few eccentric choices of his own. "Well, maybe. I hadn't put much thought into it, just went for comfort and convenience." He looked up and smiled at her. "But I'm thinking black might have become my signature color."

Grace shook her head. "Weird. I can't imagine giving up on all the other colors. I'd never be able to pick just one."

With that conversational topic exhausted, the silence in the nearly empty room stretched uncomfortably tight. Finally, Grace leaned down to pick up a notebook. "I've started a list. Looks like it's just basics right now—chairs, tables, linens. I'm not sure why Willodean thought I'd need your help." She pointed at a small closet. "Maybe to go through her memorabilia here. Some of it might be valuable. Guess it needs to be accounted for. Good thing you were available this morning, huh? Who knows what might have mysteriously disappeared otherwise?" She fluttered her eyelashes innocently.

She wasn't going to let his original judgment go easily. Charlie had a pretty good idea then that no matter what face she'd put on it, she'd been mad. He didn't really blame her either.

At her well-deserved zing, Charlie shook his head.

"There's no way my mother had anything like that in mind. She was looking for a reason to throw us together." He walked over to open the door and flipped on the light. At one glance he could see movie posters, more album cover artwork, a few Elvis statues, gold vases, and he had the old familiar feeling. His mother's collection was unavoidable. He should just get used to it.

When Grace didn't answer, he looked over his shoulder to see she'd crossed her arms over her chest tightly, like she was preparing for the worst.

"Sorry. Did you not know that already? My mother is the world's most dedicated matchmaker. She's been telling me to find a nice girl since before I started shaving." He took her list to read everything she'd already itemized. "To get off the hook, just tell her you're still brokenhearted over being abandoned by . . . what was his name?"

"Tommy Joe Huffle, car salesman extraordinaire." Grace shook her head. "She'll never buy it."

She was right. Willodean wouldn't buy it. He didn't buy it either. There was something strange going on. First of all, he hadn't seen a single tear. Maybe she was tough. He was starting to think so, even if she looked like she needed a hug this morning. But heartbreak was hard to hide. He guessed. It had been so long since his heart was in any danger that he couldn't speak from personal experience.

"She is pretty smart." Charlie looked down her list and saw she'd started numbering everything in the closet. "What time did you start?" He took a closer look and could see one side of the closet was neatly organized. The other side, the one that was a jumble of mismatched piles, looked like his mother had been in charge.

Grace shrugged and then started putting the chairs in stacks of ten. "About six. I picked up a key last night when I dropped off her keys at the front desk. And I couldn't sleep."

Charlie handed her the list. "Here. Let me stack. You count." He dragged the first stack over next to the wall. "Getting used to a new place is hard, I guess, even if you have lots of practice."

Charlie worked quickly through the furniture, arranging in even stacks and rows to make the inventory easier. It felt good to be working instead of staring at a computer screen or ignoring Tony's frowns.

Grace followed his progress, marking inventory on the list. "I think I was too excited to get started. I have a lot of ideas."

Charlie picked up two chairs and added them to the last stack. "Like what?"

She tapped a box holding a small Christmas tree. "Company parties. We could get an Elvis to play music, make it as kitschy fun or as old-school classic as desired. For the month of December, we could easily host parties during the week even if we had conferences scheduled at the same time."

"Have it catered through Viva Las Vegas?" He nodded his head. "It's not a bad idea. Just a whole lot of logistics to figure out." He raised an eyebrow. "You don't really strike me as the logistics sort. Am I wrong?"

"I'm not sure. I guess we'll see." Grace shrugged a shoulder. "If I need help, I'm sure Tony will have ideas."

Charlie closed his eyes and tried to will away the flash of anger that bubbled up. The idea that Tony would be her answer man, just like he was his mother's, made him mad enough to curse out loud. He managed to say tightly, "Oh, sure. Tony." Then he shoved another stack of chairs over.

"What is your deal with Tony? The two of you look at each other like you'd like to bare-knuckle brawl amid the palm fronds of the hotel lobby." Grace shook her head. "And the lobby would never be the same, I'm sure of that."

Then she leaned against the next stack of chairs and waited for his answer.

"We just . . . have some history, that's all." That wasn't even really true. Tony had hated him on sight, and Charlie had been going through enough guilt and regret at the time that he'd done very little to address it. The bad blood between them wasn't so much personal as tied to how they both felt about Willodean Jackson. "He thinks I should do more at the hotel, help out more."

Grace tilted her head from side to side. "Hm, is he right?" She patted the top chair on the stack. "I mean, you're moving furniture around. Seems like there'd be someone else on staff who could help if I needed it."

Charlie rubbed his forehead. "He might be right. Or he might have been right in the past. But I've made some changes. He just . . . he's good at holding grudges." He snorted. "And so am I."

Grace nodded. "Maybe you don't like how Willodean

leans on him. Almost like a son. It makes some sense that you'd want a little distance. Growing up around here couldn't have been easy. When you're a kid, all you want is to be the center of the world. Having Willodean for a mother would have made that hard and a place like this would take a lot of attention."

She planted both sneakers on the concrete floor and did her best to shove over a stack of chairs to make room for another. He ran his hand down her back while he bumped her with his hip to get her to step aside. "Let me get that." She glanced at him quickly before stumbling away, leaving only the hints of shampoo and warmth that lingered down his side. He shoved, and they both winced at the screech.

Brushing his hands like he'd just labored all day, Charlie tried to figure out a way to change the subject. The way that she just put her finger right on an old sore spot made him uneasy. Like it might be a reminder of the weird connection between them.

"You sound like you know what you're talking about."

Grace pointed at herself. "Youngest of seven. It was hard to stand out." When she wrinkled her nose at him, he couldn't ignore how cute she was. Or how nice it was to just talk with her like this, like the way he felt was okay because she'd been there too. "I had a bad habit of standing in front of the television to sing or dance or tell knock-knock jokes. I took every dare my brothers ever made. And I always regretted it. My father did a lot of shouting."

Charlie wanted to wrap his arm around her shoulder

and squeeze her close. He could almost picture a little girl who needed a hug. "Even bad attention was worth it?"

"Did you try that too?"

Charlie shook his head. "Nah, I was too serious for that. My dad died when I was young and for a while, it was just the two of us. Somehow I got it in my head that I was taking care of her. Then she replaced me . . . I liked my stepfather a lot. He taught me enough to keep my mother in hotel funds forever, but it just wasn't the same. And with all that money came this hotel and even just everyday life was . . . crazy. Still, I was a very dutiful son. Did my best not to cause trouble." Until he'd ripped everything in two.

They finished stacking the furniture, and Charlie wrote down the quantities of chairs and tables on Grace's inventory sheet. A deep frown wrinkled her forehead, and he could almost hear her thinking.

"She told me that her first husband gave her her son, and her last one brought him back. What happened in the middle, Charlie?" She shoved strands of her shiny dark hair behind one ear. "Never mind. Forget I asked. I may be insanely curious about you and about Willodean, but I do not need to know that."

She moved to brush past him. And something about her honest question and her understanding made him want to tell her, but something else about her, maybe the same things, made it hard to tell the whole truth. There was no real way to admit breaking up his mother's marriage without sounding like a villain. So he didn't answer the question. Instead, he said, "When did you and my mother get so close?"

Grace shook her head. "It's the weirdest thing. Minutes after meeting her, she knew more about my past than anybody but me, Charlie. And then yesterday, before she loaned me her car keys"—she paused to glance at him—"she told me all about her husbands."

"All about them?" Charlie asked.

"Well, no, but enough. And I told her . . ."

Charlie crossed his arms over his chest and waited. At last they were coming down to it, whatever it was that made him suspicious. The part of Grace that made it an inconvenience to be left at the altar, not devastating.

Grace paced back and forth and shook her head. "This is a terrible idea. You didn't even know me and thought I was going to rob your mother blind and steal her car." She squeaked to a halt, wringing her hands in front of her. "But you need to know the truth. I don't understand why she's determined to push us together. No mother in her right mind would, but if I tell you everything, you *will* help. You'll make it easier to spend less time together. And the way I feel . . . A little help would be good."

He had no idea what she was talking about. Now he wasn't sure he wanted to know. Whatever it was would make it impossible for him to ignore his own warnings about staying away from her and that would mean the end to their connection. He didn't understand that connection, but he didn't really want to lose it either.

"My groom . . . Well, my marriage . . . I just wanted to marry a rich man, Charlie." She shrugged. "I think

I knew it was a horrible idea, but my mother's warning about how time flies and how sorry I'll be if I don't make better choices ... the kids she's telling me I'll never have suddenly seem like something I should at least think about, decide if that's what I want ... and then this dream I have of becoming some kind of star just isn't working ... So I gave it a shot. But Tommy Joe ... well, he was happy with a pretty, quiet girl. He didn't appreciate me standing my ground on things like separate hotel rooms or having good prenuptial agreements, and I guess he decided the price wasn't worth it. So here I am."

Charlie didn't really know how to respond. Hearing his worst suspicion confirmed should have filled him with righteous indignation. The kind of person he'd been warned about and had been trying to protect his mother against all his life had just sprung up before him. A real life gold digger stood in front of him wearing a tacky sweatshirt, cheap jeans, and yellow sneakers. It was hard to see a schemer in Grace's loose hair, flawless skin, and oversized clothes. But of course she would be beautiful. She would never be successful otherwise.

Instead of angry, he was disappointed. Normally he liked being right. This time, he wished he'd been wrong. He wanted to go back to before, to talk to the woman who seemed to understand things he'd never said aloud.

"Say something, Charlie."

He shrugged. "I don't know what to say. Either that's the cleverest tactic I've seen, disarming a man with the truth, or you're not very good at fortune hunting." He snorted. "Or maybe you just aren't interested in me, the only rich man around." He didn't know which to hope for.

When he heard the elevator ding, he glanced over his shoulder. His mother scrambled off, her arms filled with files, and called a cheery "Hello, little help here?"

Before he trotted off to help, he glanced at Grace. She hadn't moved. Her arms were crossed over her chest. She opened her mouth to say something, but he turned. "Coming, Mom. Why didn't you get someone to carry that for you?"

Willodean juggled the files before handing them over. "Well, I'm not infirm yet. Besides, I didn't know how much trouble I was in until I was rounding the pool. I was committed at that point." Once she'd handed all the files to Charlie, she smoothed her hands over her fine green cashmere sweater. "Looks like y'all have made some progress. Got a budget for me yet?"

Her twinkling smile faded a bit when Charlie just shook his head and walked away. He had no idea how to deal with either his mother and her matchmaking or Grace and her . . . let down. So he dropped the files on the desk. He had no answer for the question in his mother's eyes when she followed him into Grace's office, so he just said, "Uh, yeah, Grace has it all under control. I'm going to go . . . work on the budget. Good idea, Mom." He bent and kissed her cheek and made his escape to the elevator. There was no point in staying. His mother knew everything she needed to know, and she trusted Grace anyway. If he stayed, anger and irritation would probably replace disappointment and whatever emotion it was that made him feel like he'd run a marathon. Then he'd say something they'd all regret.

As the doors slid shut, he stared hard at the carpeted floor. He didn't want to get caught in Grace's stare again. He didn't want to feel the connection. He didn't want to know that she was the kind of person who'd take advantage of someone else, someone with money. So he'd do what he said, what he always did when things got out of control: he'd work. A budget would be a fine way to get his mind back on track.

GRACE DID HER best not to stare too obviously at the closing elevator doors. Instead, she followed Willodean into her office and plopped down in her chair. And as always, she did her best to pretend that everything was just fine. She tried a happy "Good morning, Willodean," but her bright smile wasn't returned. "I hope you don't mind the jeans. Since I was moving furniture, I thought—"

"Nope. Tell me what I just walked in on, Grace Andersen, and why Charlie couldn't get out of here fast enough." Willodean leaned her elbows on the desk, and they both watched the stack of file folders slide in a slow-motion waterfall across the desk. Grace started to pick them up but Willodean stopped her. "They weren't in much of an order to begin with so just leave them."

Grace rubbed her forehead and noticed a long stripe of something on her hand that she'd picked up while moving furniture. She rubbed at the greasy streak and pretended she was entirely too engrossed to answer.

"That might work if I'd never had a teenager," Willodean said. "You don't even know each other. What have you got to fight about?"

"We aren't fighting. He was a big help." Grace pulled the first file off the desk. It was only labeled with a dollar sign. Did that mean expenses? Bills?

"Oh, no you don't. The mad in that room was thick. Don't try to pretend that was friendly conversation."

"I don't know what you're talking about." Grace tried her usual bright smile again, the one that fooled everyone into thinking she was bubbling over with happy, but Willodean shook her head.

"You can't fool me, Grace. Better actors than you have tried."

Grace shrugged a shoulder. "I wanted everything out there, I guess, so I told him that Tommy Joe and I weren't a love match, that I'd picked him because he had money." Not that it was a secret. Tommy Joe knew just exactly what his attractions were, and he used them. There was no way Grace would have considered marrying him without that understanding.

Willodean nodded. "Yeah, that would send him off in a rush. Ever since he was a little boy, he's been out to protect me. Comes from losing his daddy so young, I guess. And then his stepfather, Mason, my second husband, made sure to warn him about all the risks a rich man might face. Gold diggers, hustlers, sob stories, and just plain ol' thieves." Willodean ticked them off on her fingers. "Would have been a good idea to point out that he himself was a rich man who'd learned to gamble on one of those risks by understanding people, but he neglected that part, probably so that Charlie could keep right on protecting me. But maybe for Charlie's good, too. Anyway, Charlie's been on the lookout for anyone who'd take advantage of me for a long time."

Grace leaned forward and covered her face with her hands. "What I don't get is why it matters. I did what I did. I can't change it. And I'd much rather have the truth out there. Why does it matter what Charlie thinks? I mean, I told him so he'd step back. Why does it feel so rotten that he did what I thought he would?"

"You young people," Willodean said as she shook her head. "I could just tell you right now what you should do, how you should do it, but no, you'll have to stumble around, make mistakes, until you end up right where I want you to go."

Grace leaned back. "What do you mean? I shouldn't have told him?"

Willodean's smile was crafty. "No, ma'am. You did exactly the right thing. And don't worry. I'll initiate Phase Two. All you have to do is get the whole 'convincing Charlie to step back' thing out of your head. He'll do plenty of that all on his own. We both want him moving forward."

"You don't get it, Willodean. I like Charlie. But I am not the right person for him. If I forget that, I could mess up whatever I build here." Grace shook her head. "I don't want to do that. For once, I *want* to think about the future."

"But you like him?" Willodean leaned back in her chair, an easy smile on her face.

Grace rolled her eyes. "Well, yes, I like him."

"Even though he was pretty sure you were going to steal whatever you could get your hands on." She raised an eyebrow like she doubted Grace's honesty.

"He was just trying to protect you. I can't blame him for that." Even worse, she couldn't help the pang of envy that hit when she thought about having someone whose self-imposed job was to look out for her. She'd been doing it for such a long time now. It would be nice to just have some help now and then.

"You like him even though he's too serious. He's way too committed to his schedule. Anytime he thinks you're making a mistake, he finds it impossible to let it go. He has to tell you all about that mistake and what you should be doing instead." Willodean added, "Worse, he doesn't even like this hotel. Any time he's here for more than a day, he barks like a caged dog. Between you and me, that says a lot about his judgment and none of it good."

Grace frowned. "Is this the way this conversation is supposed to go? No, you're supposed to realize *I'm* doing *you* a favor and decide to protect your son from me."

Willodean waved her hand. "Hon, he's a grown man. And he has been almost since the first grade, if you know what I mean. I don't have to protect him. You have noticed most of the people around here look at him like he's about to hand them a pink slip, right? He can't get along with Tony, who is such a sweetheart that I can't even understand that. Charlie's not what you'd call a people person, and he doesn't hesitate to do the hard stuff. He could have had you out of here Saturday without throwing his precious schedule out of whack if he'd wanted to."

Grace straightened in her seat. "All right, Willodean. I really think you ought to be a little more . . . supportive." She didn't like hearing her talk about Charlie like this. She was his mother. She should be his biggest fan. He should have been able to count on her to sing his praises. Instead, she was just pointing out his flaws. Or maybe not flaws, but his . . . quirks.

Willodean's smile was genuine, and the gleam in her eye was sharp. "Oh, really? You'd defend him? To me?"

"I can't believe I have to, but yes. And I'm starting to understand his problem with Tony a little better too. Maybe he doesn't like feeling second best when he isn't. I like Tony, but if you're blaming all of the problems on Charlie, you're just missing the point. If you all treated him better, you might be surprised. I mean, he's been a big help to me." That was sort of true. Maybe just because he wanted to keep an eye on her, but he had helped. And she regretted telling the truth all over again at the reminder that the only way he'd help her now would be right off the premises.

Willodean straightened in her seat. "You aren't implying that I am anything less than perfect, are you?"

Grace immediately felt the heat rush to her face. "Well, no, of course not. I'd never—"

Willodean snorted. "I'm messing with you. I am not perfect. I told you about losing my son. I've been looking for a way to fix what I broke for a long time. Charlie doesn't make it easy, but I think one thing you got to get a handle on is whatever it is that makes you feel like Charlie ought to be wary of you."

"He should. I mean, maybe not now that he knows what happened. I think I've proven very well that I don't have whatever it is to be good at marrying a man for his money. But we're still too different."

"But you aren't thinking he's too good, right? Because I'll tell you, I love him more than Elvis, this hotel, or breathing in and out, but he's not perfect either."

Grace shook her head. "Doesn't matter. I've changed my mind about matchmaking. I want to work a while, get my feet under me, and find out if this is what I want. If it is, I want a chance to settle in. And if it isn't, the fewer people I disappoint when I leave, the better. I don't need a man, not now."

Willodean tsked. "Course you don't *need* a man. Don't be silly. But wanting one . . . Grace, you can't deny wanting one. And when you find the one that you want more than a job, more than a comfortable apartment, maybe even more than your own pride . . . you'd be a fool to turn your back on that. And I don't think you're a fool."

Grace couldn't look away from Willodean's sparkling eyes. She was serious, obviously meant every word, and the breathing difficulty returned along with the hard knot in her stomach.

For the first time, Grace *could* imagine wanting someone that much.

Willodean pursed her lips and gave Grace a chance to catch her breath by changing the subject. "Well, then, let's take a look at everything I've got here. You'll see I kinda have my own way of doing things." Willodean patted the folders. "And that drives every one of the people who work with me nuts. The first week I hired Laura to help Tony as assistant manager, she brought me three new forms every day. The accountant stopped cursing every time I called him and Charlie gave Laura a warm hug when I introduced them. I get the feeling you might understand where they were coming from?" Willodean raised an eyebrow.

Determined to get back to normal, Grace straightened in her chair to sort through the stack. "If you've worked as many temp jobs as I have, you learn your way around a computer and a phone. Maybe I wanted to be a star, but I played a receptionist more than I got in front of a camera."

Willodean shook her head. "I swear, every person I hire around here's like the second coming of Bill Gates or something. PowerPoint this and Excel that. Whatever happened to a good ol' legal pad and a pen? I did a pretty good business with *paper*." Her eyes twinkled as she drew out the word.

"I guess things change." Grace could feel the tension across her shoulders as she said it.

Willodean sighed. "That's the truth right there and thank goodness they do, am I right? Life would be boring if it was always the same."

Grace had always thought the same thing. There was a beat of awareness that passed between them, like the philosophy they shared connected them.

"Now then, here's the most important part, the calendar. Got the weddings listed here"—she pointed to the next two Saturdays in December and flipped the page to show a few in January—"and the two fan club meetings I already lined up are written in blue." She looked pretty proud of herself. "Charlie's been working up some kind of computer system that will talk to the front desk." Willodean shook her head like it was all beyond her. "Hope you don't mind working with him just a little to learn the ropes."

Grace tried a stern lecture to herself, but she couldn't stop the blood from rushing to her face. That was ridiculous. She'd never been a blusher, but something about the idea of having to work with a disgusted Charlie and being attracted to him anyway made it difficult to keep an even keel.

"And just hearing his name causes a reaction like that," Willodean said with a small smile. "I've been there. When you're sitting across from a man who wakes you up, makes you think things you'd thought you'd forgotten a long time ago." She patted her sliding stack of files. "Thing is, I'm rooting for you. My Charlie, he's . . . difficult, but he's worth it all."

Grace thought about explaining to Willodean again how she *should* be doing her best to protect Charlie, but she was pretty sure Willodean wasn't going to change.

"If you're set here, I'll head on back to the hotel. Tomorrow or the next day, we can talk to Charlie about a budget for basic purchases. And then the fun part . . . shopping!" She clapped her hands together. "I love that part."

Grace laughed. "Me too. Shopping with someone else's checkbook is the best way."

Willodean winked. "Smart girl."

Grace wiped her sweaty hands on her jeans. "I guess we'll have to see about that."

"You believe in fate, Grace?" Willodean leaned against the door like she was too worn out to stand.

Grace stacked a few more files. "Maybe. I've always believed in the journey. Where I land is where I was meant to."

Willodean nodded. "Good for you." She pointed at the files on Grace's formerly clean desk. "Looks like I better get out of your hair. Someone made a mess of your desk." The twinkle was back in her eye as she waved and headed for the elevator.

Grace leaned back to rest her head on the chair. The quiet of the building was nice, even if it reminded her that she was on her own again. If only she hadn't been so determined to prove her worth this morning. Charlie would still be helping with inventory. And if she hadn't been so honest, he might have smiled and laughed with her as they worked. Now she didn't know if she'd see that smile—the one that said they were together against the world—again.

It shouldn't be so hard to let that go. She'd never had it before. But it was. Some of the excitement over the new job dimmed. And in her mother's voice, Grace heard, "That's why they call it work, Gracie. Just get started." *Good advice, Mom.*

She picked up Holly's iPod, pushed play on "Jailhouse Rock," and pulled the first file off the top of the stack.

"Weddings. A very good place to start." When she heard her own voice, she had to catch her breath. It was like she'd forgotten what brought her here, but every minute she spent at the Rock'n'Rolla Hotel convinced her that step had never been about Tommy Joe Huffle or settling down to please her mother or even about finding a rich man.

That wedding had been all about setting up this collision with Willodean, and it had indeed been a very good, if not quite practical or in any way normal, way to start. No matter what else happened, working with Willodean Jackson would be an adventure, maybe one big enough to keep her right where she was for a good long while. She had no idea where this path was going, not yet, but that didn't worry her. She had enough to focus on today.

Her cell phone buzzed to let her know she'd missed a call, so Grace pulled it out of her purse to check the display. When she saw her mother's name, she knew she'd have to call her and let her know about her newest job. But not right now. Right now, fixing the mess Willodean had left on her desk was more important. And easier. She'd start with that first.

Chapter Six

On Tuesday night, Charlie knocked on the door to his mother's suite, pretty sure he knew how dinner would go. He'd been lucky enough to have a reprieve, thanks to her crowded social calendar and all the plans she and Arlene Masters cooked up. But now there would be lots of questions about Grace and innuendo and then more questions until his mother was either satisfied that his romance was on track or he lost his temper and stormed next door to the waterfall room to keep from telling her what he really thought.

Tonight he was resolved to hold on to his tongue and his temper. They'd have a nice discussion. Some of it would be about Grace, but that was only natural. He'd just explain to his mother that he wished she'd had better judgment than to push them together even if she insisted on giving Grace a job at the hotel. Then he'd tell her about his plan and remind her of the dates he had lined up.

Maybe that would distract her enough that they would make it through this without raising their voices.

"Come on in, hon. The kitchen just brought up dinner so I think it's still good and hot."

He made a detour on the way to her small kitchen to run his hand down Misty's back. She was sprawled over the length of his mother's couch and greeted him warmly by lifting one eyelid while thumping her tail against the couch cushions. The green bows on her ears shook in time with the bells on her collar. "Don't get up, sis." Misty yawned, swiped her tongue over his hand, and closed the eyelid. "I thought you'd be slaving away, Mom."

His mother snorted. "Sure you did, just like I've slaved away every time you've eaten here. If I did anything but order up Sal's meat loaf, you'd think I didn't love you anymore." She bent and kissed the top of his head like he was six years old all over again. "And that's one thing we can't have. I will always love you."

Charlie considered her and then picked up his tea glass. "Well, it would be hard to get over the disappointment, but if you wanted to try to make that casserole you made when you and Howard invited me to dinner the first time, I would eat it. Very carefully."

They both laughed. "Yeah, I'm sure I made an impression with that tuna casserole, didn't I?"

"Seemed to work out just fine, even if it was burned around the edge and raw in the middle." He shook his head. "I couldn't figure out how you did that."

"It was all a part of a master plan to break the ice, didn't you know?" Willodean winked. "That's my story, and I'm sticking to it." She patted his hand. "Guess I'll never be Suzy Homemaker, will I? No matter how many years I've got."

Charlie pulled the plate cover off and sighed with happiness at the meat loaf, mashed potatoes, corn bread, and green beans in front of him. "Just because you can't cook doesn't mean you haven't made a nice home, Mom." He picked up his fork and took a bite. As he savored slowly, he noticed she didn't answer. She was watching him and blinked like she might have a tear or two.

"What? What did I do?" He had no idea. And this was the first sign that things might not work out like he hoped.

She shook her head and took a bite. He wasn't sure if it was the corn bread or something else that cheered her up, but when their eyes met again, he was relieved to see her usual happy twinkle.

"Dinner was an excellent idea." He sighed. "Hit me with it. Whatever it is. Advice, warnings, nosy questions. I can handle it now that I've got corn bread in front of me."

Willodean pointed her fork at him. "Your daddy was the same way. I learned quick to feed him first and then ask for what I wanted. That man never could smile on an empty stomach." She watched him carefully as she said, "You could have had mostly the same thing down in Viva Las Vegas. *And* there might have been a pretty girl to keep you company."

Charlie shook his head. "We need to talk about that. Grace is not the right girl for me. And you know exactly why. I can't believe you tried pushing us together. Maybe your skills are slipping." He took a drink of the sweet tea and thumped the glass down on the table to punctuate his point. "You really ought to know better than that, Mom."

"Oh, really?" she said as if she couldn't believe her ears. "Know better, should I?" She narrowed her eyes at him. "First, watch what you're saying, Charlie Aaron McMinn. I have a feeling you're going to want to eat those words and soon. And second, you better tell me right now just what makes that pretty girl so unsuitable."

Charlie leaned back in his chair. It was about to get real. "Two words. Gold. Digger. What are you thinking?"

"You just never learn, do you?" She shook her head. "I like her a lot, so I wonder if I'm doing *her* a disservice. At least, I did warn her. Keeping your dates is a good idea, even if I have the feeling they'll look more like job interviews. Might give you a little perspective. I bet they're just female Charlies, but if that makes you happy, then that's enough for me."

Her narrowed eyes and pursed lips told a different story. Still, he was surprised to hear his romantic mother even pretend that she thought he might be able to choose better for himself than she ever would. Unfortunately, now the idea of sitting across from a perfectly suitable-on-paper woman for an inoffensive dinner filled him with dread and the slight simmer of annoyance.

Charlie rubbed his face with his hands.

"Just two days ago, you were excited about those dates. What changed?"

He could ask himself the same question. Now he

looked forward to those dates like he would an audit. While he'd worked at Willodean's desk on the budget, he'd pulled out his phone at least three times to text a cancellation. But he hadn't. He had a plan. He wasn't ready to scrap it yet.

"You do know that I married Mason Holloway because he was rich man who could take care of us, right? The only difference between me and Grace is that she's not very good at the follow through." They were quiet for a minute. "Charlie, what is it that you want? What would make you happy? That's all I want. Do you even know?"

Ouch. Charlie rubbed a hand across his chest to ease the sting of her question. "I want things between us to be like they used to be. I want you to be happy and safe. I want to find a wife because it's time. I have the house, the freedom, and I'm ready to build a nice, stable home with a kid or two to keep things interesting." He shrugged. "Is that so much to ask?"

Willodean chuckled. "Seems like you're missing a couple of important things. First, things won't ever be the way they were, but we can make 'em better. I'm already happy and safe. And, while I'm not sure why now's the time exactly, you could easily kill two birds with one Grace-shaped stone if all you want is any wife. She's right here, after all. And I know that you want to execute your plan efficiently so you can get back home and start drafting the next one."

Charlie leaned back in his chair. "Marry Grace?" He'd been sure running her off was the right decision, even if he could never make himself do it, but if he looked at it logically, by the numbers, his mother had a point. A good one. And that was enough to confuse him for a minute.

"Well, she wanted a fair prenup. You'd insist on it. She wanted a rich guy. You insist on that too." She shook her head sadly. "It's really too bad there's no way she'd say yes at this point."

"Why do you think that? I mean, maybe she'd have to work a little harder to spend money in Newport, but there's always catalogs and websites. She might be overjoyed at the opportunity." If he hadn't treated her like a thief after the family heirlooms or walked away like an offended maiden when she'd told him the truth.

He really needed to learn from his mistakes instead of repeating them enough to alienate everyone in his path.

Willodean shook her head as she unveiled the dessert, a peach cobbler with crumble crust that oozed sweetness and had his mouth watering. "Charlie, you don't even mean what you're saying."

"Maybe not."

She dumped a big pile on his plate and handed him a fork. "Eat up. You're too skinny."

He laughed reluctantly. "You haven't said that to me in a long time. You used to tell me that every night when I was in the break room of the Stardust Lounge while you waited tables and you brought me a hot fudge sundae on your breaks."

"You were the weirdest little kid. Thank God." Willodean smiled as she took a bite of her cobbler. "Any other little boy would have whined about spending every night on a lumpy couch rolling change while I waited tables. You looked like it was a big imposition to be taken away from your job to eat ice cream. And I loved you so much, Charlie, even as I was scared to death."

Charlie wiped his mouth. "Scared to death? Of what?"

"Failing mostly. I mean, after your daddy died, we were on the edge. I was lucky to have such understanding bosses that would let me stash a kid in the back while I worked. And I was lucky that the kid wanted a job to do. You always wanted a job to do. And you looked so serious. It killed me to think about what you were missing. But there was no other way. I had to work. I barely made the bills every month and the idea of you going hungry . . ." She took a bite of her pie and didn't finish the thought.

"I'm sorry, Mom. I don't remember any of that. I remember sitting on the couch with the black-and-white television, lots of money, and a sundae for payment. I don't think I was scarred for life."

"And it's not like you don't have a solid love for money and spending time on your own either, right?" Her teasing smile slipped away, and the worried frown was back.

Charlie shrugged. She had a point. "I guess maybe I understand a little better about you and Mason getting married, even if I didn't know we were poor and needed him then."

"You hated it. I know it. I knew it then, but it was so good for you, Charlie. The schools you went to were so much better, and I never had to worry about the grocery bills or what you might see or hear or worse in the back of a hotel lounge." She shook her head. "I just . . . I did what was best."

"You did." He folded his napkin. "But I guess . . . I loved what we had. I mean, I missed Dad. I knew you did too, but I liked it best when it was just you and me."

"You know what Grace said when I warned her about you? She said she believed in the journey, like wherever she ended up was where she was meant to be. And I think I know exactly what she means."

"You warned her? About me?" Charlie couldn't wrap his mind around it. He was so upstanding and predictable he couldn't imagine what sort of scene it would be that *he* was a danger.

"I'm not sure she's had a whole lot of people looking out for her. I've been where she is. And if it makes you feel any better, she wasn't surprised by anything I said. In fact, she was downright offended, told me I should be standing up for you." She patted his hand. "Even while she was trying to warn me about her, she was defending you." Her smile slipped as she added, "But the thing is that I think she's one of the ones meant to be here, Charlie, even if you aren't. You both may be absolutely right about my matchmaking this time."

Charlie nodded. "I've never loved this place the way that you do, but maybe you're right. Maybe Grace fits here."

"I know this place is a lot, Charlie. Just because I *like* a lot doesn't mean you have to."

He appreciated that she wouldn't push, but the way he felt about this hotel was about more than just the noise and the over-the-top décor. So he was going to give it one try while he was still under the influence of all the favorites Sal had provided for dinner. "This hotel changed everything." She nodded and the smile on her face said she believed it was all for the better. "And I liked things the way they were. I liked our small, old house. I liked my public school. I liked hanging out while you worked."

Willodean frowned. "But you loved Mason. And he loved you like you were his too."

"I looked up to Mason. Every day I'm thankful he was the one you picked because every day I use what he taught me. But this hotel . . . he brought that too. And all I know is that when the hotel was born, I had this stupid feeling that . . . I don't know. It was like you just disappeared. Things changed. And then when Mason died, you didn't do anything but build and decorate and promote and host and whatever it took to make this place thrive. And I missed you. And I'm such a . . . I don't know, a stick in the mud that I could never compete."

Willodean rubbed her forehead. "Son, you . . . you don't . . . I have to tell you this. It wasn't a stupid feeling and you are no stick in the mud. You are the best thing I ever did and don't you ever doubt that." She blinked. "I'm sorry. I thought Travis was the only time I put myself ahead of you, but you're absolutely right. I did it with Mason, and I did it with this hotel."

And now, maybe he'd gotten something off his chest, but his mother looked devastated, which made him feel awful. Worse. And he wished he'd just eaten and left. But he'd been doing that for a long time.

Charlie sighed. "As much as you do to make this world better, no one in his right mind would hold any of those things against you, not even marrying Travis. Please, I just wanted to . . . I don't know, explain how I feel about this place." He squeezed her hand. "I've missed you. Remember that Thanksgiving we spent raking and raking and raking leaves the year before you married Mason? Our house was so small, but that yard was huge. I remember how much fun we had. You twirled around and made a bigger mess than we started with and all I could do was laugh."

He hadn't ever told her how much he loved that place. Maybe it was time. "You know I bought it. As soon as I had enough money to feel comfortable doing something so silly just for the . . . sentimentality of it, I bought that house."

"Our first house in Memphis?" His mother tilted her head. "To do what with?"

He shook his head. "God knows what I thought I'd do. Mostly I toss the key ring around when I'm sitting at my desk worrying about whatever it is that I can't let go of."

He rolled his shoulders and tried to relax again, but he wanted to get it right. He always wanted to get everything exactly right. "You do so much for so many. Someone should do nice things for you. And I can help here more than I do." He shook his head. "I still don't know what you were thinking with Grace, though. She can't stay, and I can't change."

Willodean gripped his arm and gave it a little shake. "Now, I don't believe either one of those things is true."

She tilted her head down and stared up at him. "Here's what I know. Just because you haven't changed, doesn't mean you can't. And that's true for you, for me, for her, and most everybody I ever met. When you come up on a powerful enough incentive, you can do anything you set your mind to. I think that's just human nature, but you, my boy, you have a stronger strain than most. McMinns are some of the stubbornest cusses I ever ran across, and your daddy had a pretty good dose."

It was nice to hear her talk about his dad. They didn't do it often, but the summer he'd spent suffering on his grandfather's farm outside of Newport had shown him that both the McMinn family and his mother's family, the Longs, had their shares of obstinate perseverance.

"Right, Mom, it's a good thing you're so easygoing and laid back. Otherwise, I might have been really hard to deal with." He winked at her when she laughed.

"Maybe I know whereof I speak, Charlie, that's all. You don't give up on something you want. You got enough stubbornness, from one side or the other, to keep going."

She wrapped her arms around his neck and he took a deep, calming breath. The scent of hairspray and lavender would always remind him of his mother and home.

"I don't care what brings you back. If you want to do more here at the hotel, I want you here. But if you don't, please don't think that's the only thing that would make me happy. You are the best thing I ever did—" Her voice broke and Charlie had to sniff in a manly way to hold back a tear. "This hotel, helping people who need it, I love those things, but I want everything for you, Charlie, so you figure out what'll make you happy and you go for it. If it's Grace, you can count on my help. And if it's some boring accountant with a portfolio, I'll learn to love her too."

She expected him to say it was Grace. Definitely. But he just didn't know. He had to laugh at the way she said it, like any other option than Grace would cause her no minor annoyance. When Misty lumbered off of the couch and came to rest her head on his knee, he said, "What do you think, sis? Should I try to find some mistletoe and hang it over Grace's office door?"

Misty tilted her head up and seemed to nod. Charlie ruffled her ears and listened to the bells around her neck jingle. "That's solid advice, Misty."

His mother laughed, and he was happy to see the twinkle back.

"Do you ever wish you'd gotten a Mister like you planned when Howard took you to visit the breeder, Mom?" Charlie looked down into Misty's soulful eyes and couldn't imagine how anyone would wish for a different dog.

"No, I do appreciate his insistence that I needed a mister in my life, but she was a nice surprise. Besides, I just had no idea how much fun it was to have a dog that accessorized, you know? Howard Jackson was one smart man."

Charlie nodded. He had been. Kind too. "I'll always be grateful that Howard never met an argument he couldn't settle."

Misty heaved what sounded like an exhausted sigh and went back to climb on the couch.

"I know exactly what she means. It's hard to lounge around a hotel all day." Charlie smiled at his mother. "Oh, and I know you don't care much, but today I bought you a nice share of a company that manufactures environmentally friendly children's toys. I expect to see a pretty good return on investment within two years."

Willodean patted his shoulder. "Good job, Charlie."

Then they both laughed. She was happy to let him invest in whatever he wanted with her money, even if he tried to tell her what to do with the profits afterwards. She trusted him.

"And I've been thinking about your Christmas gift. I was going to tell you to match-make with everything you've got, but now . . . maybe not. Got any other suggestions?"

She tapped a red nail against a red lip. "Hmm, well . . . let's see, last year you got me an electric blanket. Gonna be awful hard to top that." Her face was expressionless as she said it but then she raised an eyebrow and he got the feeling she hadn't been all that impressed. What did he get the woman who had everything, including her own hotel decorated top to bottom in Elvis? "Least we got an idea what you can do for next year."

Charlie picked up the dirty dishes and slid them onto the tray in the corner. "What's that?"

Willodean chortled. "You're easy. I can tell your mind ain't really in the conversation, Charlie. You just walked right into this . . ." She clasped her hands in front of her. "Next year for Christmas, there's only one thing that will do. A grandbaby!"

"Oh, good Lord." He hadn't found the bride yet, much less . . . well, meeting his mother's timeline would be next to impossible. "How about a nice gift certificate somewhere then? Or maybe a trip to the moon?" Willodean shook her head. "I mean, the moon might be easier."

"I've already told you the most efficient way to get on with your plan. Grace is right here. We could make it work." Willodean hummed part of the "Wedding March" under her breath before she sipped her ginger ale.

"Mom . . ." She turned and waited, curiosity clear on her face. And he almost waved it off.

"Don't you want to tell me 'I told you so'? Now's a great time and, boy, do I have it coming."

His mother bumped his shoulder with hers. "Listen, Charlie, I don't know where you get it, but . . . you got to learn to let go of things, you know? I worry. I knew you were a kid when you told me Travis wanted nothing more than my money. You believed it passionately and couldn't let it stay unsaid because you love me. That's easy to forgive, son. And since then, even after Howard forced us to clear the air about Travis, his plans on my riches, and how the divorce had not much to do with you at all, every time we're together, I see you pull back. I can see you beating yourself up. We'll both be happier if you can figure out a way to let it go. Mistakes happen. I ain't going to remind you because you and I both know I made a few hundred of my own. Travis and I were adults. We split up, but that's our thing, not yours."

Remembering how out of control he'd been that

summer afternoon embarrassed Charlie every single time. "I called him a gold digger. To his face and yours. I refused to stay here and went to live with Henry for the summer. I don't think I could have made my contempt any clearer, and even after the divorce, I didn't apologize like I should have."

Willodean patted his leg. "Two things. First, spending that summer with my father was a worse revenge than I ever could've dreamed up on my own. And second, you come from a long line of people who are always right." She held a hand up to her chest. "Not that I know what that's like, of course." She smiled up at him. "Just . . . let it go. No matter what, I only want you to be happy. Everything I've done, with the spectacular exception of marrying Travis Luttrell, has been for us, for you and me."

Except for Travis and this hotel. The words rattled around in his head, but he didn't let them out.

"But a gold digger? Shouldn't you be warning me away?" Even after all that they'd been through, he would. He would still caution his mother.

"Well, now, I'd say she ain't a very good one, is she?"

"That's pretty much the same thing I said when she told me." Charlie had to consider that for a minute. "So that makes it less . . . what? I don't understand."

"She's pretty, she's smart, and she's not afraid to do hard work. Seems she ought to be married and living the high life in Atlanta by now because marrying a man just really isn't all that hard." She shrugged. "I guess I'm saying if she failed, it was probably because her heart wasn't in it. I don't believe you'd face the same challenge with her if you put your mind to it."

"What about love, Mom? Isn't that something you think I should be looking for?"

Willodean blinked up at him. "Love? Now that is unexpected coming from you. But here's what I think. I loved Mason Holloway until the day he died. It started with gratitude for everything he gave us, but he made me love him in a million different ways. I'll never forget the day you ran in to tell me he'd opened up a trading account all for you." She shook her head. "Never saw a boy so excited about stock trading. It's almost unnatural. And I remember every time y'all celebrated a good money day over dinner and how proud he was of you when he talked about you. And I'll tell you, even if you don't love a man going in, you see him fall in love with your son that way, and you can't even help it, you know?"

He watched her smile at the memory. "But we don't have that, Mom." He shook his head. "And it doesn't even matter. I can't understand why I'm thinking this way. If I look at this logically, it makes sense. It's time to marry. That much we agree on. Dating is a nightmare. I know this firsthand. She makes me feel ... different, better. And she wants to settle down with a man with money. With a strong prenup to hedge against the odds that she'll move on when she gets bored, there's no reason not to move forward."

"Of course, you aren't sure she'll say yes," Willodean said with an arched brow. "She *is* a smart girl."

He nodded.

"Here's my only piece of advice, Charlie. If you want her, pursue her. You can think about your criteria and how she matches up to that list, but if you want to be happy, you try to figure out how to be more than a bank account to her. Love, sometimes it's instant and a thunderbolt,"—she narrowed her eyes at him as he started to interrupt her—"but sometimes it's just a snowball that grows and gathers speed as it builds. You just figure out how to be a gift to her every day, and I'd say you have as good or better chances of making it stick as anyone I know."

"A gift, huh?"

Willodean waited for him to meet her stare. "And not an electric blanket, you hear me?"

They both laughed and he stood, offered her a hand, and pulled her up. She reached into the pocket of her jacket and pulled out her keys. "Think you can pass these along to Grace tonight?" Willodean blinked innocently up at him. "It would save me the *long* trip over to the staff apartments."

Charlie shook his head. "Why does Grace need your car keys? Again?" He tossed them up and caught them in the air.

"She's headed over to meet with Mike, my interior decorator, tomorrow. He's got some catalogs, things for her to look at while she's shopping for the conference rooms." Willodean tilted her head. "You aren't still worried she'll head for Sin City at her first opportunity, are you?"

Charlie leaned his head back to consider the question. "No, I guess not."

Willodean's eyebrows shot up. "Well, now that's some kind of progress, isn't it?" She pursed her lips. "You might need to worry just a little that she'll meet Mike and decide he's more her style."

"Your *interior decorator*?" He didn't feel that threatened at the idea.

"Maybe you ought to talk to KT about how much of a worry Mike would be." Willodean shook her head. "He's a hottie."

Creeped out at the idea of his mother calling anyone a hottie, Charlie decided it was time to leave. He tossed the key ring again and then leaned down to kiss her cheek. "Good night, Mom. I'll see you in the morning."

She walked him to the door and waved as she closed it behind him. As he got on the elevator, Charlie felt lighter, more . . . positive than he had in a while. They'd cleared the air. His mother didn't blame him or resent him. They still didn't see eye to eye about Grace, though.

Of course they didn't. Willodean Jackson accepted people with all their quirks and flaws, and something about her made them better. He'd seen it a million times. And he expected perfection, in himself and, if the rest of the world would just follow orders, everyone else too. Always had. Even when he'd been a little boy and he wasn't even sure what was going on after his father died and Willodean worked all hours to make the rent, he'd been certain he could control things, make them work. When he'd started making his own money, thanks to his stepfather, everything had solidified for him. Making money and a lot of it was the only control he could have.

So he'd done that. But now that victory wasn't enough to satisfy him.

He shoved the keys in his pocket as he walked through the lobby. One quick glance at the front desk showed him Tony was already on duty. They exchanged cautious chin nods and he walked on. He didn't know what he would say to Grace, but he was happy to have an excuse to see her. He had a bad feeling his mother's suggestion about efficiently snapping up Grace would keep him up all night long. He'd worry about that after he told her good night.

WHEN SHE HEARD the knock on the door, Grace lurched up to sit on the side of the bed. She'd been working on her laptop the last she remembered. She rubbed her cheek to try to erase any evidence that she'd fallen asleep on top of the papers she'd printed out to study. Before she'd fallen asleep.

As she yanked open the door, Grace ruffled her limp ponytail. Charlie raised an eyebrow, and she wished she'd taken just a minute to check a mirror.

"Did I wake you?" He pointed at the door. "You should really check to see who it is before you open the door, you know."

"No. And yes." And if she'd been awake, she would have. "What's up?" After the way he'd left, she was surprised to see him. And without an armed escort too.

Charlie fished in his jeans pocket and pulled out a key ring. "I brought these." Grace scooped them from his open hand and felt the flash of warmth that she hadn't quite gotten used to.

"Thanks." She leaned against the door and fiddled with the doorknob. "I appreciate you bringing them . . . or maybe just following Willodean's orders anyway." She tried a small smile. "Guess she hasn't quite given up."

"Willodean Jackson never gives up. Believe that." The look in Charlie's eyes was warm, teasing, and Grace couldn't help but laugh. And for a long moment after that, they didn't move. The connection snapped into place, and Grace couldn't have turned away from him if she'd wanted to. She didn't want to, no matter how much she told herself she should. Finally, Charlie shoved his hands in his pockets and shifted back and forth. "Listen, I wanted to say . . ."

Bracing herself for the worst, Grace crossed her arms over her chest.

"I'm glad you told me. About Tommy Joe and your wedding." He rubbed his forehead. "It's the weirdest thing. I knew something was off, but I didn't want to hear it. Because I feel this . . ."

"Connection." Grace bit her lip, her nerves making it hard to breathe. "Yeah, I know what you mean."

"So what do we do?" Charlie's voice was rough, like it was a struggle to ask the question.

"You don't know?" Grace tried to beat down the flutter of relief and . . . she refused to call it hope. So he didn't hate her. He might even be as confounded by the instant connection between them as she was. But so what? None of that changed his opinion or her fear.

"That's got to be a first, right? Charlie McMinn doesn't have the answer."

Charlie sighed. "Here's the thing. When you aren't around, I can tell myself that whatever we have couldn't possibly feel the way I think it feels. Because it doesn't make sense. We don't have any of the things that I'd say make people work, at least not on paper, but then you're around and you make me feel ..." He broke off and thought about it. Finally he screwed up his face and muttered, "Good. You make me feel good."

He said it like he'd just admitted an embarrassing secret.

"I think I know exactly what you mean." She stepped out and hissed as her feet hit the cold sidewalk. She leaned up to hug his neck. "The good thing is we don't have to figure it out tonight, Charlie. Maybe we could just ... take it one day at a time."

When she moved to step back into her warm apartment, he slid his arms around her waist and pulled her closer. Aware she was standing at a crossroads, a very cold place with no shoes on, Grace fought an internal battle. She should step away, but as she tilted her head up and stared at his face, she couldn't.

"Tell me not to, Grace." He leaned closer to her, his body a warm comfort on the cold night. And it was the easiest thing in the world to touch her lips to his. Charlie's chest was a hard, warm pressure against hers, his legs wrapped hers and all she could think of was how safe she felt, how comfortable. Until his mouth moved against hers. And his hand slid down over the soft knit covering her hip. Then he shifted, one leg slipped between hers while his tongue teased inside her lips and she was pretty sure she could stay right here until . . .

The door to Tony and Randa's apartment opened and bright light spilled out over them.

"Oh, God. Uh, sorry . . ." Randa slammed the door and inched around them. "I'm just headed over to . . ." And then she was gone.

Charlie leaned his forehead against hers and took a slow breath before he stepped back. When his hands slipped away, she wanted to grab them, squeeze them, pull them back to where they . . . belonged?

"So that was unexpected." He shoved his hands in his pockets and paced in a small circle.

Grace shifted from one freezing foot to the other. "Yeah, so . . ."

They looked at each other, and then Charlie shook his head. "Go back inside. You were asleep. I'm sorry I woke you. Have a good shopping trip tomorrow." But he didn't leave.

Grace slowly shook her head. "There's no way I'm going to be able to sleep now." She grinned at him and touched her mouth with one hand. Surely she looked different now. "Maybe I'll actually get the laundry done that I meant to do before I sat down to read about catering setups." She covered her lips with one finger. "But don't tell Willodean. I'm already supposed to take Friday off because I'll be working the Saturday weddings. If she finds out I'm working at night, who knows what perk she'll force on me?"

He nodded. She was a little disappointed. She wanted a laugh. "I guess I should go. You should definitely get inside. If you catch a cold, I'll never hear the end of it."

Grace wondered if either of them would ever hear the end of being caught in a first kiss right outside the apartment door, but she didn't say it aloud. If he hadn't thought of that, she wasn't going to bring it up.

"You could come in." As soon as she said it, Grace wondered what she was thinking. He should definitely not come in, not before she figured out what she wanted with Charlie. That kiss . . . it was proof that their connection could go nuclear at the right moment.

There was no coming back from something like that. They'd have to go all the way to meltdown to escape their connection if they had sex. But just the idea of never having sex with Charlie after that kiss . . . that was a heartbreaker.

"You could help me do laundry." She raised her eyebrows just to see if he'd laugh.

When he exhaled a small laugh, she felt the link between them tighten.

"Maybe not." He raised a hand. "Good night. I'll . . . catch up with you . . . later." Then he turned and left. Grace leaned against the doorjamb to watch him until he disappeared and then she slowly shut the door. She shivered and then leaned forward to thump her head against the door.

"Grace, what are you doing?" She rolled her head and laughed. Best first kiss ever with the worst possible match. Why didn't that surprise her?

"Laundry." When she thought about what she could have been doing if Charlie was a different sort of guy, the one who'd ignore his own alarms and follow her in, laundry seemed an even worse insult.

But it had to be done. And it would give her plenty of time to figure out just what she was doing with him. Maybe.

Chapter Seven

"CHARLIE, I'D LOVE to hear about your goals. Where do you think you'll be in five years?" Dr. Karen Bennett leaned back against her chair and smiled in her clinically curious way. He'd been wondering about that smile all night. Was it the only one she had? It made him feel like there was a clock ticking somewhere but he couldn't see it. That might be something he would talk to a psychologist about if they were in a session, not seated across from each other in a nice Italian restaurant lit only by the glow of candles. Romantic. But not the way he and Karen did it.

He told himself she was perfect. Beautiful in a very refined sort of way with cool blonde hair, light blue eyes, and flawless posture outlined by a fine gray knit top and pants. She was trim and her jewelry was understated silver.

The overall impression was . . . blah. He wondered if gray was her signature color.

Then he looked down at his black shoes, black pants, and black tie and figured they were at least in the same color family.

He had a good feeling the idea of having a signature color, gray or not, would get him another noncommittal hum.

He picked up his coffee cup and willed the dessert to come faster. "Well, I guess . . . I don't expect a great deal to change. I like Newport. I like my house and enjoy working only for myself." He took a sip of coffee and watched her wait for him to continue. The silence was a bit unnerving. He'd already asked her for her favorite movie, music, book, color, and whatever else under the sun that he could think of just to avoid these tense pauses. "I would like to have a family, maybe two kids, and a nice, stable relationship."

Karen leaned back as the waiter deposited two crème brûlées on the table and refilled their coffee cups. "Hm, that's not the first time you've mentioned 'stable.' That makes me curious, Charlie."

She didn't look curious. Analytical, yes. Assessing. But curious would imply a real desire to know him. He didn't see that. And then he thought about the way Grace had to do nothing more than meet his stare for him to know how she felt. And how she'd listened to him, talked to him about his problems with the hotel, and never once made him feel like a bug under a microscope.

Suddenly he was less bothered by the idea that he'd been on the verge of offering to fold her laundry just to spend time with her.

"We've done a lot of talking about me, Karen. What about you? What will your next five years look like?"

She pursed her lips for a second. Then they might have lifted in a small smile, but she took a few bites of her dessert and pushed it away. "That's easy, Charlie. I'd like to grow my practice at a rate of fifteen percent annually, find a husband who values that career, and if we make it three years, perhaps consider one child."

That was a solid plan. Cold. But clear. Easy to measure, really. His mother would be appalled. And when he imagined what Karen's reaction would be when he introduced her to Willodean Jackson and the Rock'n'Rolla Hotel, he was pretty sure the evening was over or should be. He took a sip of his hot coffee and decided he'd be willing to sacrifice his own crème brûlée to get back to the hotel. He flicked his watch over to glance at the time and then motioned at the waiter for the check. "I can see I've kept you longer than I meant to."

She folded her napkin precisely and settled it next to her plate before she pulled her phone out of her purse. "Should we see how our schedules coordinate to plan the next date?"

Ooh, sticky situation. Obviously she hadn't minded a solid therapy session with her dinner. "I just don't think it's a good use of your time, Karen." He plopped his credit card down as soon as the waiter lurched to a stop and sent him on his way.

She leaned back again, her perfect posture wilting a little in surprise even if her face never showed it. "Really? I thought we were communicating well."

The only thing Charlie was sure of was that there had been no connection. He couldn't imagine being moved to kiss her against his better judgment and in full display of whoever walked by. A week ago that might not have bothered him. The success of his plan would not have been hampered by that distance, which would've worked in favor of Karen's plan.

But he'd met Grace. And now he wanted to connect.

Karen held out her hand. "If you change your mind, text me. I would be happy to schedule a follow-up."

Charlie's lips twitched but there was no way she'd get his amusement. Follow-up was exactly right, like an evaluation of his emotional progress. Maybe that time they could have seafood or he could just pay her his copay and meet her at her office.

He shook her hand and said, "It was nice to meet you. Good luck with your plan."

She stood smoothly and navigated the tables cleanly, easily. He watched her push open the door and walk out of the restaurant.

"Here you are, sir." Charlie smiled up at the waiter and took the credit card slip to sign it. Then he slowly crossed the crowded dining room and once outside, slid into his SUV.

Then he pulled out his phone and texted the pharmacist to cancel his Thursday night date. He had a feeling that they would lack a spark too.

He shook his head as he pulled out of the parking space. Now he had a real problem. His own plan didn't interest him anymore. Stable marriage to a suitable woman sounded like the recipe for the most boring life ever. Well, except for maybe the life he was already living all on his own in Newport. Even if his plan would be easy and made perfect sense, he couldn't make himself follow it. But waiting, looking to run into the right woman in the grocery store hadn't worked.

Then there was his mother's plan. Grace. Nobody could deny that spark.

He just couldn't imagine what life with her would be like. Visions of spending the rest of his days at the Rock'n'Rolla Hotel made him cringe. He pulled into a parking spot in front of the hotel and tried to decide what to do. The best idea: go to his room and try to sleep through the sound of the rushing waterfall in the corner of his very own blue lagoon. Maybe by the time he found Grace again he'd have come to some kind of decision about her or life or the journey or something. He hoped so. This uncertainty was exhausting.

WHEN CHARLIE SLID onto the bar stool the next evening, Viva Las Vegas was doing nice business for a December Thursday. That was a good thing. He'd spent the day calling for status reports from his latest investments. As always, the news was a mixed bag, but he didn't feel invigorated by challenge the way he usually did. When he'd stopped in to see Grace, her office had been dark. Since his mother was also conspicuously absent, he had the idea that they were out together and that he should probably check his mother's credit card for recent activity. He'd known the lack of a budget for the addition, which was only a money drain at this point, not a revenue stream, would not slow his mother down for long.

Now he was in Viva Las Vegas because Grace hadn't answered her door when he'd knocked. There were only so many places she could be, and the restaurant was top of the list.

"Hi, Mr. . . . I mean, hi, Charlie. What can I get you tonight?" Cat the bartender fidgeted with her shirt and seemed to stand a little straighter.

"Cat, do I make you nervous?"

She smiled and shook her head in an effort to pretend that she was everything that was cool. And then she nodded. "Little bit. I mean, the boss's son. You know."

She tried to smile like it didn't really worry her much.

"And it doesn't help that I'm not as friendly as Willodean either." She tried to come up with an answer, but he just waved it off. "Never mind. I was hoping I could see what Sal had on special tonight. And I'm looking for something sweet."

Cat pointed at the window. "I'll just go . . . get Sal then?" When it came out like a question, he nodded and noticed Lucky was setting up for karaoke. Maybe he should get everything to go.

Distracted by Lucky's sound check, Charlie didn't notice Sal had left the kitchen until he said, "Well, now, Mr. Charlie, Cat says you're in the mood for something different. I got more meat loaf, and I know how you like it. Or could do a sandwich with some of them sweet potato fries." Sal tossed a spotless white towel over the shoulder of his spotless white T-shirt. "What you in the mood for?"

Charlie tapped the bar. "Sal, you might save us both some trouble and just teach me how to make that meat loaf for myself." Not that he'd ever be able to replicate it. It would still be nice to have the secret in case he ever needed it.

"Only two people in the world know that recipe, Mr. Charlie. I plan to keep it that way a bit longer."

"Really? I thought you dreamed it up all by yourself. We've had that meat loaf as long as the hotel's been here, haven't we?" Charlie honestly couldn't remember a day in the hotel without Sal. He was a part of the place.

Sal shook his head. "Naw, almost since it opened, sure, but it was Mr. Travis that brought this recipe. Most of the classics was all his doin' and Miss Willodean hasn't made a change. Miss Laura, now, she added a few things, but Miss Willodean put her foot down and most of Mr. Travis's recipes have stayed on the menu. Good thing since the regulars would probably riot if we took 'em off."

When one of the showgirl waitresses put a ticket in the window, Sal pointed. "I better get back to work. How 'bout I surprise you?"

"Sure. Hey, Sal?" When the cook turned back, Charlie said, "You aren't ever going to call me Charlie, are you?"

He shrugged. "Never can tell, Mr. Charlie. Sometimes an old dog can learn a new trick."

Charlie watched Sal slip back into his place like that was where he was meant to be. Every motion Sal had done a million times but it was graceful, and he whistled every now and then like he was just as satisfied as could be. Had he ever been that content? Surely he had, but no doubt it had been a while.

He did his best not to think about Travis Luttrell, apparently the chef who'd created all of his favorites in the short time he'd worked here and been married to his mother. The revelation that everything that he loved about the place, except for his mother and Misty, he owed to the man he'd insulted and run off made him uncomfortable. At twenty-three, Charlie had had the passionate conviction of youth and ignorance on his side when he told his mother and Luttrell exactly what he thought about her marrying a man ten years younger and clearly intent on making his way up in the world.

Chef Travis Luttrell had been smooth, the kind of smooth that kept women buzzing around him while men just wanted to shake his hand. And when his mother had told him they'd gotten married without telling him, of all things, he'd lost it. He'd always wanted to protect her and that felt like the biggest slap to the face. He'd been at grad school and when he came home, he had a new stepfather, one not even a decade older than he was. He'd moved his stuff out to the staff apartments, but that hadn't lasted two weeks before he was driving his car back across Tennessee to stay with his grandfather, a man he barely knew. And he'd done it because he knew it would hurt his mother.

But his mother was right. He'd paid a pretty high price in return for his grandfather's room and board. To earn his keep, something the old man had been very set on, he'd baled more hay that summer than he could have imagined. He'd done every odd job his grandfather could find: fixing fence for one old crony, mowing and mowing and mowing and mowing, and only the righteous anger had kept him there until he could get back to Knoxville to finish up his MBA. By the time graduation had rolled around, Willodean and Travis were fighting, she was destroyed, and Charlie had carried the biggest load of guilt around ever since.

From his spot at the bar, Charlie thought Lucky was looking a little better than he had when he'd visited over the summer. Then he'd been pretty sure Lucky was never sober. Now he was steady enough, but his patter had lost a little of its oomph even if he was standing upright to deliver it.

When Cat set a burger in front of him, he said in a low voice, "Lucky's looking better."

Cat leaned against the bar. "Should be feeling better too now that he can actually get off the stage without help." She shrugged a shoulder. "Got a new girlfriend; a teacher if you can imagine. She loves Elvis and hates alcohol and Lucky is quickly becoming a convert." She wiped a towel on the bar. "Thank God. We were having a hard time saving him from himself, you know?"

Charlie nodded. He did know. He'd written four checks himself on behalf of Willodean to treatment programs. Maybe all Lucky had needed was the love of a good woman.

Lucky finished his opening bit, mainly old jokes about Elvis, Memphis, rocking and rolling that every regular in the place had heard a million times already but laughed along with because tradition was a big thing at the Rock'n'Rolla Hotel. To fit the season, he was a thin Elvis Santa in red velvet. He'd skipped the bushy white beard but kept the wig, a snow-white pompadour. And then he did his own karaoke performance, something he'd stopped doing . . . a long time ago. Charlie would have asked his mother why she kept Lucky on. Drunk, he wasn't really all that pleasant to be around, on or off the stage, but Lucky was a Rock'n'Rolla tradition himself. He'd been the first, the original, the constant Elvis on staff. Maybe there were others through for the yearly Almost Famous competition, and sometimes fan clubs brought their own so that the hallways of the hotel looked like a rhinestone jumpsuit convention, but Lucky had always been here.

At least Lucky had chosen "Here Comes Santa Claus" to sing. The upbeat, cheerful Christmas song gave him plenty of opportunity to shake his hips and work the stage, something every Elvis fan appreciated. And when it was all over, the applause was enthusiastic.

"Aren't you glad to see Lucky's back in the swing of things?"

Charlie turned to see his mother had settled on the stool next to him. "Looks like he's feeling more himself."

She nodded. "Been a long time since he's looked this good. Maybe not since his wife died." Charlie had to think back but he couldn't remember a married Lucky.

Willodean said, "Maybe ten years. He just . . . it's not easy, you know." Charlie took a bite of the burger. That was twice in the span of a Viva Las Vegas visit that he'd realized there was more behind the scenes than he knew anything about. Lucky had had a hard time. He'd been a drunk and an ass because of it. Maybe he still didn't love the ass portion but at the same time, Charlie felt a little bit better, a little more open to liking the new, sober man.

"I'm surprised to see you here. Thought you had another date tonight. Hey, Sal, one Elvis!" She waved through the window at Sal who nodded back.

"You and that sandwich. I'm surprised you don't have peanut butter running in your veins at this point."

His mother slapped him on the arm and then smiled her thanks at Cat who delivered a ginger ale. "I noticed you didn't answer. Date go like you expected?"

Charlie thought about his answer. "Yep. Just exactly like I expected." He turned to face her and nodded once. "Last night's was such a boring disappointment that I cancelled tonight's. And I would have told you that if you'd been around today. I'm guessing you and Grace had to do a little shopping." His mother took a sip of her drink, but when she put her glass back on the bar, Charlie thought he could see a satisfied smile flash across her face.

When she turned back to him, though, she was all innocence again. "Did you miss us?"

She very obviously had not answered his question. They'd danced this budget dance a million times, though. Charlie decided to concede gracefully this round.

"Guess what Sal told me tonight." Charlie bit into his burger and watched Grace climb the stairs to the small stage, her hips a beautiful illustration of poetry in motion.

She wore a classic red dress he hadn't seen before. He had no idea how he'd missed her entrance. Knowing she was in the room usually made him more alert, like his skin hummed with awareness. He'd blame it on the burger.

"I can imagine Sal knows all sorts of things."

Charlie had lost track of what they were talking about so he nodded.

When his mother poked his arm, he tore his gaze away from Grace. "What?"

She sniffed and then calmly said, "You were going to share something that Sal told you, Charlie." She didn't say "Pay attention" but he could hear it in her voice.

"Oh, yeah, Sal told me all the recipes for the popular favorites on the menu came from Travis." Charlie watched her face closely as he polished off his dinner.

She shrugged and pretended not to care a bit. "I guess Sal should know."

"And I guess you do too." He took a drink of his sweet tea. "Seems like something you might choose to batter me over the head with every time I act like I'm starving the minute I walk in the door."

Willodean smiled at Cat, who slid a plate in front of her, and then picked up her own sandwich. "Nonsense. We've talked about this. Besides, you'd only say that being a good cook doesn't make him a good person."

Charlie watched her for a minute and hated that he could hear the words in his own voice. He hadn't known Lucky's issues. He didn't know a thing about Travis Luttrell except that he was too young to be his stepfather and moved fast. Since he was ready to move pretty fast with

Grace, he was starting to wonder just how bad a mistake he'd made. Sure, he'd split them up. That hadn't been his goal or at least he hoped he hadn't planned on their fiery divorce, especially now that he knew what it had done to his mother and his relationship with her. At the time, he'd thought it a happy ending or maybe the only proper choice. But he hadn't known Travis and he was starting to wonder just how well he knew the real Willodean Jackson.

"Now then, I've got a special treat for y'all. If she sings as pretty as she looks, Miss Grace Andersen, the newest employee here at the Rock'n'Rolla Hotel, is going to knock your socks right off," Lucky said from the stage.

Charlie hadn't really expected to see Grace perform, but he should have after he'd heard her singing. When the spotlight hit her, she lit up. Charlie watched Lucky and Grace closely. When Lucky kept his hands off and his eyes on his small sound board instead of shooting comically obvious leers in Grace's direction, he knew for sure Lucky had turned over a new leaf.

Somehow Charlie had forgotten just how beautiful she was. That or she was growing prettier every minute. Was either possible? He had no idea. All he knew was that, as he took a bite of burger, he couldn't describe anyone else in the room. All he could see was Grace, her curves outlined by the short-sleeved red dress. Her orange puffy coat better be hidden away somewhere or she was going to get frostbite on her extremities during the walk around the pool. Unless he went with her. Just to make sure she didn't die from the elements in the two minutes from door to door.

He wouldn't want the hotel to lose its newest employee.

When the strains of "Love Me Tender" started, he almost groaned out loud. But then he saw Grace in the bar's single spotlight and didn't care what she sang. No matter which song she picked, he'd stay to listen just to see the way her mouth shaped the words. She was wearing bright red lipstick and her dark hair and eyes, her pale skin, and tight red dress made her look like a lounge singer in the best way. But this was the Rock'n'Rolla Hotel and in Viva Las Vegas, the only music that played was Elvis music and the only people allowed on the stage knew the rules.

And when Grace performed "Love Me Tender" it was different than the countless other times he'd heard the song. He could feel heartbreak and longing, and if the breathless silence of the rest of the restaurant was any indication, every person in the room could feel it too. She didn't have a voice for radio. She had a voice for a small, dark club where people could see the emotion on her face. She was made for the Viva Las Vegas stage.

His dinner was tumbling in his stomach, and he couldn't take his eyes off her. When the last notes ended, there was silence. Charlie had to brace himself against the bar, but he started the applause. When the rest of the restaurant joined in, the spell was broken and Lucky jumped back up on the stage.

"Well, now, that was a treat. Am I right? Miss Grace Andersen is going to be planning weddings, conferences, and fan club meetings here at the hotel. So if you got an event, she'll be glad to help. And maybe you can talk her into singing." Lucky picked up his list. "I know I'm going to be calling on her to get back up here every chance I get. Next up, we've got Sidney Green who wants to do a little bit of 'Hound Dog.'"

Grace and Sidney passed each other on the stairs, and Charlie watched her wind through the tables until Willodean stopped her. Thank God his mother had stepped in. He hadn't quite regained his equilibrium yet. Left to him, he'd never have caught Grace. And that thought made it clear he needed to do a better job on his own. He'd decided last night to pursue her even though when this thing between them ended, tonight or ten years from now, it would hurt. He'd carefully considered the pros and cons. Then, when the con list was too long to ignore, he'd crumpled the paper and tossed it into the wicker wastebasket. At some point, he'd decided that, no matter how bad the bad times got, he was willing to take the risk on the good times with her. He'd hold on to that connection as long as he could.

Chapter Eight

GRACE WAS DOING her best not to look at Charlie when Willodean stopped her. The loud lecture going on in her head about how he was a single man with absolutely no obligation to her at all in any way, shape, or form distracted her. So what if he'd been out on two dates while she ... well, she'd been pretty sure she wasn't going to sit around thinking about that. Karaoke and loud conversation at Viva Las Vegas had seemed the perfect way to spend the evening. That was before she saw Charlie at the bar. But she'd already put on her best dress. She was committed. If she hadn't been so busy pretending to be oblivious to his stare, she'd have successfully avoided him for one more night. Willodean had told her to take Friday off and given her a Graceland ticket. It would get her out of the hotel and help her on the job, neither of which she told Willodean but no excuse was necessary. Willodean expected everyone to make the pilgrimage to Graceland at the first opportunity.

The forced separation from Charlie had seemed a blessing after she'd spent most of the night replaying the kiss and going in circles in her head about what she wanted to do about it. When faced with a decision, she usually went with her instincts. She hated indecision, but she'd almost decided to talk to him about . . . dating for now, not forever. Could he even go with the flow like that?

This time she wasn't sure whether it was her instinct or her desire to have Charlie's lips on hers again telling her to take the risk. Either way, she was scared. And then Willodean had casually mentioned his date while they were out shopping. And she'd been mad about losing sleep over him. Of course that's all it was.

"You were wonderful up there, Grace. I bet Lucky'll try to get you to start things off every night," Willodean said as she hugged her. "And you look so nice too."

Grace turned her back on Charlie and smiled. "Thanks, Willodean. Sometimes I get this crazy urge to stand up in front of people to entertain. This may be the perfect setup for me. A real job during the day and a handy stage to get out the urges when necessary."

Willodean subtly shifted and Grace did too so that Charlie completed their circle. Grace met his eyes but quickly looked away. She'd nearly forgotten the words up on the stage when she looked up to see him watching her so intently. But instead of nervous, he made her feel confident and really beautiful. She had no idea how he did it either. He had looked pained when she'd started to sing, but maybe it had more to do with the song choice than her voice.

When Willodean had told her over lunch during their shopping that Charlie was headed out for dinner that night with one of his dates and that she hadn't gotten the progress report from his date the night before, Grace had felt it like a hard shove, a push that might wake her up if she was sleepwalking. And since then, she'd tried to tell herself it was all for the best. Charlie and his schedule could never be what she needed.

Even his mother, the local matchmaker, had agreed.

The urge to get up on a stage, to perform, had been immediate. That was nothing new. She'd been entertaining as a way to handle her uncomfortable emotions for a very long time.

Then he'd shown up and made everything better. The jerk. The hot, deluded jerk.

If there'd been anyone in the restaurant under retirement age, she might have angled for a drink, just to show she could.

But maybe not. She'd only known Charlie for a few days, but it was hard to imagine finding someone she enjoyed just being with any more. Talking with him was easy. She didn't worry so much about being charming and happy and entertaining. With him, she could just be Grace. The hot, deluded, *dating* jerk.

"Guess I'll be heading back to my place then." She awkwardly waved toward the door to the lobby.

"Aren't you having dinner, Grace?" Willodean poked Charlie in the ribs, and his comic "oof" for effect showed a little less tension between them. Despite her annoyance with him, that gave her a warm glow. She wanted them to get along. "Charlie here will vouch for the meat loaf for sure."

Very aware of just how little money she had left between her and negative bank balances until she was paid again, Grace shook her head. "Nah, I'll probably whip something up at home."

Charlie didn't say anything, but she had a feeling that he could see all the way through her.

"Guess I'll go. Besides, I wanted to talk to Tony about how the booking system for the hotel and the conferences will work." She glanced at Charlie who was in conversation with Cat and had to wait for him to notice her attention. She could feel the stupid little frown on her face, which was absolutely ridiculous. Charlie could talk to whomever he wanted to. Clearly. "Or maybe Laura would be better." She had a feeling it would be easier to talk to Laura than Tony, but only because she would use more words.

Willodean stared at Charlie hard until he shook his head. "No, I'll do that. Tomorrow morning."

Even though she hated his stuffy, bossy voice, she nodded reluctantly. "Fine. I'll go to Graceland in the afternoon." She took a step and then said, "I'll meet you at nine."

Without another glance at Charlie, Grace smiled at Willodean and left the party that was Viva Las Vegas, enjoying the silence of the quiet lobby as she strolled across it. Instead of Tony, Laura was behind the desk, but she wasn't alone. Misty was in an undignified sprawl under a palm frond strung with white Christmas lights, and there was a very handsome man in his own undignified sprawl in the lobby chair closest to the desk.

"Hey, Grace, how's the first week going?" Laura asked as she stopped in front of the desk.

Grace shrugged. "Lots of questions so far. I mentioned that I'd stop by to talk to Tony about showing me the booking system, but Charlie's going to help instead. Could you leave him a note or something? I don't want to disturb him tonight." She tried not to imagine what it might be like to knock on Tony and Randa's door on one of his few nights off.

Laura's smile said she knew what Grace meant. "You bet. And if you need any help later, let me know. I'm pretty good with that stuff."

Misty leaned against Grace's leg so she reached down to scratch under her chin. "Willodean says you're the author of all the forms the hotel uses."

"She dreams in spreadsheets." The good-looking guy rolled up out of the chair and walked over to lean against the front desk. "Other girls wrote fan letters to television heartthrobs, but she probably sent a love note to whoever created Excel." He held out his hand. "Please don't tell me you're one of the spreadsheeters. It would be nice to have a new addition to the seat-of-the-pants crew."

Grace slipped her hand in his with a sad shake of her head. "Sorry. I love a good function."

There was silence and then Laura laughed and said, "And now you've probably made a fan for life. KT appreciates geeky humor."

KT . . .

"KT Masters. You must be Grace, the new event planner."

Grace smiled up into eyes that showed nothing but good humor and satisfaction with the world. That was a very attractive trait.

"My stubborn fiancée has told me all about you."

KT Masters. The actor. Of course. She'd come all the way to Memphis to have a star sighting in the wild, and she was glad she hadn't missed her opportunity.

Laura shrugged. "Well, not all. I mean, I don't know that much. Except that . . ."

"I was abandoned at the altar by the rich man I was going to marry." Grace made a face. "That's probably enough to start with, isn't it?"

KT waved his hand. "Listen, you're better off. Any guy that's going to leave you in a wedding dress is not working with all his faculties. I mean, if I were lucky enough to get a woman to say yes and actually set a date and then show up and put on a pretty dress in front of all our friends and family, I would certainly be there, no matter what else happened. I wouldn't let her go." He narrowed his eyes at Laura, and she returned the favor. "But that's just me, I guess."

Laura's lips were twitching as she shook her head. "He wants to get married. Soon. And what KT Masters wants, KT Masters gets and the rest of us fall in line."

KT pouted. "Aw, now, don't be like that. You know I can make you want it too." He wagged his eyebrows at her, and Laura's blush was immediate.

Grace was trying to figure out a way to get out of the conversation, to disappear from the lobby, and just basically make her sad, spinsterish way back over to her beautiful new apartment for a satisfying bowl of noodles when KT laughed and put his hand on her shoulder. "Sorry. It's just fun to tease a beautiful woman."

Grace watched Laura and KT communicate with their eyes and was happy Misty gave her hand a lick. She laughed at the dog and the spell was broken.

"Grace, I'm glad I caught you. Where's your coat?" Charlie shot a narrow-eyed look at KT whose hand slowly dropped off her shoulder.

She had no idea what to say to that. "Um, well, I left it over in . . ." And the fact was that it was none of his business. He might know the answer if he hadn't been out on a *date*. She motioned down at her dress. "It didn't really go with the outfit."

KT said, "And covering up that dress would have been a shame, a terrible shame." Grace laughed at his outrageous wink and then at the way Laura rolled her eyes.

Charlie grumbled and set a to-go container on the front desk before he shrugged out of his jacket. "Here." That was all he said. He thrust his jacket toward her and said, "Here." Like maybe she was lucky to have his help or . . . something.

"Charlie McMinn, I was hoping to run into you." KT held out his hand. "Got a project I want to talk to you about." Then he held up a hand and in a stage whisper said, "Privately."

"I'll be here the rest of the week. I'm in my usual room. Call me when you have a minute." Charlie wrapped an arm around Grace's shoulder, and she knew her expression matched the surprise on Laura's and KT's faces.

KT whistled. "That's how it is, huh?"

Charlie didn't answer.

Misty yawned long and loud, and they all laughed.

Charlie took the opportunity to guide Grace away from the desk. "See you tomorrow, Laura. Call me, KT."

As they walked down the hall toward the door that led to the pool and staff apartments, Grace was aware of two things. First, Charlie never moved his hand. Even through the layers of her dress and his jacket, the one that smelled like clean man and leather, she could feel his hand, strong and steady in the small of her back. And second, a small smile tugged at the corner of his lips. It never bloomed into a grin, but she could see that he was pleased about . . . something. She really shouldn't care because he was dating and that was the best solution to this odd attraction between them. But that didn't change the fact that she did care. She hadn't seen a smile like this from Charlie, and she wanted to know what it was about.

"You seem . . . happy tonight. Did you get some good news?" She couldn't remember being this in tune with another man ever. When he was grim, she wanted to know why. And when he was happy, she wanted to celebrate with him. She'd spent a lot of time looking out for herself. Being connected to someone else was strange but good. And then she remembered. "Oh, I bet it's because you had a wonderful *date*." She hadn't meant to emphasize the last word but she did and ended it with a snap of her teeth.

Since even she could hear the bite in her voice, she was certain Charlie couldn't miss it.

"The date was . . . over before it started." They paused in front of the door. "I cancelled it after last night's complete snoozefest. Maybe a waste of time because . . ." He shook his head and looked outside but there was nothing to see. The fact that he'd avoid her gaze made her think there was more to say and it mattered to him. A lot. Finally he huffed out an impatient sigh. "When I'm here, I usually get the Angry Boss treatment." He looked at her and then waved his hand. "You know, the guy everyone dreads coming into work because he sucks all the joy out of the room. I worked for that guy for ten years before I moved to Newport. And I hated him. Obviously, I should have felt a little more sympathy."

Grace blinked. That wasn't the answer she'd expected.

He shook his head. "Never mind. It's stupid. I am the boss's son. So what if none of them jump when she comes around or refuse to call *her* by her first name." He rolled his eyes. "It's just nice to be needed. I usually feel like the outsider. First I'm helping you. And then KT. If Tony had been around and cracked a smile, I would have thought you were all in on an elaborate prank of some kind."

Grace leaned a shoulder against the door. "Honestly? You're happy because people need you?" She stared out at the pale concrete just outside the door and tried to wrap her head around that. It just didn't seem . . . normal.

"I think it's really more about being included." When Grace looked up at him, he scrunched up his nose and scrubbed a hand over his face. "Never mind. How did this conversation get so off track?" He straightened his shoulders and propped a hand on his hip. The pose made him bigger and stronger and Grace was struck again by how cute he was when he pretended to be all tough. Obviously he was a big marshmallow inside. He wanted to be included.

But she wasn't quite ready to let him off the hook. "And last night's date was just . . . fine." Her teeth did the closing with a click thing again.

He nodded. "Fine. Awkward. Boring. Horrible. Horribly boring in the way most first dates are." The disgust was clear on his face. "I hate dating. I brushed off a second 'appointment' hint and then cancelled the date I'd set up for tonight. I had this plan, this list of criteria, and they both matched at an acceptable percentage." His face was serious when he quietly added, "Even though I want the same thing, a nice wife and a stable home, I'm not sure my heart's in the plan anymore."

"For some reason, it sounds strange to hear you talk about your heart." She looked out the door to see the clear night sky. "What brought on this understanding?"

"I think it was when I had to stifle a yawn as I outlined my own life goals."

Grace's mouth dropped open. "That sounds horrible."

Charlie's dry chuckle was an agreement. "But I do have a heart, you know."

She glanced up to see that he was serious.

"Of course you do. I mean, I know that. I just wasn't sure you did." She shook her head. "Matching percentages sounds more like you. Strategic plans with performance measurements and deadlines. That I could believe. But your heart . . ." This close to him she could see the question in his eyes and she couldn't look away. "That sounds a little bit more like me talking."

"You do know we're standing under mistletoe, don't you?" He pointed at the plastic sprig hanging over the door.

"Is that why you decided to have our heart to heart here?" She couldn't ignore the crazy way her heart beat at the promise of another Charlie kiss. She hadn't quite resigned herself to not having more, obviously.

Charlie reached up to smooth her hair back. "Nah, that's something a planner would do. I'm turning over a new leaf. I'm going to take it . . . day by day."

The zing of anticipation she felt at hearing him say something so perfectly in line with everything she wanted stole her breath. Intent on his mouth and the excuse of the mistletoe, Grace took a step closer and watched him retreat the same distance.

"So that song you sang . . ." He didn't finish the thought but his opinion was clearly not a positive one. And she was reminded of why he would have trouble being included. He had no idea how to talk to people. Or when to shut up and kiss them.

Grace raised both brows. "Yeah? What about it?"

He grimaced. "I hate that song."

Grace tried to ignore the sharp jab of hurt that hit the

center of her chest. This wasn't personal. He was talking about the song, not her performance.

But it felt very, very personal.

She snapped to attention, ready to walk off in a huff, but he grabbed her arm. "Wait." He closed his eyes and slid his hand down her arm, leaving a streak of heat behind that sent a good shiver all the way through her and made her hate his leather jacket with a vengeance, to hold her hand. His thumb traced back and forth over the skin of her wrist. "But I . . . for a song I hate, I couldn't take my eyes off of you. You were great. I think you might have found the stage you were made for."

Grace tried to ease some of the tension in her shoulders. "Aren't you going to say I have the voice of an angel? I mean, every other man who was trying to make some progress with me liked to trot that out."

Charlie frowned. "I'd say you have the voice of . . ." When he paused, she had to brace herself. Whatever it was, it would probably be a doozy, a backhanded compliment of massive proportions. "Your voice is seductive. Makes me think of hot nights and cool sheets." When Charlie raised both eyebrows her direction and waited for her judgment, she couldn't help the laugh that bubbled up. He wasn't smooth. But he was very cute when he tried.

Grace nodded. "It was actually the right stage. Not too big, not too small. Just right." She put her hand on the door to push it open but he stopped her again.

"Give me one more shot at this." Grace frowned up at him and waited. He took a deep breath. "What I should have said is that your face . . . that's the face of an angel, but your voice reminds me of hot nights and cool sheets." Grace wanted to laugh again, but he wasn't joking. His eyes were locked on hers, and his lips were a hard line, like whatever he was saying and, more important, whatever he was thinking, mattered a lot.

Grace licked her lips. "Yeah, the whole angel thing's just a line anyway and not a very good one." She shifted inside his jacket. "I'd rather have honesty."

"I hate that song because I've had to listen to it on repeat with every tragedy my mother ever suffered." He rubbed his temple. "And God knows that's way too many. When my dad died, 'Love Me Tender' was on morning, noon, and night. And I've never been able to say to her, 'Please stop playing that damn song,' because she was hurting, it made her feel better, and she should have that, whatever it is. But now when I hear it, all I can think of is . . . helplessness. So I hate it. The only thing that could have kept me in my chair was your voice and the way you looked lit up by a spotlight. So . . ." He shrugged awkwardly. "That's honest."

She met his stare and could tell that he was having a hard time with it. He fidgeted, but he didn't retreat. He looked vulnerable but so strong too. And she could imagine a little boy or a young man listening to his mother mourn the best she could and had to blink back tears. "Guess what? I'm never going to sing that song again, Charlie. I want you to be my number one fan." She gave his hand a squeeze.

Charlie tangled his fingers in hers and then shoved

open the glass door. When they stepped out into the cold night, Grace had to bite back a gasp.

"You really need your stylish orange coat tonight," Charlie said as they hurried around the pool.

She didn't want to let vulnerable Charlie go, but they had to catch their breath so she would happily talk about coats or weather or whatever it took to keep him around.

Grace hurried to open the door. "I wouldn't have frozen if you hadn't come along, you know, Prince Charming?" She pulled him inside after her, unwilling to debate on the doorstep over whether he should come in before they froze solid. "I'm a grown woman, been taking care of myself for a long time. I thought about the coat and discarded it on the way out." She pointed to it.

Charlie shook his head. "Well, maybe you could do a better job of taking care of yourself. Maybe you need someone to convince you to think of your health instead of the line of your dress." He rubbed his forehead. "Not that it's not a very fine line. Of dress. I mean, it is."

Grace shrugged out of his jacket and hung it over her coat on one of her few hangers before she ran a hand over her hip. "You like? It's one of the dresses I brought along in case I made it to a nice restaurant." She looked down at it. "This red dress has always been lucky for me."

Charlie nodded. "Were you wearing it when you met Tommy Joe Huffle?" It was hard to tell what he was thinking from his expression. "And just exactly what sort of luck were you looking for tonight in the bar?"

Grace crossed her arms over her chest and tilted her head while she tried to convince herself he wasn't saying what she thought he was saying. What difference would it make if she had worn it over to Viva Las Vegas to look for a man?

"What do you mean, Charlie?"

"I mean . . ." He shook his head. "I was just thinking that it works for you. It should bring you all the luck in the world, but if you were wearing it when you met him, maybe you ought to get a new one. You know, better karma or something."

"I thought you were about to ask me if I wore it over to Viva Las Vegas because I was hoping to get lucky enough to pick up a man." Grace raised her eyebrows at him. "And we would both know you don't have any right to ask me a question like that, right? Because . . . date, Charlie."

He rolled his eyes. "I'm really getting the impression you don't like that I went on a date last night. I thought it would clarify things. And I was right. There's no need to go on another." He huffed out a breath. "And between you and me, it wouldn't matter one bit what you wore over to Viva Las Vegas. If there were any eligible men, you could pick them up in that ratty sweatshirt and your baggy jeans. That dress would be overkill if that's all you wanted, a man."

She wasn't sure she believed him. The look on his face said he knew it had been a good answer, but she didn't want to be that girl, the crazy jealous type. If she was going to, she owed him advance warning. So she let it go and tapped the to-go box in his hand. "Is this your second dinner?"

He looked down at it like he'd completely forgotten he

had anything in his hand. Then he held it out to her. "No, this is for you."

Grace held both hands up like it was too hot to touch. "No, thank you. I have my own dinner. I don't need yours." But she wanted it. Instant noodles for dinner every night had gotten old fast.

He shrugged a shoulder. "Good. It's not dinner. It's dessert. I thought you might—"

He stumbled to a stop when she grabbed the box out of his hands. She popped the lid open and sighed. "Oh, it's the banana pudding. How did you know?" She'd craved it since she saw the menu in Viva Las Vegas but could never justify the expense.

His small smile was back. "Had a hunch. You have to eat your dinner first, though. My mother never had many rules, but that was one she enforced."

Grace nodded and went to put the container in her refrigerator. "Did you have a sweet tooth?"

He nodded. "Still do. Dessert's something you have to spend some time with, savor it." When she thought of his kiss, she understood.

Charlie was ready to bolt again. "I guess I should let you eat your dinner." He shuffled a step closer to the door. "I like what you've done ... added some color." He pointed at the two brilliant blue throw pillows she'd picked up on clearance to brighten up the place and the purple throw Willodean had given her for the couch.

She raised an eyebrow. "This is where you tell me how silly it was to spend any money at all on home décor when I can barely feed myself. Right? It wasn't cost effective maybe. But I wanted it to feel like *my* place. For the first time, it feels right to put down roots. Small roots."

"No, the place needed some personal touches." Charlie crossed his arms over his chest. "That's how I feel at home. It's mine. I picked all the paint and flooring and fixtures. And everything I could, I did myself. There's no other place like it. It fits me perfectly. Peaceful. Quiet. Out in the middle of the woods."

It was hard to imagine and she had nothing to say to keep the conversation going, but Grace didn't want him to leave. Not yet. Not without a kiss for sure. She trailed him step for step across the tiny room and waited for him to stop. He yanked his jacket off the hanger and slipped it on before he ran his hand through his hair.

"Listen, maybe . . . you and I, we could try a date. Have you ever been down to Beale Street? Music, people, food, drinks. A girl like you would enjoy every minute. Let's go tomorrow night."

A girl like me? If only he'd left that part out, the words to remind her that he hadn't always been her fan. Grace crossed her arms over her chest and stepped back while she considered his . . . offer? Order?

"I don't think that's a good idea. Besides, we've got weddings to perform on Saturday so . . ." She didn't meet his eyes.

"So . . ." Charlie ran his hand through his hair again and huffed out a frustrated breath. "I'll be over in the morning to show you the system."

He turned the knob and pulled open the door but paused. Then he closed it again and turned to face her.

"You make me crazy, Grace. But I'm not leaving without a kiss. Until you tell me not to, I'm always going to kiss you good-bye. I don't want to miss a chance." He stepped closer and wrapped his arm around her waist before settling his mouth on hers. Grace's breath caught on a gasp and he took advantage, his tongue teasing hers while he slid his hands over her hips. The sudden flash of heat convinced Grace to stretch up against him, wrap her hands around his neck and bury her fingers in his hair to anchor herself to him. She didn't want space between them. More than anything she wanted to get closer. When he pulled back to catch his breath, Grace rested her head on his shoulder for just a second. And it was just as nice as she thought it might be that first day in Viva Las Vegas. He was strong. And warm.

"I hope ... I've just spent so much time thinking about that kiss, Grace. I had to see if it was a fluke." He steadied her as she stepped back.

"It wasn't."

His harsh laugh covered the sound of the door opening, but the blast of cold air woke her up.

"What are we going to do about it?"

He shook his head. "I'll see you in the morning."

After he shut the door, Grace paced in small circles between the couch and the bed. She was going about this all wrong. Instead of letting him think everything was about forever and all or nothing, she should explain to Charlie that they could explore this thing between them. As long as he understood that she had zero interest in anything long term, surely they could keep things light and easy until everything between them ran its course. And it would. Charlie would eventually get back to his plan, but maybe there was a way that they could be friends anyway. She could keep her job as long as she wanted it.

And she could have Charlie too.

Grace flopped back on the bed, resigned to another long night of going in circles.

CHARLIE FORCED HIMSELF to take one step and then another until he was back inside the warmth of the hotel. He leaned against the wall in the hallway next to the *Blue Christmas* album cover and tried to make himself think clearly and rationally about everything.

He'd meant to take his time, give her a chance to get to know him and maybe forget the first Charlie she'd met. To him, a dinner date was the natural first step.

She'd turned him down. And if that wasn't enough, the kiss had . . . The second kiss was even better than the first.

Now that he was away from her, he had to consider his own reaction to her logically. He was the guy who made decisions based on black and white criteria: cost, potential return on investment, pros, cons, quantifiable determinants of possible success.

Here, he knew he liked the way she looked. And that he was easy around her. But it wasn't something he could tie dollars to or facts or anything that he could stack up and count. He was easy around her. Even crammed into his mother's office with the whole group of people who looked at him as the prodigal son, he'd met her eyes and felt calm. And okay. That was a huge factor, no matter how impossible it was to measure.

But the part he was forgetting in his study of this unusual phenomenon was what she thought about him. She might think he was the biggest stick in the mud there was, gold jacket and Elvis hair notwithstanding. And she probably should. Those were the exceptions to his rule of quiet country life with his computer, his projects, and himself. Lots and lots of time with himself. He should give up thinking about what he thought about her and devote a little brainpower to figuring out how make a better impression on her. Obviously. His Beale Street offer had been an honest attempt to find something she'd like even if he hated every minute.

How did people do this? Dating was impossible. Being single was impossible. And being married . . . from what he could tell, it was also impossible. All of a sudden, he wanted to be home where it was quiet and he could think without the distraction of Grace or his mother or the never-ending Elvis music that even now he could hear coming from Viva Las Vegas.

"Should I be worried you're lurking down this hallway?"

Charlie opened his eyes to see his mother standing in front of him. She'd added jingle bell earrings, so he had no idea how she'd managed to sneak up on him. Obviously he couldn't hear her over the voices shouting in his head.

"Just thinking."

"Seems an odd spot." Willodean raised her eyebrows

and glanced out the door. "But I guess I know what you're thinking about anyway."

"Actually I was thinking about how ready I am to get back home." When his mother's smile disappeared, Charlie wanted to apologize. But it was the truth. After all their conversation, he didn't want to hurt her but he also wanted to make her understand he hadn't changed his mind about spending a lot of time at the hotel. Charlie pushed away from the wall, and they headed for the lobby.

"Mom, do you ever think about visiting me? The place . . . it's nothing like what you remember. I've made it over from top to bottom."

His mother nodded. "I know and I should. It's not very brave of me to sit over here in Memphis and moan about missing you when all I'd have to do is jump in the car. I know that. There's just something about that place. And I'm thinking that being so very different might make it even harder to go back."

Even to spend time with me? That question teetered on the tip of his tongue, ready to tumble out, but he bit it back. The answer didn't really matter. That's what he had to learn. He might want her to miss him enough to put aside her own concerns, to pursue him, like he had followed her a few thousand times growing up in her Elvis-themed dream, but at some point he was going to have to get a handle on those feelings and understand that the way things used to be wasn't the same as they were today. And the very same was true of tomorrow. He didn't want to regret things he should have said or done.

"Sure, I can understand that. And I do like the chapel. It's peaceful. You know I like peaceful."

Willodean patted his shoulder before she stepped onto the elevator. As the doors closed, she said, "Can't quite imagine how a son of mine could be happier tromping in the woods with a camera or hammering nails than living every day with meat loaf on speed dial, but I'm guessing I can just go with different strokes for different folks."

Reminded again that he was the one who didn't fit around here, Charlie leaned back against the elevator. "Just because I like a little peace and quiet doesn't mean I'm not fun, you know. If you knew the companies I'd gambled on lately, you'd be surprised. In the past six months, I've invested your money in solar panels, low-calorie ice cream, and flying alarm clocks. Just for the fun of it!" He waited for her to be surprised. Instead she looked a little sad and a little amused, all at the same time.

"We've got to get you out of those mountains more, Charlie."

He had to laugh as much as he hated to. When the elevator doors opened, he followed her down the Hawaiian hallway.

"Any progress on my gift, Charlie? Or anything I can do to help with next year's idea?" He didn't answer but watched the wheels turn in her head. "Maybe by pushing you and Grace together?" Willodean blinked. Then she hooted. "I believe I do feel an I-told-you-so coming on."

Charlie shook his head. "I can't believe we're having this conversation. But there's something about her. I shouldn't feel this way, this crazy attraction because she's just all wrong for me, but when I'm with her it's like everything settles." He scrubbed both hands down his face. "It's hard to explain."

When he glanced at his mother, it was clear she was biting back an answer. And if she wanted to celebrate by spiking the ball in the end zone or even crow about being right while he was wrong, he'd deserve it. He could already taste his pompous speech about how ridiculous the idea of love at first sight was. He'd been certain of the world and his place in it when she'd tried to explain why she'd married Travis three months after she'd hired him to cook in Viva Las Vegas.

Maybe it would do him good for her to replay the conversation. He still wasn't sure he believed, but he was beginning to think an instant connection, even if it might not qualify as love, was totally possible. Could happen. Had happened already. On his part anyway.

But his mother showed great restraint. Instead of reminding him of stupid things he'd said when he was young, she asked, "What in the world are you doing here with me? Didn't I tell you to take her out to dinner? I mean, you're handsome, smart, and rich, but don't be lazy enough to think that's all a good woman needs." She frowned in concentration and then wagged her head from side to side. "Okay, well, maybe that is all a lot of good women do need, but you can do better, can't you?"

Charlie flopped back against the wall right next to the painted hula girl frozen mid-wave. "I asked her out. I thought she'd jump at the chance to see Beale Street.

Girl like her, used to the bright lights of big cities, has to be going a little stir crazy staring at the walls of a studio apartment."

Willodean frowned, her black brows forming a sharp V over calculating eyes. "She turned you down. That might not be a good sign. Thought she was smarter than that." She pursed her lips. "Wait. You didn't happen to say 'girl like you' when you asked, did you?"

Charlie didn't know whether she was doing it for effect or it was an honest display of loyalty, but it was nice that she'd automatically take his side against her newest adoptee. He rubbed his chest and did his best to call the warmish feeling there heartburn. He was old enough to fight his own battles, but it was nice that he could count on his mother's support if he had to.

"Maybe." When his mother shook her head, he got it. Grace's change from warm welcome to cool breeze made more sense. He thumped his head against the wall. "She mentioned having to be at work early Saturday like it was an excuse."

"Girl doesn't know you very well, though, does she?"

Now his eyebrows formed a sharp V. He couldn't see them, but he knew enough about his own face to know that his mother's was stamped all over it. Their frowns were nearly identical. "What does that mean?"

Willodean shrugged. "Well, I mean, you know ..." She trailed off and looked out around the hallway like someone might burst in to save her from this line of conversation. After five seconds of wishful gazing, she said, "It's not like you're a real party animal. You can still do

Beale Street on a school night because your schedule means you have to be tucked in bed by ten."

Charlie straightened, ready to hotly defend himself. But there was no defense. She was right about his schedule. "Actually, I'm a big boy now. I stay up until eleven." When he looked at his mother, her eyes were twinkling again. He fought back a smile.

"Well, it seems you might have a problem, Charlie. Those other ladies won't work and Grace won't have you. Not like this anyway."

"Like this?" He glanced down at his clothes, all black, of course. Maybe he could try some color. Like maybe blue. He'd always thought blue was his favorite color.

"Never thought I'd have to say this, but you better make up your mind. One day she's a gold digger intent on robbing me or you or both of us blind unless you save the day and the next she's this mysterious siren who makes you do things you never thought you would." Willodean shook her head. "And neither one's very flattering, Charlie. Maybe try treating her like one of your matches, but instead of checking off the boxes you think you should go for, think about what you want. That thing you said about her making you feel settled . . . that's no small thing."

Then she hugged his neck. "Best part is that tomorrow's a whole new chance. You can try again, do better."

He patted her back and tried to rub away the ball of discomfort brewing in the center of his chest. He waved as his mother closed the door and stepped inside her own blue lagoon next door. He couldn't believe how many missteps he'd made with Grace. She'd said she didn't hold grudges, but there might be a limit to how many chances she'd give.

Still his mother was right. Again. As long as the sun rose in the morning, he had a chance to do it better. When he thought about that kiss, he decided he wasn't ready to give up, not yet. He'd just keep trying like the old Charlie. This crazy rush he felt? He knew better than to get in a hurry. He'd slow down. Take his time. Show her a better, more polite Charlie. She might not know what to think, but good businessmen knew that the first answer wasn't always the final answer.

Chapter Nine

GRACE WAS SITTING at her desk the next day and trying not to stare like an idiot at the way the muscles in Charlie's forearms flexed as he worked on her laptop. They'd said their awkward good mornings, and she was little bit relieved to see he'd had as much trouble sleeping as she had. Charlie was tired, but there was something about him that was a little different. Something very . . . nice. She picked up the coffee he'd brought her from Viva Las Vegas and took a sip while she considered asking him to go on a date herself, but this time to Starbucks. Beale Street hadn't been that hard to turn down, but she hadn't forgotten how badly she needed designer coffee.

And she'd been pretty stern when she lectured herself about how, instead of getting mad, she should have asked for an explanation. "Girl like you" could have meant any number of mostly inoffensive things. She and Charlie had moved past suspicion.

If only he'd kissed her this morning or tried to. Or even moved close enough to make it easy for her to kiss him, she knew they'd be back to normal. Or better. But he was a polite, cheerful stranger this morning. Very solicitous. It was weird.

After a very quick demonstration of the software, where she'd asked what she considered very logical questions, Charlie was working up some forms to help her track special requests, and he'd already called two different project management and software firms to request quotes. Since he'd invested small sums in both, they were both happy to take his call.

It was nice to have the help she needed. The research alone to find people capable of working out a system like this would have taken time.

She leaned her head back on her leather chair and glanced at the lists she'd pinned to the bulletin board behind her desk. She loved that every brainstorm she'd had to address increasing bookings in the conference area and chapel led to another brainstorm and another, but the lists were getting a little out of hand.

Willodean obviously agreed. She refused to come over again until Grace got a little less brainstormy. But Charlie had seemed pretty impressed when he stopped to read the first list, her ideas on spreading the word about the chapel.

Reminded of Charlie, she watched him work. The rolled sleeves of his black flannel shirt showed muscled forearms that rippled as he typed. And it was hard to ignore how far gone she was if she was lusting over a man working on a database. He didn't seem to notice she was in the room. Charlie was pretty good at focusing.

When her phone rang, she didn't even glance at the caller ID. "Hello?"

"Well, Grace Andersen, I was convinced I was going to have get on a plane to Vegas so I could claim your body." Her mother's voice was as dry as ever. Grace didn't think she'd ever heard her mother in a panic. Today was no different.

"Ah, hi, Mom." Grace watched Charlie's head shoot up, and she shrugged her shoulders. Of course that would get his attention. "Sorry I haven't called you this week."

"And I guess you forgot about last week too." She hadn't. She'd been busy last week, what with getting married and all. Plus, she hadn't wanted to run the risk of telling her mother about the wedding, Tommy Joe Huffle, or anything else that might cast a cloud on what was supposed to be a magical day. It was hard to keep a secret from Ann Andersen.

Grace cleared her throat. "Well, I was sort of waiting for the right time to give you some great news. I guess this works."

Her mother said, "You're coming home." She could hear a thread of happiness in her voice. Or maybe it was I-told-you-so. Grace wanted to go with happiness.

"Well, no, but I am closer. I've got a great new job in Memphis." She turned her chair to look out into the empty lobby of the second floor and waited.

Her mother sighed. "Doing what now?"

Grace took a deep breath. "Event planning for a hotel. I think I'm going to be really good at it too."

"For how long, Gracie? How long will you stick this one out?" In her head, Grace could see her mother slowly shaking her head.

She wished she knew the answer. She didn't so she ignored the question. She'd gotten pretty good at that. Her mother hated it, but it was hard to argue with someone who refused to engage. "Good news is that I think I can make it home for Christmas this year. I'll get a bus ticket, so if you or Daddy could pick me up in Knoxville, I'd love to see everyone."

As she said it, she realized it was true. Always before she'd hated the idea of going home without a television series or a movie role or even a national commercial to show for her time. But now, it seemed like she'd decided this might be her success.

"Of course we'll pick you up. We've missed you." Her mother didn't say anything for a minute, and Grace was sure she could hear a million unspoken bits of advice floating around. "And you know we'll send the money for you to get home any time you need it. That part hasn't changed, Grace." The certainty that this was how her whole adventure would end turned her mother's generous offer into another reminder that her dream had been silly all along and the longer it went, the sillier it got.

Grace squeezed her eyes shut and tried to tell herself that it was just the way her mother talked. The crushing guilt could only hit her if she let it. "Uh, okay, Mom.

When are you celebrating? I can't wait to have some of your turkey and dressing again."

"Christmas night. Both Kevin and Christy have to celebrate with in-laws on Christmas Eve. It won't be a full Christmas dinner. Your father bought two dozen pork chops, so that's what we're having."

Of course. Not even holiday tradition could stand in the way of Andersen practicality. "Well, I've just started this job, but I think my boss will be happy to give me a day or two to celebrate."

"We'd like to have you, but don't screw up a good job over it."

Grace shook her head and had to take a deep breath before she could answer. Instead she squeezed her eyes shut, shook her hand out, and forced a smile. "Of course not, Mom. I'd never do that." Not now.

Instead of listing all the perfectly acceptable paychecks she'd already lost, her mother was silent. If Grace concentrated, she thought she might hear her mother biting her tongue. Maybe that was a sign of growth.

"You just let us know when to pick you up, and we'll be there. You could try giving me a call. Now that we know the phone works."

Grace laughed at her mother's deadpan delivery. Like she had a million times before even when she wasn't exactly sure her mother was joking. That sarcasm was a lot more like her mother. "I'll do that. I can't wait to see you all. I guess I'll need to get some Christmas gifts, though, and in a hurry."

"Oh, no, we don't exchange gifts anymore. No one has

the time or the money to waste on exchanging scarves and the like."

Grace nodded. She should have expected that too. So maybe she'd never been thrilled at whatever hand-me-down had been washed up and wrapped for her on Christmas morning, but the package itself, with the bright paper and ribbon . . . that had been exciting. That had represented the hope and the possibility of Christmas.

But the whole conversation reminded her that, even though she'd been away and she had changed, home had stayed exactly the same. No matter how much she wanted it to be different, she had a feeling she'd be just as out of step as ever when she sat down at the table, the lone Andersen who would have chosen turkey even if it wasn't on sale and wrapping up scarves for fun.

Her mother cleared her throat. "You need to get back to work, but tell me more about this job. Event planning. Like throwing parties? You'd like that." Her tone said she had no idea why, but Grace was happy to have her interest.

"Sure, parties, conferences, meetings, weddings. The hotel, the Rock'n'Rolla Hotel, is inspired by Elvis so the events will all be a lot of fun." She braced an elbow on her desk and rested her forehead on her hand.

"Elvis. A themed hotel." After a beat, her mother added, "Now that sounds more like you."

And Grace fought the urge to explain or cry or argue or . . . she didn't even know but there it was, the tone of voice that said she was doing it all wrong again.

"I could do well here, make a place. Give me a chance. You'll see."

Her mother sighed again. "Of course, Gracie. It's just that . . . at some point, you have to settle. You have to find something permanent."

Grace glanced over her shoulder to see if Charlie was eavesdropping as shamelessly as she would be in the same position. He continued to type away on his computer, his e-mail program open now. "The thing is, this place feels permanent to me. I fit here. And I'm doing an amazing job already." She glanced at the lists again and nodded as she said it. It was all true.

"Well, if you make it for Christmas dinner, bring pictures. We'd love to see more of the place." That was her mother's attempt at being encouraging.

"Mom, I'm coming. Count on it." And the first picture she was going to show them was of this office. Maybe she could get Charlie to pose too.

"Good. Can't wait to have you home again." Reading between her mother's lines, Grace wondered if her mother thought once she made it there, Grace might not want to leave again. Picturing her mother's slight frown and her father's mostly confused look around her, she knew she would always want to leave again. Visits home were something to cherish, to look forward to, mainly because they were brief and rare. The idea of moving back home made her stomach hurt.

"I'll check the bus schedule and call you after I buy my ticket to let you know when and where, okay? I'm working now so I should get back to it."

The bus ticket was going to eat up most of the check she'd planned to keep after paying down her hotel and wedding bill, but it would be worth it. That alone would please her mother and pleasing her mother was rare enough that she was happy to give up the idea of another shopping trip.

"You do that. I miss you."

Grace could hear the truth in her mother's voice. And it made her happy and sad. They were so different. They'd always have trouble talking to each other, but she never really doubted her mother loved her. It was just hard to believe her mother liked her sometimes.

"Love you, Mom."

Her mother said, "Love you, Gracie," and Grace ended the call. She plopped the phone down on the desk and scrunched up her face and waved her hands around while she paced back and forth in the tiny spot in front of the door.

"Should I have left?"

Grace opened her eyes to see Charlie watching her, his lips turned up at the corners because he was no doubt amused by her weird habit.

"Making the face helps me get rid of fear or whatever. Always has. I started it with stage fright, but now . . . it helps cheer me up." She put her hands to her cheeks. "And my mother . . . sometimes I need a little cheering up after I talk to her."

He nodded. "I get that." She knew he did. Probably more than anyone she knew, he understood how hard it was to love someone so much and never see eye to eye.

"You don't think Willodean would mind if I took two days at Christmas to go home, do you?" She wrung her hands as she realized she had to ask these things in advance. She was working in the real world, and she wanted her job and her nice apartment to be waiting for her when she came back.

Charlie gave her the are-you-kidding look. "She'd buy you the ticket and send you herself if she knew you wanted to go. She'll be happy to give you the time off."

"Money for a bus ticket . . ." She plopped down in her chair. "Good thing we won't be exchanging gifts. They'll just have to enjoy my shining presence as the best Christmas gift ever. Or I could sing 'Love Me Tender' for them. Far as I know, nobody in my family hates it." Out of the corner of her eye, she could see him open his mouth and close it again. "Spit it out, whatever it is you're dying to say."

"Let me give you the money for the ticket."

His voice was all business, the same bossy tone she'd heard every time he'd warned Willodean about trusting her, and she hated it.

"You don't even have to pay me back." He slapped his forehead. "Forget that. I'll just take you home. Sevierville's not that far from Newport." He nodded like he was satisfied everything was settled properly and turned back to her laptop.

"Not so fast." She waited for him to turn back around. "You're forgetting some things. First, a *girl like me* doesn't take handouts. Never have, never will. I'm happy to work a little extra to pay for a bus ticket.

Maybe I can pick up a shift or two at Viva Las Vegas."
Charlie shook his head and started to answer, but she
held up her hand. She was surprised he waited. "And it's
Christmas, Charlie. You need to be here at the hotel, not
six hours away. Besides, my mother might not survive
the wondrous surprise of such an upright gentleman es-
corting me." Of course she would. If anything showed
on her mother's face, it would only be mild surprise. But
he didn't know that.

"It's fine. I'll go home and come back. Everybody's
happy." He nodded as he said it and pointed at the laptop
like her silly independence was ruining his work flow.

"No way. I'll buy a bus ticket today, after I talk to Willodean." For some reason, the idea that he would go so
far out of his way to help her felt weird. She was so used
to doing it all on her own for herself that it was hard to
imagine a world in which a man would drive across the
state of Tennessee so she could have Christmas at home
with her family, especially this man, the one who'd been
ready to call her in for grand theft auto.

He sighed. "You don't have to prove anything anymore, Grace. I believe you never intended to take advantage of anyone, you always pay your way, and even if
you'd married Tommy Joe Huffle, he would have gotten
the better end of the deal." He got up and walked over to
sit on the corner of the desk. "I was wrong."

"You didn't even stutter as you said that. Who are you
and what have you done with my Charlie?"

"'My Charlie'? I like the way that sounds." She liked it
too and the way the corner of his mouth turned up. "And

when I said 'girl like you' last night, all I meant was fun, social, not anything else."

Willing to take him at his word all of sudden because of her improved mental outlook, Grace nodded. "Okay, but still . . . work, you know?" She didn't know if she meant only Saturday or the fact that he was the boss's son or both or something else she hadn't even thought of. She just wanted him to be sure.

"Yeah, I know. We will. And then maybe, after work is over tomorrow, we can reevaluate, okay?" He reached over to turn the laptop. "Let me show you what I've set up so far to make sure I'm on the right track." He clicked and pointed and talked about the changes he'd made to the forms to make her job easier and the preliminary calendar software he'd gotten from one of the firms he'd contacted. And she was impressed.

She was also happy to have his help. Men who got excited about software projects and offered to drive her six hours out of their way with no strings attached were rare in Grace's world. And she was certain that Charlie would have no idea what she was talking about if she pointed out his specialness. He was his mother's son that way.

If he kept it up, she was in serious danger of rolling to a stop right here in Memphis, Tennessee. That idea scared her to death, but for the first time ever she could see how that end could be the beginning of something fabulous.

Chapter Ten

ON SATURDAY AFTERNOON, Charlie had decided that spending time with Grace but not being able to touch her was a surefire way to drive himself insane.

They'd worked a full day of crazy weddings, and he was glad to have had her help. The last couple, retirees who'd rekindled an old flame through Facebook, had gone whole hog with multiple songs, readings from the Bible and their own really bad poetry, and he'd needed her help to keep everything on track. They'd worked well together. But he could just tell she was getting ready to cry when the groom, a short man in a blue tuxedo, had broken up and had to grab a big white handkerchief from his pocket to make it through. He'd raised both eyebrows at Grace and watched her sniff and pull herself together. Then he'd winked to see the corners of her mouth turn up.

Now he pulled down the streamers fastened to the ends of the pews while he waited for her to return from helping the bride pack up her stuff. He figured there would be a big party over in Viva Las Vegas as soon as the bride and groom appeared. They looked like they knew how to celebrate.

"All right, I think everything's locked up. We can call this Saturday finished." Grace sat down and then immediately stretched out on the pew with a tired sigh. "And I think I'm going to celebrate my first week with a hamburger from Viva Las Vegas and the romance novel Randa left on my doorstep." She turned her head. "What about you? I know you're planning to leave early in the morning."

He couldn't tell how she felt about it either. He wanted her to be as melancholy at the thought as he was, but whatever she'd done to convince herself that they were better as friends was working.

"Yeah, pretty early."

Grace eased up to face him, her elbows propped on the back of the pew. "Tired, Charlie?"

He nodded. "Yeah, a little, but instead of the party at Viva Las Vegas, I was wondering if you'd like to share a pizza. I'll pick it up. Know a great place . . ." It was pizza. Who could turn down pizza?

He thought she was going to, but instead she said, "Okay, sounds good. I need to know a good pizza place since I don't cook if I can help it."

"Really? I thought you were some sort of chef or something?" He tried to remember the list of her jobs. There was something about cooking in there.

"Raw foods chef. No real cooking required, although

I've always wanted to take a cooking class. The last time I tried to make rice on the stove, I nearly boiled myself to a three-alarm fire. I didn't lose my job that time, but my roommate strongly encouraged me to never cook anything ever again." Her face was at once sad and amused when she smiled up at him. "I would love to be able to make a chocolate cake without having to call the fire department."

"Why haven't you done that? Seems a simple enough goal." He tried to come up with any reason he'd volunteer for a cooking class and couldn't.

She shrugged. "Never had the time. Or money. And finding both at once . . ." She smiled brightly. "But I have *not* given up yet."

A terrible thought crossed Charlie's mind. "You said you didn't think you were a vegetarian anymore, right?" He tried to be open-minded when he said it, but the truth was that it would be a hard thing to let go of what might be the perfect woman, except for her difficulties in settling down and financial planning, but giving up the perfect steak would be nearly impossible. He was a big believer in the power of the perfect steak.

"For about six months, I *was* a vegetarian." She pursed her lips and then busied herself with picking up his pile of streamers.

"And then what happened?"

She motioned vaguely as she shoved them in a garbage bag. "That boyfriend dumped me. I consoled myself with a hamburger the size of my head. Beef and I have been on solid footing ever since. Men may come and go, but the perfect medium rare steak is a joy forever." She nodded once and they both laughed and Charlie started to wonder if the story of the man who proposed to the woman because she was pretty enough to stop him in his tracks and she loved a good steak would make the rounds as the most romantic thing ever or the stupidest.

"All right. I'll be back . . ." Charlie flipped his watch over to check the time. "How about eight? I'll stop and de-Elvis too." He pointed at his crunchy hair. He'd gotten rid of the gold jacket half a second after the last guest filed out of the chapel, but the hair took a little more effort.

They walked out through the dark lobby and Grace locked the door. "Another clear night." Then she shivered. "But I guess it's too soon to give up on snow, right?"

Charlie nodded. "Way too soon to give up."

She shot him a quick look and then she frowned.

"Get inside. I'll come bearing pizza soon." Grace narrowed her eyes at his order, but after another shiver, she headed for the staff apartments. She waved and stepped inside her apartment. Charlie looked up at the dark sky and something clicked in place. It was too soon to give up on snow and on convincing Grace to give them a shot. This was the time to take one more chance.

BY THE TIME Grace heard the knock on the door, she'd changed her mind at least ten times about what she wanted from Charlie and whether yes or no was the right answer to his offer to bring over pizza. They were doing pretty well as friends or friendly coworkers. When she remembered his kisses, though, she wasn't satisfied with that. She wanted more. Having Charlie McMinn and his pizza in her tiny apartment should make it easy enough to have what she wanted. And that was the scary part.

Grace paused in front of the door and smoothed a loose strand of hair behind her ear. Then she straightened her shoulders, wiped her sweaty palms on the jeans she'd changed into as quickly as she could after she left Charlie out by the pool, and opened the door.

And as soon as she saw Charlie standing there, holding a pizza box and two cups, she was glad she'd said yes.

"Hi." For some reason she felt as nervous as she had when Russell Pickens had stood on her doorstep in a rented tuxedo with a bedraggled corsage. She'd traveled a lot of miles since her senior prom, but a handsome man holding a pizza seemed to hold a lot more promise than even the high school quarterback had that night. When Charlie's warm breath clouded the air around him with his answering "Hi," she remembered the crucial step of getting him inside: moving out of the doorway.

"Come in." She stepped back and took the pizza box and cups while he shrugged out of his jacket.

Pointing theatrically at the single stool Tony had brought her from some hotel storage area for odds and ends, she said, "Well, have a seat." She displayed her inherited plastic plates with a flourish. "You can have this smiley face or that one." As she settled across the bar from him and watched him pile gooey pizza on top of both, she asked, "What's in the cup?"

He took a huge bite of pizza and held up one finger.

Eventually, he said, "Sorry. We're past my normal dinnertime. My stomach was pretty sure I was starving. It's sweet tea, as is only appropriate with barbeque pizza." He tilted his head to study her face. "Besides, that *was* what I was drinking the day you drained my glass in Viva Las Vegas approximately thirty minutes after we met."

Grace's lips twitched as she fought down the satisfied smirk that wanted to escape. She'd done it because she knew it would make an impression. And it had. "I bet you hated that. I'm surprised you didn't lecture me on all the wasting diseases I could get right then and there."

Charlie's laugh was low and quiet. In her small apartment, it was an intimate sound and she could feel the ripple all the way to her toes.

"Not gonna lie. That was a shock. And most people would have gotten an angry set down for sure. You might be the only person in the world who could get away with it." He picked up his cup. "But not this time. That's why you have your own. And, if you'll let me know what you'd pick if you were *ordering your own drink*, that's what I'll get the next time."

Pretending to consider the matter even as the idea that there would be a next time worried and thrilled her, Grace took a bite of her own pizza, and then washed it down with tea sweet enough to make her teeth hurt. She shivered and nodded. "That's absolutely perfect. I haven't had tea like that in such a long time."

They didn't talk while they devoured half the pizza. Eventually Charlie leaned back with a sigh. "All right. I think I'm going to make it."

Grace laughed. "Care to explain what it is with you and your schedule?"

He balled up his paper napkin. "The schedule is greatly tied to food, meal times, and spacing them properly so that my usually sweet disposition doesn't take a nosedive with my blood sugar." He shrugged. "Well, and the schedule is also my way of ordering things."

Grace pushed around the crusts on her plate. "Someone has mentioned to me that schedules matter to Charlie McMinn." Willodean's warning made a little more sense now.

"Maybe. It's not like I expect other people to stick to my schedule."

Grace just blinked at him and waited.

He sighed. "Okay, that's not exactly true. But the truth makes me sound a little bit like an anal stick in the mud. And who wants to go with the truth in that case?"

Grace laughed. "When you aren't here at the hotel, being disrupted, what does a good Charlie day look like?"

He ticked points off on his fingers. "Run at six, breakfast at seven, work at eight. Lunch at noon. Dinner at six. Bed at eleven."

"And what about when you're wheeling and dealing, investing like the shark you are."

He tried a modest shrug. "That doesn't take up much of the day. I'm pretty good at it."

"Of course you are. I would expect nothing else." Grace took another bite of her pizza. "And the routine never gets boring? Do you ever want to shake things up? I like variety."

"Boring? Maybe. But I'm not big on making a change just to make a change. A good reason? Then I can be flexible." He said the word like he was unfamiliar with it. "But for you? Liking flexibility's going to be good as an event planner. Lots of events, different times of day." He nodded encouragingly.

He was trying to be positive, relate to the free spirit. It was kind of cute, especially since it looked so odd on him.

"Are you excited about going home for a visit? How does it feel to be this close?" He took a sip of his tea. "Tea this good ought to have brought you back home sooner."

Grace shrugged. "You might have a hard time understanding this, but I just couldn't fit in with my family. I'm the youngest of seven, and they couldn't be any more regular if they tried. Schedules and budgets and multitasking were all very important. My mother would be a big fan of your schedule and would give me the most confused look if I dared to deviate from it. Imagine it. Six normal kids and one oddball that was determined to be grand. And nothing about that's changed, so while I'm looking forward to it, I'm dreading it too."

Charlie leaned both elbows on the bar. "Or maybe you spent your formative years as the only person on a schedule in a house with a woman who'd rather roll the dice than analyze and who adopts new people like it's going out of style when all you want to do is sit with her and tell her about the bully at school who likes to pick on rich kids but she can't talk because she's got a hotel to decorate and every visit is a reminder that things will never be the way you want."

The tense silence stretched between them, and Grace knew more about Charlie in that minute than she'd known about any other man she'd dated, no matter how long they were together. Before she could get her mouth in motion, he took a deep breath. "So maybe you convince yourself to build your own world, run it all on time because it makes you happy even if you can't quite convince everyone else to run on it too. And then you feel like a total ass when you tell a beautiful woman that you like to eat your dinner at six every night because you have mommy issues."

He started to stand, but Grace stopped him by wrapping her hands around his and squeezing them. "Stop. Wait. You don't have to feel that way, Charlie. Here's the thing about being a rolling stone. I've met a lot of people. Some of them weren't nice, but most of them were just doing the best they could, you know? You run into some people along the way that teach you that no matter what the past looks like, where they started, the who they are now is just your . . ." She looked into his eyes and tried to figure out what to say that didn't sound like kooky new age nonsense or romantic words that would send a guy like Charlie running out into the night.

One corner of his mouth turned up. "You want to say soul mate or something like that but not say soul mate. Right?"

Grace squeezed her eyes shut. "I worked my way into a corner, and I couldn't figure a way out but that was the gist of where I was going. I think what I mean is that there are people for whom the connection is instant. And we can leave it at that. I felt it with Willodean." She watched his face close off and then decided to throw it all in the ring. "Not like I felt it with you, of course, but still. With you, it was like we had a private joke that the rest of the world didn't get. To me, at least. And I've never felt that."

Surprise flashed across his face before Charlie rubbed his forehead. "I think I know what you mean."

Grace slid off her stool, picked up the plates, and put them in the kitchen's small sink. Then she shoved her hands in her pockets because she had no idea what to do next. The apartment had a television, but it had been so long since she watched anything she didn't know what was on. She had no radio. "I wish I had a deck of cards."

Charlie frowned.

"So that we could play something, poker or gin rummy or hearts." She shrugged her shoulder. "Dinner's over, but I don't want you to leave."

She did her very best to keep her eyes from straying to the full-sized pink elephant in the room, but the bed was hard to ignore as just about the only other things to look at were her blue pillows and the modern wall art of her bright orange coat.

"I wouldn't mind folding laundry." He rolled his eyes. "Or whatever."

This time when their eyes locked, the room was just as quiet but the tension felt different, lighter. She had the feeling they were on the same team again. She took a step toward him. She had no idea why except that he might be as magnetic for her as the call of the open road. She could never resist the possibility of the untraveled path, and there was something about Charlie that made her feel that same fluttery excitement and low-grade fear of the unknown.

"Maybe Tony has cards. I could go ask."

Charlie rubbed the back of his neck. "Or . . ."

When he didn't continue, she made the "keep going" motion with her hand. "Or what?"

"If I was at home tonight, I'd take advantage of the cold and clear. Head out in the woods—"

"On purpose?" Grace couldn't imagine what sort of boredom it would take to convince her to head out into the woods at night. No boredom would do that. Nothing short of an ax-wielding maniac would convince her to do that.

"Not big on the great outdoors, huh?"

That could be classified as an understatement along the lines of "Elvis has a lot of fans" but she didn't want him to go either. "Well, not really, but maybe I just needed someone to show me the ropes." She was pretty sure that was not true. It was the same as saying "Oh, sure, I love football" on the first date when she could barely name the local team mascot much less follow all the downs and yardages and penalties and positions. She'd done that one time and suffered every game until Super Bowl Sunday before she took a job in Los Angeles as a masseuse.

Charlie nodded. "Right. Well, I was going to say we could see if we could find any constellations, but it is pretty cold and—"

"Now that is something I can happily try, Charlie. Besides, outdoor Memphis is hardly the same as east

Tennessee. There I might see bears. What's the worst that could chase us here?" Ax-wielding maniac was the answer even in Memphis, but she wasn't going to say that. Her positive image had already taken one hit. She didn't want to add overactive imagination to it. She had a feeling that was not a quality Charlie would embrace.

"Maybe too much light pollution to see stars, but we could try." He tilted his head. "Want to?"

"I'll just grab my very warm orange coat. Aren't you glad I got it now? We don't have to worry about being shot on accident."

"You know you're smack dab in the middle of Memphis, right? Hunter orange probably won't save you from a stray bullet here." Charlie's voice was dry as he asked the question but she could hear the hint of amusement. Exactly the reaction she'd been going for.

She sniffed. "Maybe you're right, but my motto is always safety first."

He didn't argue. He wanted to. She could see it on his face. If she were giving out points, he'd have earned some by letting that whole comment pass by. "Maybe we could sit by the pool? It's clear, no trees."

He shook his head. "Too much light. We'll need to go where it's dark." The small smile on his lips and spark in his eyes combined with the husky promise in his voice made her shiver. Just like that. He could touch her without lifting a finger.

"Okay, well, how about we take this ugly pink blanket then? We should be warm enough, right?"

He nodded. "Pink's not your color?"

"Youngest of seven, remember? We had a boy's room and a girl's room. And my oldest sister Ellen loved pale pink everything. It was the color of the room forever. My parents were big on getting a lot of mileage out of whatever they bought. Every hand-me-down I had was pink. And not exciting pink. Girly, cotton candy pink." She rolled her eyes. "Pink's fine but pastel's not in my world." She pulled the blanket off the bed and quickly folded it while he slipped on his jacket.

"You know," he said, shooting obvious glances at her new coat, her new pillows, and her clothes, "I would have guessed that about you. The bed was the part that didn't make sense."

"Came with the place." She licked her lips and did her best not to look at the bed. The room shrank again now that they were both talking about the bed. Maybe it was because she'd spent a lot of time in that bed trying to *not* think of Charlie or his broad shoulders, his intense focus, or the way he kissed. If they ever ended up in that bed together, things would never be the same between them. *She* might never be the same. The instant connection between them would take sex, something she'd always enjoyed, and turn it into something else, something she'd never forget.

And it scared her to death to know that wherever her path took her, she might measure her future against the memory of Charlie. It scared her more to think of never having him in the first place.

After Charlie slipped into his coat, she shoved the folded blanket in his arms and took her only piece of modern art off the wall and put it on. Without a word, Charlie opened the door and motioned her through it. He pulled it shut, and they both took a minute to adjust to the night.

"C'mon, let's try the green space. I think that will be our best shot." He wrapped his hand around hers and pulled her along. While she carefully watched every step she took through the trees and grass in the field behind the hotel, she was conscious of the heat of his hand and the way he traced his thumb over her skin every once in a while, not like he had a pattern or a rhythm but like an unconscious habit.

"This is probably good." He pulled her in front of him and then unfolded the blanket before wrapping it over his own shoulders and sliding his arms around her waist. Grace jerked in surprise but grabbed his hands to stop him when he moved to step back. Maybe Charlie had changed his mind about getting closer. Even if this was the extent of his boldness, she wanted to savor it. "Let's see how cold it gets."

"You don't think someone will shoot us, do you? My safety orange is now completely hidden." And she'd never be cold again. There was something about standing in a dark field with Charlie's arms wrapped around her that turned up her temperature, even through his leather jacket and her puffy coat. That was some kind of connection.

"Not unless they're out hunting big pink bears, probably not." He squeezed her closer and she could feel the happy contentment pass between them.

"I should have warned you. I've never been able to see constellations."

She could feel his shrug, and he fidgeted for a minute. "Luckily, now there's an app for that. All you have to do is point the phone at the sky, and science will show you what you should be able to see. Clouds and light pollution might get in the way, but having a picture to know what you're looking for can help." He handed her the phone and grabbed the slipping blanket as she aimed it at the sky. "Most people can find the dippers easily enough." He tapped the phone screen. "There. The Big Dipper. Do you see those four bright stars there?"

And with the help of the screen she could. She could see exactly what he was pointing at. "You see the bowl and then the handle." He motioned and then shifted, his chest rubbing against her back as his breathing picked up. "And then the Little Dipper. You can see that." He pointed again.

She nodded. "This is amazing. There's an app for everything, right?"

His laugh was quiet and close to her ear. The warmth of his breath melted through her to pool in her abdomen, and she decided this was a hobby she could totally get into. She and Charlie could travel the world with his handy phone. He could show her the stars, and she'd just melt against him.

"I hate to point it out, knowing how you feel about bears, but if you can find the Big Dipper, you can also see Ursa Major." His arm shifted against her shoulder as he pointed again. "Hope that bear doesn't make you want to take off for civilization."

The warmth in his voice made her want to smile. And kiss him. And the two urges together were enough to confuse her into silence.

"Did you know Ptolemy listed Ursa Major in the second century in a list of forty-eight constellations? It's mentioned in the Bible. Shakespeare wrote about it. Van Gogh painted it."

"So what you're saying is that Ursa Major is kind of a big deal?"

Charlie turned her in his arms and frowned down at her. "Major. It's a major deal."

He wagged his eyebrows at her and she laughed.

"Am I boring you with more than you ever wanted to know about stars?" He shifted slightly, the movement of his thighs against hers a distraction she couldn't ignore. They swayed together and Grace was happy to have Charlie dancing like this, holding her, their breaths mingling in the still night.

"Believe me, I'm not bored at all. You just keep talking. I'm going to rest my head against your chest. I could stay here all night." Except her nose was cold. And her ears. When he rested his cheek against hers, she decided she could sacrifice a nose to the cause.

"We'll freeze if I move into what I know about Ursa Minor, and if I hit the zodiac, just forget about it. They'll find a frozen pink lump in the morning." His voice was low and irresistible. He slowly slid his hands down to her hips to squeeze, test, and Grace wanted more than anything for this to be their beginning. Right here. A fresh start. Here they weren't so mismatched. When it was just the two of them, they meshed together perfectly.

They stood there quietly for what might have been forever. Understanding that they could stand there until the end of time and for whatever reason Charlie would never make the move she wanted, Grace turned her head and pressed her lips against his in a quick, soft brush to test the waters. "Charlie, you said you'd always kiss me good-bye unless I tell you not to. Maybe you ought to add hello to your list too." She smiled up at him. This moment was perfect. She didn't want to lose it. His arms tightened around her, and he rested his forehead against hers.

"We have nothing in common, you know. I want trees and quiet, and you need applause and probably love every second you spend inside that hotel." He pressed his lips against hers, this time teasing with his tongue while he ran hot hands over her hips. "But that matters not one damn bit right now. I can't imagine any place I'd rather be. Please tell me you feel the same."

Grace opened her mouth and closed it again, confused about how to answer him. He'd said a mouthful very, very efficiently.

"I don't make friends all that easily. I probably don't have to tell you that, but I'm glad you showed up here in Memphis, Grace. I'd call you a friend, except I've never wanted to kiss any of my friends the way I want to kiss you. Walk away now if you don't feel the same."

Grace frowned up at him. "You're so smart, Charlie, but sometimes . . . I have something very important to tell you. Are you ready?" She waited for him to nod.

"When a woman moves toward you, she wants a kiss. When she follows you out into the dark Memphis night to see the stars, she wants a kiss. And if she presses up against you like this, you better kiss her again for good measure. Got it?"

Charlie tilted his head to one side, a frown of concentration showing how carefully he considered her words.

Grace rolled her eyes. "Don't think about it, Charlie. Just do it, okay?"

She could see the decision on his face. The frown smoothed out, his dark eyes heated up, and his tight lips eased. One corner of his mouth quirked up. She raised both eyebrows in a dare or silent invitation and then she couldn't remember what they were talking about. His lips were warm perfection on hers. When he pulled her even closer and slipped his thigh between hers, she gasped. Charlie took advantage and invaded her mouth with a teasing glance of his tongue against hers.

Every shift of his body sent a flash of heat down to pool between her thighs. The cold night air was crisp and clear, and she could smell Charlie's laundry detergent and something else, a clean, male scent that made her think of steamy showers. His arms around her tightened, and she wanted to be closer. When he pulled back to gasp for air, she leaned her head against his shoulder and closed her eyes.

"Like that? Is that the kind of kiss you're talking about?" Charlie's voice was low and rough next to her ear, and the shiver that ran down her spine had nothing to do with the temperature.

She nodded and then pressed a kiss against his neck right next to the collar of his flannel shirt. "You start slow but really build up speed, Charlie."

She could feel his rumbled laugh all the way to her toes and hear the smile in voice when he said, "You may know me better than I thought."

When he stepped away this time, she forced herself to stand her ground. She didn't follow him but looked up to see his eyes. "Thanks for showing me the stars."

He frowned again. "You're talking about the Big Dipper, right?"

Grace shook her head as she took his hand. They were quiet as they walked slowly back to the staff apartments, the ugly pink comforter draped across their shoulders. When they made it back inside, Charlie brushed some grass off and folded the comforter. "I hope you have another blanket. You're going to get cold without one tonight."

Grace watched him, and she could tell he was honestly worried about her getting cold. It was in no way an obscure come-on or a prelude to an offer to keep her warm all night. And she liked him even more for it. "I'll just toss it in the dryer, knock off any creepy crawlies." She forced him to let go of the comforter and tossed it on the couch.

He stepped back closer to the door, like he was going to leave just that easily. Like the kiss under the stars had been both hello and good-bye for the evening. And she couldn't have that.

"Wait." He closed the door so quickly she would have

laughed if she weren't so nervous. "Take off your coat." He frowned like he didn't appreciate her orders any more than she did his but he did it. And Grace scrambled out of hers before she tossed both on the couch. She tangled her fingers together and paced as she tried to figure out the best way to make her case.

"So, maybe we've gone about this the wrong way, Charlie." Even the wrinkle on his forehead was cute, but he didn't answer her so she went on. "I mean, we've been treating this"—she motioned between them wildly—"thing between us like it's life and death, all or nothing, now or never. But what if it isn't?" He straightened and took a step closer. "What if all we have to figure out is tonight? I can't believe I didn't see it! I don't worry about the future. I let each day take care of itself. Why would I get all wrapped up in what-ifs and when-this-happens?" She crossed her arms over her chest. "I blame you. You're the only thing that's changed."

Charlie took a deep long breath, scratched his chin, and said, "Just exactly what are you saying?"

Grace felt a hysterical laugh bubbling up, but it wouldn't help her case so she squashed it. No matter what sort of free-spirit nonsense she was spouting, she felt like she was about to take a leap of faith. But Charlie was here. And she didn't want him to leave tonight. If she thought about the next six days without the chance of running into him somewhere in the hotel, she felt sad and maybe a little lost. But she was going to give up the future and focus on right here, right now. And if he didn't step away from the door and kiss her, she was going to take matters into her own hands and soon . . .

Charlie's mouth quirked into a lopsided smile. "Are you asking me to stay, Grace? I'm not sure I can forget about all the rest, but if you want me, I'm staying."

He caught her as she bumped against him, her arms around his neck and her lips pressed against his. She'd never been so happy for her compact living space as she was then. She pulled him with her step by step without taking her lips off his. When she stumbled up against the bed, Charlie laughed and stepped back. "I like the destination, but maybe we should slow down."

Grace nodded. "Sure. In a minute." She toed off both shoes and then pulled her sweatshirt over her head in one smooth movement, afraid to give either of them much time to think about anything other than that moment. Before she could get her pants undone, he grabbed both her hands and guided her back onto the bed.

"Slow down. Believe me, I'm not going anywhere tonight." Grace thought for a split second about telling Charlie to turn out the lights, but the gleam in his brown eyes as he leaned back to take a long look at her flimsy black bra was worth a little exposure.

"It's a good thing I didn't know this was under that sweatshirt, Grace." His finger was a featherlight pressure as it outlined the cups of her bra. "Makes me curious about the rest."

She gasped a laugh as he leaned back and in his normal efficient manner unbuttoned, unzipped, and yanked off her jeans. He stood and lifted one foot up to rub it, a seduction all on its own after a long day in her business-like heels. He tossed her sock away and then conquered her completely by doing the same with her other foot. Sprawled on the bed, unable to move, Grace was happy to see him reach for the buttons of his shirt. Maybe he was a conqueror, his eyes memorizing every curve of her body, but she was ready to do a little exploring of her own.

She pushed the straps of her bra down and reached to unfasten it, glorying in the way his gaze was locked on her. When she slid her fingers in the waistband of her panties and slid them off, she thought he might have stopped breathing altogether. And whatever fears she had disappeared. Maybe her whole life she'd been looking for the place where she stood out, where people noticed her. As long as she had one hand on her bra and Charlie was around, she had the feeling he'd see nothing else. Tonight she'd found what she was looking for.

Chapter Eleven

GRACE ANDERSEN IN a wedding dress was so beautiful it hurt. Grace Andersen in a bright red dress on a stage was magnetic. Grace Andersen in an orange coat on a winter night made a man warm and think about futures and happily ever after. But Grace in nothing . . .

Charlie didn't even have the right words. Instead of telling her how beautiful she was or how pretty her hair looked spread out on the pink sheets she hated or how lucky he felt to be this close, all he could say was "Wow."

Grace reached out and helped guide him down. He heard a hitch in her voice as he settled against her and loved the way she squirmed when he rubbed his chest against hers. When their eyes had met in the mirror of the bridal suite, he'd been amazed by how beautiful she was. She'd glowed. But here, pressed tightly against his chest, her perfect skin hot against his, he was certain there was not another woman in the world like Grace. The way she bit her lip and whispered his name made him feel like a god.

Her legs shifted restlessly against his as he leaned up on one elbow to paint a light trail of kisses from her collarbones down between her breasts and around her belly button. Her gasp was a laugh and she said, "That tickles. We aren't playing that sort of—"

He wrapped his hand around her breast and covered her mouth with his at the same time, their bodies perfectly aligned and her satin skin as beautiful as he remembered from their very first meeting. While his fingers teased her nipple, he caught her sighs and impatience with his kiss. He wanted to laugh with happiness because this was . . . If he'd missed out on this because of his own stupid plans, that would have been a sad ending. Each squirm brought her closer against him and their tongues tangled and tasted until he was lightheaded. She wrapped her arms around him, her fingernails sharp encouragement to do more and faster.

"God, Grace," Charlie said as he eased back to watch her face while he explored her other breast. He leaned down to suck that nipple into his mouth and had to fight back a groan when she buried her fingers in his hair to pull him closer. Her legs twisted against his, and each shift of her hips was a hot caress against him.

She frowned when he pulled back, resting between her thighs to memorize her.

Trailing her fingers down his chest, she said, "Don't stop now, Charlie."

As if he could. Their eyes met and he knew everything would be different because of her.

The idea didn't scare him the way he might have expected.

She was beautiful spread out before him. He smoothed his hands down over her sides, squeezing as he went to feel muscle and satin skin, before he gripped her hips and ran his thumbs over the curve of her abdomen. She squirmed beneath him until his finger teased through her curls and then down into her heat.

She arched under him and wrapped a hand around his forearm, to stop him or encourage him he wasn't sure, but he didn't stop and she didn't either, her hips moving against him eagerly until she forced her eyes open. He met her stare and absolutely nothing else mattered but Grace. Pleasing Grace. Loving Grace.

Winning Grace.

He kissed her hard on the lips then grabbed one of the condoms he'd been carrying in his wallet for who knows how long, opened it, and slipped it on. She sighed when he settled against her and then they both held their breath as he slid into her.

Charlie rested his forehead against hers and was happy to note her breaths were as ragged as his. He wanted to stay here with her forever. He shifted and felt the sharp points of her fingernails again. And then he moved. She groaned. And his control was gone. She wrapped arms and legs around him and held on as they worked against each other. When she arched, he pulled her hard against him and buried his head in her shoulder until the shudders stopped.

He was still gasping for breath when he realized his grip was hard enough to leave bruises. He forced himself to loosen his hold on her even though he hated every brush of cool air against his sweaty skin. Finally he rolled to the side and pulled her with him, her hair a beautiful sweaty tangle.

When he could talk without panting, he looked down at her. Her eyes were closed, dark eyelashes fanned over pink cheeks, but her hand moved in languid strokes over his side.

"You didn't fall asleep on me, did you?" He ran a hand down her arm and frowned at how cool she felt. He eased her back and watched her eyes drift dreamily open. When she blinked up at him, the sharp intelligence he normally saw in her eyes softened with hazy satisfaction, and he felt like a god again. Maybe if he could make her eyes do that every day, they could overcome fighting about schedules and the millions of other things that would pop up.

He had to tear himself away, but after stopping in her bathroom, Charlie flipped off all the lights, grabbed the blanket on his way back to the bed, and slid in next to her.

She sighed heavily as she rested against him. "This night has not gone like I expected."

He pulled her closer. "But in a good way, right?"

She stretched against him to kiss his cheek. "Thanks, Charlie."

He had no idea what she was thanking him for, and he didn't really want to get into his sharing again so he smoothed her hair over her shoulder and pulled the blanket up.

They were quiet for so long that he thought she'd fallen asleep. "So, if I have the chance to sing again, I know what not to sing. Do you have an Elvis song that you do like?"

" 'Heartbreak Hotel' maybe."

When she raised up on an elbow to frown at him, he laughed.

"You really have a problem with this place, don't you?"

He was surprised she'd gotten that from his answer, but she was damn smart.

"I did. Maybe I still do. A little." He rolled his head on the pillow. "Listen, my mom . . . she's great. You know it. I know it. The world knows it. And until this place came along, I had plenty of her time, even though she's always been a person with pet projects, usually people." Grace raised her eyebrows at him, and he kissed her forehead. "Of which you are my very favorite." He laughed at her frown and saw her lips twitch in response.

"With this visit, I think things are changing a little. My mom and I've talked. You're here." Charlie glanced away, afraid to see her reaction to that. "And even Tony's loosening up a little."

Grace rested her pointy chin on his chest, and he did his best not to wince.

She wiggled closer to look down in his face. "I think Willodean's lucky to have so many people who love her and are willing to fight over her, defend her. I hope she knows she's lucky."

Charlie watched a shadow cross her face and rubbed his hand down her back.

He wanted to ask her what that shadow was about,

why she didn't think she had anyone to fight over her or defend her. But she ran a hand down his chest, and he forgot where he was going.

Since he was laying all his cards out on the table, he was going to go for the whole hand. "You know how my mother thinks she's some awesome matchmaker?"

Grace nodded.

"Well, the thing is, I might be her nemesis, the one man in the world who can offset her abilities."

Grace frowned at him. "Maybe you should have told me that sooner, like before we got naked."

"I broke up her third marriage, her only failure, with my own powers. All I had to do was shout insults about her younger husband, call him a fortune hunter, pack my stuff, move all the way across the state, and refuse to talk to her for entirely too long. And poof! Next I hear, Travis Luttrell is no longer my stepfather."

Grace perked up. "Travis Luttrell? He was number three? Even I've heard of him. He was on one of those cooking competitions." She shook her head. "He's really good-looking and handy with a grill."

Charlie tried to remind himself that he was holding her. In bed. And she was naked. And they'd successfully rocked each other's worlds. There was no need to be jealous. There was no reason to feel like she'd just said his enemy was a really great guy. He didn't even know Travis Luttrell, not really.

"But they were adults, you know? They made their own decisions and with you taking your ball and moving across the state, it should have been easy to stick together.

The fact that they didn't . . . well, you didn't help, but I'm not sure you can take all the credit either." Grace didn't turn away from him, just watched his face carefully.

Charlie felt a little of his worry ease. He'd expected her to think he was a bad person. Really, what had his mother's marriage meant to him anyway? He was a grown up. She should have been free to do what she wanted. But Grace accepted him. Believed he was still okay.

Of course she did. Her ability to forgive easily might be number one on the list of things that made her perfect for him. He'd already proven he'd need it.

If it was possible, in the dark apartment Grace was even prettier than in the wedding dress. It had to be her hair. The snarls and tangles looked like she'd been twisting under him in passion. He liked the look.

He pulled her closer. "You make me feel like a damn hero, Grace Andersen."

She smiled down at him. "I like that. You make me want to be a hero myself."

"How many chances are you going to give me?" She straightened up, and he could see the confusion on her face. "How many times can I say the wrong thing or act like a possessive asshole before you move on?"

Grace snorted. Then she brushed his hair off his forehead and he liked the mix of woman who'd refuse to take his crap and still touched him tenderly. "Jeez, it's like you're two people. A pushy, demanding rich guy who gets what he wants. And this other guy, the one who's so . . ."

He didn't want to hear whatever she came up with to fill in the blank. "Just the one guy, Grace."

She nodded. "Well, here's the thing. I like you. Chances are good you'll never run out of second chances for saying something dumb. But I'm done thinking of forever. I only want to concentrate on one day at a time."

Her answer lightened the tension in his shoulders. "Anything I should know about? Something that would get me tossed on my ear with no chance of return?"

She frowned at him while she thought about it. "Well, sure. But . . . I don't have a list. Just . . . don't be a jerk. And if you are, remember that women love grand gestures, okay? You apologize. If that doesn't do the trick, try something on a larger scale." She nodded at him and waited for him to acknowledge her advice. "That can't fix everything, but I can't think of many things that a public profession of love wouldn't address. Just don't give up."

Love. He hadn't thought it. She hadn't said it. They weren't at love yet. But there was something about watching her lips form the word that made him want it.

"Apologize? McMinns don't usually apologize, mainly because we're almost always right."

Grace rolled her eyes. "Guess you'll have to decide how bad you want it, Charlie. When you mess up, that is."

It was probably a good thing she was already thinking of "when" he messed up, not if. Because it would happen. And then he'd have to fight his genetic predisposition to further escalate or to walk away. He wondered if he could make a better decision this time. He didn't want to spend the next fifteen years ducking Grace every time he visited the hotel.

The idea that he could just *not* mess up didn't really

occur to him. Maybe he was making some progress with his perfectionist tendencies.

When Grace settled over him, Charlie did his best to ignore the small warning bell going off in his head. The fact that he'd told her the worst things about himself, things he'd change if he could snap his fingers to do it, and she'd still laughed with him and kissed him and shared everything with him made it clear she wasn't just any girl. He'd had sex before. He couldn't imagine laughing in bed with either of his fiancées. He'd been about to marry them and was still unable or unwilling to be himself or talk about his mistakes like he had with Grace after less than a week.

It seemed pretty clear to him what he had to do. A smart man would hold on to her. All he needed was a plan. When she slid her hand under the cover and scraped her nails lightly in a blazing trail down his thigh, he decided he'd get right on that. First thing in the morning.

Chapter Twelve

WHEN HIS PHONE chirped an alarm, Charlie shifted and smiled as Grace muttered next to him. He was wrapped around her and didn't want to move. But he was anxious to get home. The sooner he went, the sooner he'd be back. The sooner he'd have another chance to convince Grace to think about the future. With him. Maybe she'd miss him so much while he was gone that she'd be a little more open to some real planning.

Unfortunately, her independence came with some stubbornness. He could see how all this needed to happen. Convincing her would be the hard part.

Even after just one night, he knew he wanted to wake up next to her again. He wanted to feel like this: rested, content—maybe even happy—every day.

"Good morning," he whispered.

Her eyelashes fluttered open before she twisted around to glare up at him. "Who says? And why is it so early?"

He waved his watch. "Schedule. I'm headed home today. Remember?"

She scooted up and shoved her wild hair away from her face. "You really need to get a hold of what Sunday means, Charlie. Rest."

He kissed her lips and slid from the bed. "Maybe next weekend. I'm going to miss you, you know. I'll be in a hurry to get back. That's the first time I've ever said that about this place."

Grace rubbed the sleep from her eyes and tried her bright smile. "I'm going to miss you too. And I'll be anxious for you to get back. That's the first time I've said that to any man. But there's plenty of work to do. I'll be fine, of course. Randa's asked me to help her shop. I do like spending someone else's money."

He knew she was teasing and maybe doing her best to show him nothing had changed, that everything was normal, but he couldn't let the opportunity pass. He wanted everything settled. He wanted to get his plan in motion. Having Grace in his quiet farmhouse would make everything perfect. Surely she would see that.

He traced a finger over her delicate features and waited for her to face him. "Marry me. Next Monday, we'll stand up before a justice of the peace. We'll celebrate Christmas here, then we'll go back to Newport and surprise your family with the news. I'll pay off your credit cards and give you a nice, new limitless one. Imagine going home for Christmas with fancy gifts and the steadiest of all boyfriends, a rich husband. Trust me, I'm good at this planning stuff. You don't have to think a thing about the future. I'll just take care of it."

Grace straightened up and yanked the sheet with her. "God, Charlie, way to ruin a mood. I've already explained this to you. Slow down and just . . . enjoy today. You have to listen! Don't push me."

He told himself not to overreact. "How did I ruin the mood? With a marriage proposal?" And maybe his tone wasn't quite as conciliatory as it should have been. He didn't feel like getting along. He wanted an answer. He wanted Grace. More than that, he wanted her to just say yes, pack up her stuff, and come with him. After years of making decisions involving big investments, he'd learned to go after what he wanted. Only his mother had ever derailed his plans.

Besides all that, he'd been trying to ignore the low-level anxiety that bubbled when the thought about leaving her here, in this hotel, near the interior decorator built like a linebacker.

Charlie was afraid that if he went away, the idea that she'd be better off with someone who actually stayed in Memphis might occur to her. And he couldn't stay in Memphis. After a week in this hotel, he was ready to spend some time hiking in the woods around his house, get sawdust in his hair by building his mother a small coffee table, and do some online shopping so that he could spoil Grace with gifts she'd love, and maybe . . . bore himself to death. No wonder she didn't jump at the chance to come home with him to Newport.

She huffed out a sigh. "Yeah. With a marriage . . . that

wasn't even a proposal and you know it. We've known each other a week. You hate gold diggers. You hardly know me, and I know you well enough that I understand this is just . . ." She slapped a hand on her thigh. "I don't even know what to call it, but it's not . . . I know what I want. We aren't there yet and now you've rushed it. Rushed me! And after we just talked about this! One day at a time, Charlie. That's all I can focus on for right now."

Charlie held up both hands to surrender. She had a point. But she just wasn't seeing the whole picture. This happened to him a lot. He had a great idea, jumped ahead, and then had to remember to bring everyone else with him. "Wait. You're right. I did rush. But calm down. Let's look at this logically." He knew the right thing to do here. For *both* of them. But he'd said it all wrong again. He took her hands in his and tried his best reasonable voice. "Grace, I . . . listen, you don't plan for the future. I get it. So you're worried, unsure. But I do and I was fully prepared to set Willodean on the matchmaking trail when I came to Memphis this time. That was going to be my Christmas gift to her."

He smiled at her. She didn't smile back. "But then there was you. And me. And this. Maybe my spreadsheets tell me that it's time I get married, settle down. I want kids. I want a wife. I need a hobby. I wouldn't mind if it was you." Just as soon as he said it, he knew he should never have said that last sentence. Or the one before it. Grace stiffened further and yanked her hand away. "You're at the same point. Or you were. You wouldn't have landed in Memphis otherwise. I don't do patient well, especially when it's so clear how this will work out if you would just . . . go along."

She jumped up to pace beside the bed. "So we should just . . . take a chance, roll the dice, because we're both ready to get married? And I should just believe you because you've used that smarmy, talk-down-to-the-little-lady tone with me. The one that I absolutely hate?"

Charlie decided to take one more run at logic. "When you told me about your plan to marry a rich man, I was mad and sad. But after a minute of consideration, I can see opportunity. I'm a business man at heart. And really, with an airtight prenuptial agreement and an honest good-faith effort from both of us, a marriage like that could work. There's really very little risk."

Grace's eyebrows shot up before she huffed angrily. "Do you even hear yourself, Charlie?" Her lips were a tight line as she shook her head. "Just because it's *logical* to you, doesn't make it right for *me*. And I can't imagine spending years with someone who would treat me like I'm the one with a problem every time we disagree."

He held up his hands to try to calm her down. "Just . . . think about it. The prenup wouldn't take very long to draw up. Maybe a romantic Christmas wedding instead of the justice of the peace? We could do it here."

Grace covered her face with her hands before she laughed. "You really don't get it. I like you. I am thinking of next weekend with you, but that's as far into the future as I'm willing to go right now. And I can't even imagine what would convince me to try with a guy who's writing his open door into a legally binding contract. I don't think . . . someone who's pretty sure it won't last . . ." She shook her head. "How sad does that make us? Besides, I'm not sure I do want to be married anymore. Maybe I never did. Maybe all I wanted was the beautiful dress and my time in the spotlight. But I think I could be really good at this job. I want to give it a chance, give myself a chance to see if this is it, the thing I've been looking for."

An angry response boiled on the tip of his tongue. He didn't roam around. He stayed. He didn't want an escape. He just didn't want to have any regrets. Things happened. People changed. That was all. The end. But she looked so miserable he forced himself to slow down.

"All right. I understand what you're saying." He didn't but it seemed like the right thing to say. "Nothing has to change today. I just want . . ." He pulled her back against his chest. "I just want you in my life. I want to take care of you, but . . . I guess I get it. *You* don't want that."

Grace heaved a sigh. "Charlie, that's not what you want." He started to argue but she shook her head and said, "No, you want me to do what you want and when you want it. I get it. Who doesn't? But you aren't listening to me. I'm staying here. Memphis is where I should be, not Newport. Not ever." Some of the tension eased out of her shoulders. "If what you wanted was me in your life, you would think about . . ."

"I'd think about moving to Memphis? You've got to be kidding me. I thought you understood, Grace." He started to yank up the blanket. "I've told you how I feel about this place. How can you even think I could move here? I mean, even for you?"

Grace's shoulders slumped. "I guess . . . I think this shows where we are pretty well, Charlie."

He thumped his head against the wall. "I'm not going to apologize for . . . offering you everything you wanted when you landed in Memphis and more. You could make us both so happy, Grace. Why are you being so . . . why can't you embrace the *journey* this time?"

Grace sniffed. "Are you mocking me now, Charlie? One disappointment and you have to . . . turn it into this?" She shook her head. "How can you feel so right and be so absolutely wrong for me? Maybe you better go."

Charlie stood up and yanked on his clothes. "You're going to change your mind. Well, you should change your mind. You'll think about this and we'll talk when I get back." He had to fight the panicky feeling welling up. Just the idea that the only way to have Grace was to settle in at the Rock'n'Rolla Hotel made his heart pound. Grace didn't move, didn't acknowledge his words. When he was dressed, he wrapped his arms around her and kissed her cheek. He whispered, "I promised myself I'd never leave without kissing you good-bye." Then he left her apartment and wondered where the hell he went from there.

WHEN GRACE FOLLOWED Charlie out to the lobby, she had the overwhelming urge to cry. That impulse was followed by a lot of mental tough love because it was crazy to be attached to Charlie like this after a week. In fact, for her, it was crazy to be that attached to him period. The fact that Charlie could make marriage sound like signing a mortgage said so much about him, none of it really endearing. And her own feelings left her vulnerable. And feeling vulnerable gave her itchy feet because it was harder to hit a moving target. She'd told herself he could leave without her this morning, that making a cleaner break would be easier, but she'd heard his whispered words in her ear and she couldn't let him leave without one last kiss.

So she watched Charlie hug his mother's neck. He and Tony shared a tense shift of the chin upward. And KT clapped him on the back and said, "Drive safely." They shared a wordless exchange and KT said, "And we'll see you next Friday."

Charlie smiled. "Yep, I'll be here, ready to suit up for Saturday weddings." His eyes met hers, and she could read the promise on his face. He was coming back. He wasn't giving up on his plan. And a little of her fear eased. There was something about him that made her believe his promises. Right now she was so angry at him for ruining their time together, for being so certain his way was the only way and that she'd come around just exactly like he expected, but she couldn't stay away.

Even though she knew he was coming back, she was going to miss him. And after the holiday, he'd be off wedding duty in the chapel. Willodean had found a Baptist preacher with a strong set of sideburns who'd jumped at the chance to work in the chapel when needed. So Charlie would have very little reason to come back.

She wanted him close. He made her feel steady. Solid. Grounded. Content.

The logical part of her, the one she'd frequently done her best to drown out, told her those weren't the best reasons to marry someone.

That same part was happy to give her a list of other reasons why she shouldn't marry him.

She shivered as she trailed behind him toward his SUV. He tossed his suitcase in the back and then turned to wrap his arms around her. They leaned against each other until Grace could feel the cold burning the end of her nose.

Do you really have to go? That's what she wanted to ask him. But she wouldn't.

Don't go. I'm afraid. She couldn't say that either because she couldn't be afraid. Strong. Happy. She would be fine without him. She had a great job, a place of her own, and thanks to Willodean's insistence, she had a nice budget to spend on event setup. She had her own purpose and she was coming to understand how important that was.

She was even thinking of spending some of the next check on a can of paint for her apartment. She'd never painted, never had her own place or enough desire to make it fit her like she did here in Memphis.

But she wanted Charlie too.

"I guess I have to go." His face looked set but there was something about his eyes that said maybe he wasn't sure either.

Determined to be happy, even now, Grace straightened. "Text me. Call me. Think of me." She stretched up to put a smacking kiss on his lips. She would just pretend everything was going to be okay. *Don't give up on me.*

He ran his hands over her hips and then took a step back. "Yes, ma'am."

Grace stood on the sidewalk and watched him wave and drive away. She was still standing there when Randa joined her on the sidewalk. "Ready to go?" She waved a key ring. "I have Tony's keys. We can buy anything we want!"

Grace forced a smile but she didn't fool Randa.

"Come on, Grace. It's just a week. Absence, fonder, all that jazz." Randa squeezed her shoulder and jingled the keys again. "Besides, there's nothing like a little retail therapy to take a girl's mind off a man, is there?"

Grace laughed. "Possibly alcohol, but this will accomplish more."

"Christmas gifts!" Randa clapped her hands together. "It's been . . . well, I've never had a chance like this, a time to buy thoughtful gifts for people who will appreciate them. This is going to be good."

Grace nodded and Randa tugged her off the sidewalk toward Tony's truck. Randa had enough money to make the trip fun. There was no sense in moping. Charlie would be back. She'd cope. And this was just the latest leg of the journey.

CHARLIE WAS PRETTY sure he'd made a mistake about fifteen minutes outside of Memphis but tried to tell himself that going home would help him decide what to do. When he got to the quiet of his old house and had a chance to think, he'd see the best way to talk to Grace to convince her that she was overreacting.

But he didn't believe it any better when he parked beside his porch, rolled out with a groan, and stretched to ease the stiffness in his legs. He walked around and tried to figure out the right words to fix it from hundreds of miles away. Words other than "You were right."

Made it home. Miss you. He hit send and then pulled all his luggage out and staggered up to the glass-paned door. His key was in the lock when he heard the tone that said he had an answer.

I hate that we fought. Already anxious for Friday. Misty is too.

He smiled, shoved his phone in his pocket and decided not to worry too much about the future. Maybe she was right. Things weren't where he wanted them to be, but he was home again. He'd think of something. When his plans were in danger, he always thought of something.

CHARLIE HAD EXHAUSTED all of his Christmas good humor and optimism about his ability to figure out a way to win Grace by the time he stepped away from his computer on Thursday. He'd followed up on both investment deals in the works, called for updates on the four companies he'd been working with, updated all of his records, and identified two new opportunities. He lived for this. Literally. But now, he wished he had a floor to sand or a wall to paint. He was contemplating the kitchen cabinets when he finally realized what he was doing. If he ripped them out just to have a project, his mother should have him committed.

He was bored. There was no other way to put it. He'd been bored before his last trip to the Rock'n'Rolla Hotel but there was something about knowing that Grace was there, the only person in the world who could make working weddings fun, that made everything he did at home seem ordinary. Grace was special. Grace was in Memphis.

And he wanted to be where Grace was.

Understanding that he'd be willing to give up his careful plan for the future for one girl, a girl who liked to dance to Elvis songs, insisted on wearing all the colors, and had listened to his worst mistake without once making him feel like a failure, was hard.

He'd stayed in Newport this long out of sheer stubbornness, hoping he'd come up with a way to have her and his old boring plan too.

As far as business went, it had been a good week. As far as Grace ideas, not so much. His way was still the simplest way. She should move here.

He took up the key ring for Willodean's dilapidated house in Memphis and flipped it on one finger while he surfed the Internet to see if he could at least come up with an inspired idea for his mother's Christmas gift.

He'd already paid for a dessert cooking class at a Memphis restaurant and ordered Grace a standing mixer. He'd seen one in the photos advertising a pastry class and then he'd found one in neon purple. Since he'd ordered it gift wrapped and shipped to the hotel, he was pretty sure he was the best, most efficient gift giver ever. Grace would finally get the chance to take her cooking class.

Maybe she'd share her first chocolate cake with him. He hoped it was the kind of present that said he was listening when she talked about something she'd always wanted to try. It had mattered enough for him to remember. She mattered enough that he'd listen to her and try to give her everything.

That was a lot of pressure for a kitchen appliance but he thought it was a sign of his own development that he could come up with it. He hoped she'd agree.

But that left his mother. With her gift, he could use some help.

Thinking he'd give her plenty of space, he'd texted Grace once or twice earlier in the week. And she'd replied. She'd spent just about every minute since he'd left shopping, first with Randa and then Mike, Willodean's decorator. When he'd read that, he'd felt the old familiar jealous monster rise up. Mike was a good-looking man. Maybe. Charlie wasn't a judge. He just knew KT growled every time Mike hugged Laura although they'd been friends a long time. The thought of Grace hugging Mike helped him understand KT's urge.

He'd been hunting the Internet for the perfect grand gesture for his mother with no luck. He'd almost bought her pink Cadillac in Nashville but took his finger off the button when he realized it wasn't big enough. Throwing money at the problem wouldn't work.

He sighed and rubbed his tired eyes as he leaned back in his desk chair. Maybe he'd just fall back to his old standby: a plane ticket to Hawaii. Really, who could complain about a gift like that?

And then he wouldn't need to spend any more time working on this.

Resolved to just buy the ticket, he sat up in time to watch one of the Web ads change over to a colorful shot of the best looking fried chicken, mashed potatoes, and greens he'd ever seen in his life. Luttrell's, voted best Southern food in the state, was having a special midnight seating for Christmas, complete with champagne. *Travis* Luttrell's.

And just like that, the grand gesture he knew he had to make was crystal clear. He had apologized and his mother had forgiven him, but something kept it from being settled for him. He was sure he'd made real progress with the whole Rock'n'Rolla family on this last trip. He didn't want to feel out of place anymore. It was time to face his mistake head on. He'd apologized to his mother, but he really needed to talk it out with Travis.

He picked up his phone to text Grace. *Just had the best idea for my mother's Christmas gift, the grandest of gestures.*

He waited anxiously while images of her out on the town with Mike flashed through his mind.

He had to let out a sigh of relief when he saw her answer. Maybe she really didn't hold a grudge. *Great! Is it bigger than a bread box?*

He laughed. *Much bigger.*

Don't forget my gift! You know what I want . . . snow! Or maybe Charlie McMinn singing his favorite Elvis song in Viva Las Vegas. The smiling emoticon showed she understood just how likely that was to happen. About as likely as snow for Christmas.

It wasn't the sort of romantic answer he'd been hoping for, the one where just being in his arms was enough. Or something like that. He was still thinking about how to answer her when she texted again. *Bought my bus ticket. I'm leaving on Sunday, so I'll miss the staff party but it'll be good to see the family.*

He tossed the key ring across his desk and shook his head. And just like that he understood something really important about himself and about her. He could change. And she was worth it. The idea of having someone to celebrate the holiday with had filled him with anticipation and . . . a strange glowing warmth that he might call love if he had to give it a name. And now that he knew she wouldn't be there, everything was wrong. But he had to learn not to push Grace, so he just texted: *Can't wait to see you.*

Watching her open her gift would still be nice on December 27. She would be worth the wait. He could go with the flow. He wished there was some way to get her snowflakes. He was willing to consider Memphis all over again. Finding a few snowflakes seemed easy after all that.

Her answer was gratifyingly fast. *I miss you.*

Me too. When he sent the last text, he tossed his phone on the desk and forced himself to leave it there. There was something that made him want to say "I love you." But not in a text.

And if it was true and he said it, she might leave skid marks on the way out the door. That was the very last thing he wanted. She was too important to walk away from when he was angry, and she was too special to try to manipulate or change into the person he'd thought he wanted. To keep her, he'd have to do the changing himself.

Instead of worrying that issue, he picked up his desk phone, called the hotel, and made a very special reservation with Tony's help and encouragement, then he dialed the number for Luttrell's in Nashville, Tennessee, and asked to speak to the chef. Nashville was an easy drive from Memphis. Since Grace was leaving Sunday and his meeting with Travis was Monday afternoon, he decided to combine business and . . . not pleasure, scheduled another meeting, and booked a hotel. He still had a lot to figure out about Grace, his mother, Travis, and how to get what he wanted, but had a feeling that swallowing his pride was going to be the biggest challenge.

Chapter Thirteen

GRACE HAD BEEN staring at the clock off and on since two seconds after she walked in the door Friday night. It was payday and life was good. She'd splurged on dinner at Viva Las Vegas. Randa had bought her a can of paint, a nice red that would make a great accent wall, as a house-warming gift. And Charlie was coming back.

She was trying to convince herself that she was reading, but she hadn't turned a page in fifteen minutes. At each pop of the building, she started, tense and ready to throw open the door. When she finally heard the knock, she nearly convinced herself she was hallucinating.

Then she jumped up, tripped over her electric blue throw pillow, and fumbled with the door before yanking it open. She landed hard against Charlie's chest, her arms wrapped around his neck. "I've missed you. I don't like when we fight."

"And I hate it, Grace. Just ... if we can, let's always

make up this way." Charlie's laugh against her neck sent shivers down her back. The soothing circles he rubbed on her back made it easier to breathe. "How many times do I have to tell you to check before you open the door?" He squeezed her tight and straightened. "And put your shoes on before you step outside."

Grace felt the tears burning her eyes but sniffed them back. That was not the greeting she wanted after missing him for six days. She leaned back to say something flirty and fun, but Charlie covered her mouth with his in a hot, hard hello. He managed to walk three steps across the threshold and slammed the door shut without breaking the kiss. When they were gasping for breath, Charlie leaned back. "Hello."

Reluctantly Grace stepped back and forced herself to let go of him. "Is that a blue shirt?"

Charlie shrugged out of his coat. "Like it?"

"I do." She pulled him over to sit on the couch. A blue shirt? On the man in black? She wasn't sure whether it was a good sign. Maybe it was bad. Or no sign at all. Suddenly nervous for a different reason, she said, "So . . . did you get all your shopping done?"

Small talk. When in doubt, talk about nothing. What she really wanted to know, whether he could ever ease up and just be with her without the constant need to strategize, was too dangerous. She didn't want to fight again and she couldn't run away. Small talk was the answer.

He tilted his head to the side and tangled his fingers through hers. "Almost. I've got to go back to Nashville

Sunday to pick up my mother's gift, but then I'm set. Not that you'll be here on Christmas."

Grace smiled. "But then I'll be back. And I have something really exciting for you."

"Really?" His surprise was not flattering. But she'd come up with the perfect gift, one that didn't cost a dime. She was going to spend New Year's with him in Newport. She'd spent a lot of time thinking about his "proposal" and missing him enough to reconsider. She owed it to Charlie and to herself to at least see what he would have to give up, but every day she spent working with Willodean was a confirmation that she'd found her place. She was good at her job. They had one new fan club meeting set for January, and she'd sent out a quote for a small conference in February with the chance for a follow up in August. And she fit with the funny Rock'n'Rolla family better than she ever had anywhere else. She'd had dinner with Willodean twice and helped Randa cook a nearly inedible meal for Laura and KT, KT's grandmother Arlene, and Laura's daughter, Holly, before she'd lost spectacularly to Willodean in her Elvis trivia game.

It had been a good week for friends. The next week would be about family. And then she'd spend some time with Charlie. Her ties were getting stronger all over.

"You'll just have to wait and see what kind of surprise I've got lined up. I'll be home on Thursday." The distance between them worried her, but having Charlie's hand in hers felt just right. He looked tired but solid. Strong. And that something that had had her jumping at small noises and nervously chewing her fingernails calmed. Grace relaxed against the couch for what felt like the first time since he'd left Sunday morning.

But the fact that she was still dressed worried her a bit. Had he changed his mind about her? Had he missed her as much as she'd missed him?

"It's too bad it's so cloudy." She went to look out the window beside the bed. "I was going to lure you outside to wow you with all my lunchtime research."

Charlie raised a brow. "Go ahead. I can be wowed from here." She had no doubt he meant every word of that.

"Well, I was going to tell you about Polaris, the pole star or North Star, which is in the handle of the Little Dipper."

Charlie stood, flipped off the overhead lights, and walked over to stand behind her at the window. In the reflection, he nodded his head like he was impressed. "What do we use the North Star for?"

"No idea." Grace laughed when he did. "I ran out of time to read Wikipedia entries."

"Since we're not going to have determine what latitude we're at, that's probably fine." Charlie stepped closer and she could feel his heat through the thin knit of her new orange sweater. They both looked out the tiny window at the solid clouds covering everything in the sky.

"There's probably an app for that anyway, right?" Grace shivered at the warm gust of air that drifted over her nape when he laughed behind her.

"Probably. What else were you going to tell me?" He rested his hands on her shoulders and waited.

"Polaris is part of the Little Dipper and Ursa Minor, which used to be described as more like a dog's tail." Grace held her breath as she leaned back against him until he wrapped his arms around her waist. With a sigh she let her head rest against this shoulder.

"Impressive. Is that all?" His hands were warm against her abdomen, and she wanted to tell him to forget the stars. Forget the clouds. Forget the window. And definitely forget Wikipedia. All they had to remember was the bed behind him. Not that it would be easy to forget. It loomed pretty large in her mind.

"Um, well, the dog made me think of the Dog Star so I had to look that up. Some people call Sirius, the brightest star in the sky, the Dog Star."

"Why do they do that?" He ran his hands up and down her arms, raising goose bumps on her skin and then chasing them away.

She turned and stared up at his face. He looked serious even though they were playing, and she had the idea that they were on the same page again. "No idea. I forget. Why did I bring this up again?"

Charlie licked his lips and then closed his eyes for a minute. "They call it the Dog Star because of its position in Canis Major." He swallowed audibly. "And you brought it up to save me from making a total awkward ass of myself while I tried to figure how to apologize again. You were right. I did push. I won't do it again." He brushed his lips against hers. "Thank you."

"Well, I'm not sure that's what I had in mind. And I'm not quite as sure now that I was so right. Maybe I overreacted. I've just . . . gotten so used to being independent above all else. Yes, I've needed help, but I never took a handout. But this is different." She ran her hands up and down his broad back. "And you are so tempting. But . . ."

Charlie said, "There's no rush." He shoved a hand in his pocket and pulled out a key ring. "I have a real gift, but I wanted to show you this."

Grace tried to tell herself not to overreact all over again. *Just wait.*

"Newport's pretty boring now. And I loved renovating my house. So I'm going to take this key and I'm going to start a new project. Here in Memphis." He shook his head. "It has very little to do with you. I was bored in Newport, convinced you guys were having a party without me. If I was here, you'd have to party with me."

He shook his head. "I'm going to tell my mom at the Christmas party. I'm going to stay at the first house we lived in, renovate it. Considering the shape it's in now, that project should take a while to complete. And I'm looking forward to getting started. I won't be at the hotel, but I will be here in Memphis. Day by day, I'll be here."

Grace felt the flutter of happy nerves in her stomach. "You've surprised me, Charlie. And I would have doubted that was possible."

He laughed. "I'm glad. Maybe I can do the same for Willodean Jackson." His smile disappeared. "I can't believe we're going to be apart on Christmas. All week I've been looking forward to sharing the holiday with you."

The sinking feeling she'd had ever since she booked the ticket was back. She hated to miss the party. More than that, she hated to be away from Charlie this soon. And she desperately wished he could be with her for her return home. This trip to see her mother again after so long was absolutely one of the times she wished she had a partner to take on the world with her. But . . . she wasn't ready to give up her independence completely. She could do this by herself. Showing up with Charlie would say to her mother and his, and probably the rest of the world, that this was a serious thing, like long-term serious. And she wasn't ready for that pressure.

So, to chase the sadness away, she ran her hands under his shirt, tracing her fingers around his waistband. "Let's make the best use of our time, Charlie. Weddings tomorrow, but the rest of the time, it's just you and me. Right?"

She wanted more than a kiss from Charlie. And their conversations always went more smoothly when they weren't talking.

She stretched up and gave him an open-mouthed kiss, her lips light against his until he muttered a curse and took over. At first his lips were hard, demanding, but he pulled her body tight against his and softened the kiss. It became more of a seduction, his tongue a flirting tease that tempted her into responding. Each brush of her tongue against his sent a shock through her.

She knew her fingernails were sharp points as she clutched his shoulders, but when he moved his hands over her hips, she couldn't do anything but hold on to him for strength. He was the only thing left in the world at that point and she couldn't let go.

As he inched up her sweater, he pulled back to look

into her eyes. She could see the question and hoped he could see the answer in her eyes. It was yes. Tonight, whatever he wanted, it was going to be yes. She owed him the words though. "Yes, Charlie. Straightforward. It's yes."

He rested his forehead against hers. When Charlie gripped her thigh in his hand, his thumb a torment on the sensitive skin, Grace's laugh was shaky.

He brushed his lips against hers and said, "What's funny? It's you and me. I want to laugh too." She rolled her head against his shoulder and shivered as he kissed a hot trail over her jaw and down her neck.

"It's just ... words we have trouble with. This, though ..."

Charlie's thumb swept higher on her thigh, grazing the seam of her jeans. His voice was harsh when he said, "This we're pretty good at."

Grace laughed and then pushed back on his shoulders. Charlie took one step back, then another, and plopped down on the bed. He blinked up at her like he couldn't quite figure out how he'd made it there, but he never let go. She was glad.

Then Grace tilted her head back to look up at the ceiling. She squeezed her eyes shut, scrunched her face up, and waved her hands. Charlie didn't laugh this time. And Grace decided to go for it. "Thank you for coming back, Charlie. Thank you for giving me one day."

He wrapped his hand around her nape and kissed her softly. "And another one tomorrow. And the day after that. I'm starting to believe those new days are never going to run out for us, Grace." He shook his head. "It's amazing."

For the first time, Grace wanted to make the plans she'd been so afraid of. Tomorrow was going to be a good day. She believed Charlie. And she believed he would help make every new day better.

Chapter Fourteen

CHARLIE ROLLED TO a stop in front of the upscale restaurant, Luttrell's, and wished he'd found a way to convince Grace to join him. He could then have taken her on to Sevierville, but committed to his promise to himself not to push her again, he'd only smiled as he'd left her apartment that morning. And he was trying to be happy about seeing her after Christmas. He had a few things to keep him busy anyway. First was taking care of his mother's gift.

He'd changed his mind at least once every hour since he'd managed to get Travis Luttrell on the phone, but once he'd set up this meeting, he couldn't back down. It was time to face his past, maybe apologize if he could get it out, and put it all behind him. He didn't want to drag around his guilt anymore. And he had to talk to Travis to understand everything that had happened, his part in it, and then . . . maybe make some amends there too.

Damn it.

As Charlie stepped into the beautiful restaurant, he thought he might see a bit of the Rock'n'Rolla Hotel spark here, but everything was starkly modern from the black brick floor to the silver fittings. Lush greenery and black-and-white photos reminded him of the hotel. These photos covered some of the country's greats. He could see Johnny Cash, Hank Williams, and Patsy Cline photos on the walls. But there was still a nice tribute to the King of Rock and Roll in the form of black-and-white photos of Sun Studio on the wall of fame.

He glanced down at his black pants and shirt and realized he fit right in. He tried to picture either Grace or his mother here and knew they would not be impressed, even though the backdrop would make them both shine.

"Never thought I'd see you again."

Charlie turned to face the man he'd honestly hoped never to run into, especially like this, and held out his hand. "I bet. And you might want to sit down because I'm here to apologize."

Travis Luttrell, older but still as tall and energetic as Charlie remembered, sniffed as he looked down at Charlie's hand like he was considering leaving him hanging. His blond hair showed some gray and he had a few more lines on his face, but the chef was tall and fit and the spark in his eye might have matched Willodean's. Charlie tried to figure out what he'd do if Travis refused to talk but couldn't come up with a new plan.

Finally Travis sighed and shook Charlie's hand with

a punishing grip. Then he motioned over his shoulder. "Apologies are handled in my office. Come on back."

They wound their way back through the dark restaurant, and Charlie could hear clinks and clanks and shouts of a kitchen getting ready to open for dinner. They stepped into a small office, and Travis closed the door before he dropped into a chair behind a spotless desk.

"Neither of you like cluttered desks, that's for sure."

Travis raised an eyebrow but didn't answer.

Charlie sighed. "Fine. I'm an asshole. It's a revelation that's been sneaking up on me for a long time, but I've done my best to keep my head down and ignore it. I shouldn't have accused you of being only after her money. I didn't even know you. I shouldn't have come between you. I was grown. My mother should . . . she should have had the chance to have everything she wanted." He rubbed his hand over the crease in his brow. "But I just . . . I'd spent a long time trying to protect her, and I was worried."

He met Travis's hard-to-read stare head on. "If it makes anything better, I've regretted my part in the divorce ever since I had a chance to cool down. That summer I left, I worked like a dog. And even after you two split and I went back to Memphis and the hotel, I could hardly face myself and the memories."

"But you're just apologizing *now*." Travis tapped a finger on the desk just like his mother did when she was thinking. Then he sighed. "And that sorta makes perfect sense to me, Charlie."

"It was hard to convince myself I was wrong." Charlie

rolled his eyes. "But I should have handled myself differently. I was young. Stupid. I have gotten a little wiser."

Neither one of them said anything for a long minute. Then Travis said, "There's a girl, am I right?"

Charlie snorted. "Is it that obvious?"

"When you see an asshole converted right before your eyes, there's usually a woman involved." Travis shook his head. "But you . . . I understand making a mistake and not wanting to face it. I should never have given up so easily, but it was easy to blame you and blame her and then regret leaving for . . . what's it been? Twelve years since the divorce? Living with her was exciting, but it was a constant battle too. We didn't see eye to eye on some important stuff, and I could never learn when to pick my battles."

Charlie watched Travis's serious face and had the flash of understanding that his experience could teach him a lot about what *not* to do with Grace.

Travis leaned back in the chair. "Guess I'm an asshole too, one that doesn't know how to say sorry." He held out his hand. "Maybe I'll take a page from your book. 'Course, it's not you that deserves the apology, is it? Even after it ended, I still think Willodean was the best thing that ever happened to me."

Charlie shook his hand and said, "This girl, she mentioned how women love grand gestures. This is my shot at giving my mother the grandest. I've got a hotel room reserved for the next week. If you'd like, you can use it, come and see what's changed. Maybe . . . I don't know, maybe you two could catch up."

"Catch up? We're different people now, Charlie." But the look on Travis's face said he wouldn't mind the chance.

"Is that your wife?" Charlie pointed to a framed newspaper article on the wall. It was a local celebrity kind of piece with a photo of Travis and a pretty blonde seated at the restaurant bar.

"Ex-wife as of almost two years now."

Charlie glanced at his watch. "I know you've got to get ready for dinner, but I appreciate you taking the time, Travis." He stood. "I hope you'll think about coming for a visit."

Travis stood too. "Willodean . . . she'd hold a pretty mean grudge, I guess." He shook his head. "I'll never forget the way she nearly brained me with my own frying pan when I told her what I thought about your outburst." He rubbed his neck.

Charlie laughed. "Yeah, she's pretty good at letting you know immediately how she feels, not nursing grudges. I don't know how much it matters, but I just learned that the meat loaf Sal makes special for me every visit is your recipe. All the crowd favorites at Viva Las Vegas are yours. Still on the menu."

"That must have burned." Travis's face showed an amused satisfaction.

"Not gonna lie. That meat loaf sat like a boulder on my stomach for a while. Next time I had the chance, though, I forgot all about it." Charlie shook his head. "You were talented, but I didn't want to see that. I'm sorry again. The world needs that meat loaf in it." This time the apology came easier. He wondered if he was getting the hang of it.

Travis gripped the armrest of his chair. "Well, as long as we're sharing our souls, there might have been some truth to what you said. I might have pursued Willodean for what she could bring me. Viva Las Vegas was the chance I'd been looking for and she gave it to me. I loved her for that. But you know this. There's something special about Willodean Holloway, something that you don't find anywhere else. At least, I haven't been able to."

Charlie thought about correcting Travis about his mother's last name, but he did not want to get into what happened after their divorce or Howard Jackson since things seemed to be going so well. He already felt lighter, better, like maybe this time when he walked into the lobby of the Rock'n'Rolla Hotel he could see it for the place it was today and not his past mistakes.

"Think about coming for a visit. I know restaurants are busy places, even at Christmas, but I think she'd be happy to see you. Sal definitely would and he's my meat loaf supplier so I'm interested in his happiness."

Travis didn't look convinced but he slowly nodded. "I'll give it some thought, Charlie. It's not every day a man gets a chance to correct his mistakes."

"I know that's the truth." Charlie thought about asking Travis if his mother had been easy to get over. He didn't want to know the answer. If Grace never settled, if she never decided to stick here with him, he'd have to do some serious getting over her. One look at Travis's thoughtful face and he had the idea that some women were impossible to get over. It didn't surprise him that his mother was one. She changed people. He had a feeling

Grace would be the same. And he felt another sympathetic tie to Travis Luttrell.

"This girl, the one who's giving you all the good advice . . . she sounds a little like your mother."

Charlie nodded. "Yeah, well . . . it's too late to let that stop me, you know? She's not logical, she's not easy, and she doesn't follow direction. Plus, I think she's really getting into Elvis."

"But she's exciting. And beautiful. And worth it." Travis clapped one hand on his shoulder. "You miserable man. Good luck with that. You'll never get over her, so be careful not to lose her."

They walked out of the restaurant together.

"When you come back through town, stop in for dinner. I think you'll like the menu." Travis rocked back on his heels to look up at the sky. "Looks like snow coming in."

Charlie nodded. "Hope it waits until after Christmas. Got a lot of miles to cover still." And he wanted Grace back in Memphis before they were snowed in. "I'll be back for dinner tonight. I'm in town until Christmas Eve."

Travis frowned.

Charlie shrugged. "There's a small research lab I want to take a look at."

"At Christmas? All right, Scrooge McMinn."

Charlie laughed. "They won't be complaining once I write the check."

Travis laughed. "I guess not."

"Will we see you this week?" Charlie wasn't sure what he hoped for, a yes or no. This might be his best lesson in trusting the journey. He fought down the urge to tell Travis what he should do.

"Could be. Maybe I'll come down the chimney like Santa." Travis said, "Won't that be special?"

Charlie shook his hand again. "I have a feeling that won't be the only special thing this Christmas."

Chapter Fifteen

GRACE DID HER best to ignore Lucky's impatient waving from the stage. It was past time for her to step up there and sing for the staff gathered in Viva Las Vegas. There were only a few guests in the hotel on Christmas Eve, and the restaurant was closed for this special Christmas party. Everyone was there. Willodean had hired caterers so the waitstaff and kitchen staff all had the night off. The music had been loud, all Elvis's hits, but now Lucky had taken the stage.

She was happy she'd changed her plans. She'd waved good-bye to Willodean and gotten on the bus determined to prove her independence by enjoying a visit with her family without the pressure of having to prove herself. No matter what her mother believed, she was good at her job and she was going to keep it.

But before they'd reached the first stop, the over-whelming feeling of homesickness that hit any time she thought about the hotel was impossible to ignore. She wanted to be home for the holiday. And that meant Memphis. And Charlie. Even before she'd made it to Jackson, she'd called her mother to explain her change of plans and Willodean to see if she could get a ride home.

She hadn't called Charlie. She hoped he'd be pleasantly surprised.

"We've got a special treat. Miss Grace Andersen's going to do a song or two." He motioned toward her, and the whole room turned to see where she was. With a sigh, she moved through the crowd even as she wondered what had happened to Charlie. She smoothed nervous hands over the skirt of her red dress.

"All right. How about some Christmas fun?" Grace said after she stepped up and took the mic. When "Santa, Bring My Baby Back to Me" played, she sang for all she was worth. She pulled from her acting experience, her modeling experience, and even her event planning experience and sang and danced with Lucky and pretended that she had the holiday spirit, even though it all felt wrong without Charlie.

She could see couples dancing at the bottom of the stage. KT and Laura bopped, Tony and Randa did an awkward sway, Mike and Cat the bartender barely moved as they stared into each other's eyes. *It is like Noah's ark in here*, she thought as she searched for Willodean and Misty in the room.

Lucky spun her around once violently as the song came to an end, and loud cheers from his girlfriend broke through the applause.

Grace tried to catch her breath as she watched Lucky vault off the stage to stop the cheers. "I have one more song, a special request from a friend," she said and added through gritted teeth, "who is not here . . ."

Just as Charlie walked in. Even more surprising, he was wearing his gold lamé jacket and slicked-back hairdo. He looked surprised to see her on the stage, but his smile grew as she waved. Willodean and Misty were at his side. Willodean was as pleased as could be, and her green sequined dress sparkled like her eyes. Even Misty seemed to be wearing a huge doggy grin as she sat on Charlie's foot.

"Sorry, everybody," he said as he smiled at her, "snow's here a little sooner than expected. Took me a little bit longer than I thought, but I wouldn't miss this."

She felt the weird lurch of anticipation at the word *snow*. Or maybe it was the look in Charlie's eyes or the new lightness in the way he walked. Something was different, and she was happy to see it.

Grace said, "All right. This one's something you can dance to."

Grace sang "Hound Dog" with everything she had and laughed along with everyone who watched Charlie spin his mother in a circle around a very drowsy Misty. She hadn't thought he had it in him, but the smile on his face and the laughter in Willodean's voice were priceless.

Breathless, she handed Lucky the microphone and floated down the stairs, the adrenaline rush of standing on the stage and the excitement of seeing Charlie again all rolled up into one big fluffy ball of excitement.

"All right, now that we're all here, we can get to the main event ..." Lucky's voice trailed off and everyone swiveled to see what he was staring at. Grace could see an older blond man covered in snow hovering in the door to the restaurant. "Travis, is that you? Travis Luttrell?"

Viva Las Vegas was probably almost never silent, but everyone in the room froze then turned to see Willodean's reaction. She sounded shocked as she said, "Travis, what are you doing here?" She took two steps toward him and then came to a stop with her hands on her hips.

"Charlie invited me for a visit." Travis shoved his hands in his pockets. "Thought I'd take him up on it. Didn't know there'd be a blizzard too. Looks like I may be snowed in for a bit." He shrugged a shoulder, and they all watched snow fall off to land on the floor with a wet plop.

Willodean crossed her arms over her chest. "Well, now, ain't that some kind of thing."

Travis stepped closer and bent to kiss her cheek. "I've missed you, Willy." He took one of her hands in his. "You're still wearing the emerald I got you. And I always did like you in green, matches your eyes."

When Willodean blushed a bright red, Grace wanted to do something, anything to break the tension in the room, but she like everyone else was frozen to the spot.

Eventually Sal crossed the room with his hand held out. There was general manly back slapping for a minute and then Willodean glanced back at Travis. Grace couldn't tell what she thought about the latest arrival at first. Then Willodean swung around to look at Charlie.

"You just can't leave it alone, can you?" She shook her

finger at him. "You just got to be doing something all the time."

Grace met Charlie's satisfied smile with one of her own. "You were listening. Very nice grand gesture."

He kissed her lips and nodded like he'd known all along just the right thing to do. Helpless man. He was so cute when he was cluelessly cocky. "This one was all for me. But the look on her face was pretty priceless."

Willodean put one hand on Misty's head and said, "Travis, I'd dearly love to show you all the changes we've made, but we got a party to finish first." Then she turned back to Lucky on the stage and shot him a "get on with it or else" look.

Lucky cleared his throat. "Ah, well, now we all know Christmas is a time for miracles. Lord knows it's a miracle I've made it to this one myself." He glanced down at his schoolteacher girlfriend and waved at her. "Another one we're about to witness is a wedding."

Everyone in the restaurant started to chatter. Willodean clapped her hands. "Oh, I do love a surprise." She glared at Charlie. "Mainly when they happen to other people."

And KT towed a sputtering Laura up on the stage. "Ambush seems to be the best way to get this done, Lola." He held his hand over Laura's mouth. "Where are my maid of honor and best man?" His grandmother stepped up on the stage to stand next to him, and Laura's daughter, Holly, bounced up the steps to grab her mother's hand. "And Charlie? Better get up here. I won't be able to keep her still for long."

Charlie squeezed Grace's hand before he joined them on the stage.

KT knelt down. "Laura, will you marry me tonight?"

Laura clasped her hands over her mouth but nodded wildly. "Yes. Let's. A Christmas wedding. Let's do it."

KT whooped. "A real Christmas miracle!"

Grace looked to Willodean for a clue and noticed that she was beaming from ear to ear. And behind her Travis Luttrell hadn't taken his eyes off of her.

Maybe Noah's going to be paired off too.

As Charlie led the ceremony, she listened to him talk about sickness and health and as long as they both shall live and felt . . . peace. Maybe this was exactly the place she'd always been looking for. When KT slid his ring on Laura's finger, she launched herself at him, her happy laughter contagious. The whole wedding party erupted in cheers and Lucky hit play on "Teddy Bear." KT spun Laura around in a circle and everyone toasted to their happiness.

Charlie managed to elbow his way back to her. "Sorry I almost missed your song, but you got your snowflakes. But why are you here? You should be home, right?"

"I didn't want to miss this party." Grace leaned against him. "And you're here. I am home. Everything I wanted for Christmas in one package. I can go tomorrow. Maybe you could take me?"

Charlie grinned. "I'd love to!" He frowned. "But the weather's pretty rough. We may be stuck here."

Grace shrugged. "Well, I was going to save this for later, but would you like your Christmas present?"

Charlie looked around at the crowd and frowned. "Uh, I guess?"

She wrapped her hands around his neck. "Here's my grand gesture for you. Let's spend New Year's in your house in Newport. I can visit with my family, show you off, but we can escape too. Tromp around in the woods if we have to."

Charlie kissed her sweetly, a smile on his lips. "That sounds like an excellent vacation. And then it's back to work. Here in Memphis." Grace nodded. This was where she belonged. She studied Charlie's face and could not see one bit of worry over giving Memphis another try. And he didn't have to say a word to convince her that he was happy to take it one day at a time. Charlie had changed. Or he was trying to. For her.

That made her own change that much easier. Staying in once place would be easy. Charlie would draw her. Their connection made it impossible to consider leaving him. The last question she had about Memphis was gone. The job she'd been searching for was here. Charlie was here. And the family she'd waited for was right here, chattering, laughing loudly, celebrating, and probably driving Charlie just a little bit crazy already.

After everyone had congratulated the bride and groom, Lucky cleared his throat. "And now, we've got one more bit of business to take care of." The tiny stage spotlight clicked on to highlight Tony and Randa who were refilling drinks behind the bar. It took Randa a minute to realize everyone was watching them. She slowly set the last glass of punch down and smiled awkwardly.

"What now?"

Tony, looking a little bit uncomfortable but absolutely determined, pulled a black box out of his pocket. Randa's eyebrows shot up and every bit of color drained from her face. Tony must have noticed because he wrapped a hand around one arm as he cleared his throat. "Randa Whitmore, would you do me the honor of marrying me?"

When he flipped the box open, Grace managed to contain her gasp but Randa didn't. "Good grief, Tony, why is it so big?"

The shine on the diamond was fairly blinding.

KT opened his mouth to say something, but Laura clapped her hand over it.

Tony sighed. "You deserve the best, Randa, but I want you to marry me anyway."

Randa laughed and wrapped her arms around his neck. "Oh, I'll marry you, Tony Ortega, but let's get a ring I can carry on my own, okay?" Grace thought she could see a smile on Tony's face before he kissed Randa but it was hard to tell. And then the kiss got so passionate it was awkward to watch them. The uneasy partiers in the restaurant all turned to look at Lucky.

When Charlie started winding his way up to the front of the room, Grace had to force herself to stand very still. Willodean walked over to stand next to her and wrapped an arm around her waist. Nervous, Grace said, "Do you know what he's doing?"

Willodean shook her head. "No, but the boy does like to go big. Better brace yourself."

When Charlie took the mic and Lucky stepped up to

his sound system, Willodean squeezed her tighter. "Well, good Lord, I think he's gonna sing." The wonder in her voice told Grace this was as unusual as she thought it was.

Charlie said, "A very special lady made two Christmas requests. The first one, snow . . . well, I'll try to figure out a way to take credit for that." The crowd laughed. "But the second one she probably thought was even less likely. But for Grace Andersen, I'm willing to do just about anything, even stand up here on this stage and sing Elvis."

The music played, and Charlie, dressed and coiffed as a very handsome young Elvis, ignored everyone in the room and sang to her. No one moved. No one spoke. And no one would have believed he had it in him. Grace knew how hard it was for Charlie to do it and that was all she needed.

He was rigid. He wanted what he wanted when he wanted it. But he was standing on a stage singing an Elvis song. For her. Because he understood the power of the grand gesture. When the last quiet notes ended, Charlie handed Lucky the mic and made a direct path for Grace.

Everyone in the restaurant pivoted to watch him. And when he put his hand in his pocket, Grace nearly expired on the spot. Whatever he wanted, it was yes, but if that was an engagement ring, she was going to need a brown paper bag to breathe into.

"Grace, you look scared to death." She could see the amusement on his face. "But I'm not asking you to marry me. Not again. I understand what you meant now. And even if I know I love you and I know that you love me, that doesn't mean we have to get married. Or move. Or anything else except be here now and enjoy that." He held out his hand and showed her a key ring. He glanced over at his mother. "Mom, I like tearing down and building, so I'm going to . . . do that. With our first house. Grace will work here. We'll date and I'll figure out how to focus on just one day. I can help here more, spend more time with you. I want to be a part of the Rock'n'Rolla family, even if I don't call the hotel home."

Charlie smiled down at her as his mother kissed his cheek. Willodean stepped back and said, "I ought to murder you, but I do gotta say, you have a bit of your mother's showmanship, son."

Then she and Charlie turned to look at the staff gathered in Viva Las Vegas and Willodean said, "I thought this was a party!"

Everyone clapped and the noise was crazy as they all turned to look at Lucky. He raised both hands. "That's all I've got. Unless anybody else wants to propose. Make a baby announcement? Come back from the dead?" Everyone laughed. "No? Then let's dance!" He hit play, leaped off the stage, and spun his schoolteacher around in a circle.

Grace and Travis followed Charlie and Willodean out into the quiet lobby. Misty padded along behind them and slid down to sprawl on the floor with a satisfied grunt.

"So instead of letting me find you a wife," Willodean shot a glance at Grace, which she did her very best to ignore, "you decided to give me an ex-husband for Christmas. I think an electric blanket might have been an easier thing to return, Charlie." Willodean crossed her arms over her chest.

Charlie shook his head. "No, I did that for me. I've felt awful for so long, let it stand between us way too many years, and nothing was going to make that better but to try and repair it. Howard taught us both that, Mom. Besides, I owed Travis an apology too."

She nodded reluctantly and glanced over her shoulder at Travis. "Can't hurt to show him around, but you know it ain't going to be a match made in heaven. That split we had? You weren't here to see it but it was awesome. Powerful."

Grace thought Travis looked like a man with his own plan and she wondered if maybe Charlie had gotten a touch of his mother's matchmaking skills.

Charlie smiled. "Travis tells me you're both different people now. Maybe that's the only way to look at it."

Willodean patted his cheek. "When did you get so smart?"

"I think it's in the genes."

Willodean harrumphed but she didn't disagree.

"What do you think, Mom?" He held out the key ring and jingled the keys. "Will you come and visit once I get the old place fixed up?"

Willodean frowned. "That place was tiny and the neighborhood ain't so good, Charlie." She waved at the lobby. "Why would you go to all that work when you could live like a king here? Or even buy a nice new mansion outside of town. You aren't thinking of moving Grace into that place, are you?"

"It's for me. I need the project. I need the connection. I've just . . . I don't know, I love the place in Newport. I love that it has history. I love that I worked hard to restore it and it's everything I chose. And I want to do it all over again, but here. In Memphis. I might even volunteer, maybe with an organization that rehabs old places. I could spend some time with Habitat for Humanity or even the Red Cross. Maybe I got a touch of your desire to help people too. It just looks different on me."

Willodean looked from him to Grace and back. "If it gets you back here, I'll be happy to visit y'all in the new, fully restored, pest-free house." She patted Grace's arm. "Y'all don't do anything I wouldn't do. Come on, Misty, let's get back to the party." She wrapped her hand around Travis's arm. "Come with me, Mr. Luttrell." She shook her head. "Doesn't look like you've aged one day."

Travis leaned down. "I'd say exactly the same to you. I think you might have gotten prettier."

Willodean tsked. "Still a silver tongue, I see."

Travis's laugh was low. "Never doubt it, but I'll be happy to give you a demonstration."

Before they disappeared back inside Viva Las Vegas, Grace heard Willodean's wicked chuckle.

When she glanced up at Charlie, he looked a little uncomfortable but determined to get over it. Their eyes met and she couldn't look away. "Merry Christmas, Grace."

She wrapped her hands around his and squeezed. "I was afraid you were going to do something crazy like propose."

He shook his head. "No, ma'am. I'm much too cautious for that. And I was listening."

Grace smiled up at him. "Good."

He leaned down and rested his forehead against hers. "Thank you for helping me understand my problems with my mother. I need to be here. And I want as much time with you as I can get. Forget marriage. I *can* learn to be patient. Just . . . spend your time with me."

Grace nodded. "Done."

He pulled her close and kissed her.

"When I meet your parents, should I throw around boring rich guy words like 'derivatives' or 'annuities' or 'tax breaks' just to impress them?"

The mental picture she had of Charlie wowing her parents was beautiful. He would charm them by being himself. Maybe some of that shine would land on her too. She smiled at him. "Definitely. My mother will think she's in heaven."

He laughed. "Done."

"I'm so glad you'll be with me, Charlie." She tangled her fingers in his and leaned against him. "If you're there, I won't feel so alone."

Charlie wrapped one arm around her. "No matter what, Grace, you'll still have Memphis. We both do."

Grace shook her head. "It's the craziest thing. I thought I was going after what I wanted. I thought performing in front of thousands would satisfy me, but I think, even if I'd made it big, I would always be searching for this place. I know I would always be searching for you."

Charlie closed his eyes and took a deep breath. "I never thought I'd say this, but thank God for this hotel." He shook his head. "Don't tell my mother I said that."

Grace laughed and blinked away a tear. "Never. It's you and me against the world, Charlie McMinn."

They were quiet and he asked, "Should we go back to the party?" They could hear a rousing round of "Jingle Bell Rock" and the clinks of happy partiers.

"Maybe instead you could show me your gift. Let's go watch it snow. That is what you got for me, right?"

Charlie wrapped an arm around her, and they walked down the hall to the door to the staff apartments. "Here you are without a coat again. But I do love this dress."

Grace coughed and reached into the meeting room being renovated as the new gift shop to pick up her coat. "Maybe I'm learning a little too, Charlie. I was hoping you would show me the stars tonight. Snow's even better."

He held her coat for her and then pulled her close after she had it on. "Let's see if I can't do both. Snow first, stars later."

Want more fun, flirty romance from
Cheryl Harper's Rock'n'Rolla Hotel?
Read on for excerpts from

STUCK ON YOU

and

CAN'T HELP FALLING IN LOVE

now available from Avon Impulse.

An Excerpt from

STUCK ON YOU

LOVE'S IN THE limelight when big-shot producer KT Masters accidentally picks a fight with Laura Charles, a single mother working as a showgirl waitress in a hotel bar. When he offers her the fling of a lifetime, Laura's willing to play along . . . just so long as her heart stays out of it. If she can help it, that is!

Laura said, "Excuse me, Mr. Masters." When he held up an impatient hand, she narrowed her eyes and turned back to the two women. "Maybe you can tell him the drinks are here? I've got other customers to take care of."

The pink-haired woman held out a hand. "Sure thing. I'm Mandy, the makeup artist. This is Shane. She'll do hair. We'll both help with costumes and props as needed."

As Laura shook their hands, she privately thought that might be the best arrangement. Shane's hair was perfect, not one strand out of place. Mandy's pink shag sort of made it look like she'd been caught in a windstorm. In a convertible. But her makeup and clothes were very cute.

KT said, "Hold on just a sec, Bob. Let me go ahead and tweet this. Gotta keep the fans interested, you know."

Laura glanced over her bare shoulder to see KT bound down the stairs, pause, snap a picture, and then type something on his phone before shouting about taking down the electronic display in the corner. Lucky would not be happy about that. As KT waved his arms dramatically and the director nodded, Laura smiled at the two girls. "Guess I'm dismissed."

They laughed, and Laura turned to skirt their table as she reached for the drink tray. Being unable to move, like her feathers had attached themselves to the floor, was her first clue that something had gone horribly wrong. And when KT Masters bumped into her, sending the tray skidding into the sodas she'd just delivered, she knew exactly who was responsible. She tried to whirl around to give him a piece of her mind but spun in place and then heard a loud rip just before she bumped into the table and sent two glasses crashing to the floor. She might have followed them, but KT wrapped a hand around her arm to steady her. His warm skin was a brand against her chilly flesh.

The only sound in Viva Las Vegas was the tinny *plink* of electricity through one million bright white bulbs. Every eye was focused on the drama taking place at the foot of the stage. Before she could really get a firm grip on the embarrassment, irritation, shock, and downright anger boiling over, Laura shouted, "You ripped off my feather!"

Even the light bulbs seemed to hold their breath at that point.

KT's hand slid down her arm, raising goose bumps as it went, before he slammed both hands on his hips, and

Laura shivered. The heat from that one hand made her wonder what it would be like to be pressed up against him. Instead of the flannel robe, she should put a KT Masters on her birthday list. She wouldn't have to worry about being cold ever again.

"Yeah, I did you a favor. This costume has real potential"—he motioned with one hand as he looked her over from collarbone to knee—"but the feathers get in the way, so . . . you're welcome!" The frown looked all wrong on his face, like he didn't have a lot of experience with anger or irritation, but the look in his eyes was as warm as his hand had been. When he rubbed his palms together, she thought maybe she wasn't the only one to be surprised by the heat.

They both looked down at the bedraggled pink feather, now swimming in ice cubes and spilled soda under his left shoe. No matter how much she hated the feathers or how valid his point about their ridiculousness was, she wasn't going to let him get away with this. He should apologize. Any decent person would.

"What are you going to do about it?" She plopped her hands on her own hips, thrust her chin out, and met his angry stare.

He straightened and flashed a grim smile before leaning down to scrape the feather up off the floor. He pinched the driest edge and held it out from his body. "Never heard 'the customer's always right,' have you?"

Laura snatched the feather away. "In what way are you a customer? I only see a too-important big shot who can't apologize."

He opened his mouth to say ... something, then changed his mind and pointed a finger in her face instead. "Oh, really? I bet if I went to have a little talk with the manager or Miss Willodean, they'd have a completely different take on what just happened here and who needs to apologize."

Laura narrowed her eyes and tilted her head. "Oh, really? I'll take that bet."

An Excerpt from

CAN'T HELP FALLING IN LOVE

LOVE GOES UNDERCOVER when business strategist Randa Whitmore arrives at the Rock'n'Rolla Hotel in search of a new acquisition for her father's hotel empire. Too bad Marine-turned-hotel manager Tony Ortega can see right through her Elvis fangirl alibi. Randa's prepared to bring out the big guns—just so long as she can stay objective and out of Tony's muscled arms. After all, it's just business, right?

Tony smiled and Randa watched his face closely to see if his eyes were locked on her legs. She fought off the twinge of doubt when Tony quickly glanced away from her. She yanked out the seat belt and clicked it while she told herself to think about books. Handsome men might be hard to understand, but books would never let her down. "Tony, I'm in. You can close the door."

He muttered something that sounded like "No guts, no glory." Then he straightened his shoulders and stepped closer. "You were too fast in the bookstore. I wanted to do this."

His face was determined as he leaned towards her, and

she lost her breath because it looked like he was going to kiss her.

Then he did, his lips a warm shock against hers.

This kiss was a sweet hello. His lips settled on hers in an easy slide. When she gripped his shoulders and tried to pull him closer, he smiled against her lips and his tongue was a quick tease over her bottom lip before he rested his forehead against hers. Randa didn't move. She was afraid to. He was going to step back, and she didn't want him to. She wanted to stay right here with him. Finally he took a deep breath and leaned back just enough to look her in the eyes. "There's this one other thing I've been dying to do."

"Yes." Randa nodded her head. She had no idea what it was, but she was ready.

Tony squeezed his eyes shut for just a second. The sound he made when he opened them again was somewhere between a laugh and a moan. Maybe it was both. Randa understood exactly what that felt like.

He pressed forward to kiss her again, his hand a hot support against the back of her head and his lips aggressively seductive. This time he coaxed her lips open and teased her tongue with his. Each tentative touch sent a shiver of awareness through her. She wanted to press her breasts against his chest, get closer, so much closer, but the seat belt pinned her down. Her breath was long gone when Tony ended the kiss, his breath coming in quiet pants as he stared into her eyes, but when his hand rested on her knee she tried to gasp. And when he touched her thigh, lightly rubbing his hand on bare skin, she lost her mind.

She actually bit her lip to keep from moaning like a porn star. Because a man touched her thigh. It was a little like she was back in high school but so much hotter.

Seduced in front of a bookstore. Did it get any better? More private, certainly. But better, no way. Tony's eyes were hot as he stared down at her.

Randa squeezed the hand on her thigh and said, "Satisfied?"

The look in his eyes was predatory. Tony shook his head. "No way. Not even close."

Randa licked her lips. "Good. Me either."

About the Author

Whether she's writing, reading, or just checking the items off of her daily to-do list, CHERYL HARPER loves her romance mixed with a little laughter. When she's not working, you will find her ignoring housework, cursing yard work, and spending way too much time with a television remote in her hand.

You can visit her online at www.cherylharper-books.com.

Visit www.AuthorTracker.com for exclusive information on your favorite HarperCollins authors.

Give in to your impulses . . .
Read on for a sneak peek at six brand-new
e-book original tales of romance
from Avon Books.
Available now wherever e-books are sold.

ONCE UPON A HIGHLAND SUMMER
By Lecia Cornwall

HARD TARGET
By Kay Thomas

THE WEDDING DATE
A Christmas Novella
By Cara Connelly

TORN
A Billionaire Bachelors Club Novel
By Monica Murphy

THE CUPCAKE DIARIES:
SPOONFUL OF CHRISTMAS
By Darlene Panzera

RODEO QUEEN
By T. J. Kline

An Excerpt from

ONCE UPON A HIGHLAND SUMMER

by Lecia Cornwall

An ancient curse, a pair of meddlesome
ghosts, a girl on the run, and a fateful
misunderstanding make for the perfect chance
at true love in Lecia Cornwall's latest novella.

"I'll have your decision now, if you please."

Lady Caroline Forrester stared at the carpet in her half-brother's study. It was like everything else in his London mansion—expensive, elegant, and chosen solely to proclaim his consequence as the Earl of Somerson. She fixed her eyes on the blue swirls and arabesques knotted into the rug and wondered what distant land it came from, and if she could go there herself rather than make the choice Somerson demanded.

"Come now," he said impatiently. "You have two suitors to choose from. Viscount Speed has two thousand pounds a year, and will inherit his father's earldom."

"In Ireland," Caroline whispered under her breath. Speed also had oily, perpetually damp skin and a lisp, and was only interested in her because her dowry would make him rich. At least for a short while, until he spent her money as he'd spent his own fortune—on mistresses, whist, and horses.

"And Lord Mandeville has a fine estate on the border with Wales. His mother lives there, so she would be company for you."

Mandeville spent no time at all in his country estate for that exact reason. Caroline had been in London only a month, but she'd heard the gossip. Lady Mandeville went through highborn companions the way Charlotte—Somerson's countess—devoured cream cakes at tea.

Lady Mandeville was famous for her bad temper, her sharp tongue, and her dogs. She raised dozens, perhaps even hundreds, of yappy, snappy, unpleasant little creatures that behaved just like their mistress, if the whispered stories were to be believed. The lady unfortunate enough to become Lord Mandeville's wife would serve as the old woman's companion until one of them died, with no possibility of quitting the post to take a more pleasant job.

"So which gentleman will you have?" Somerson demanded, pacing the room, his posture stiff, his hands clasped behind his back, his face sober. Caroline had laughed when he'd first told her the two men had offered for her hand. But it wasn't a joke. Her half-brother truly expected her to pick one of the odious suitors he'd selected for her and tie herself to that man for life. He looked down his hooked nose at her, a trait inherited from their father, along with his pale, bulging eyes. Caroline resembled her mother, the late earl's second wife, which was probably why Somerson couldn't stand the sight of her. As a young man he'd objected to his father's new bride most strenuously, because she was too young, too pretty, and the daughter of a mere baronet, without fortune or high connections. He'd even objected to the new countess's red hair. Caroline raised a hand to smooth a wayward russet curl behind her ear. Speed had red hair—orange, really—and spindly pinkish eyelashes.

Caroline thought of her niece Lottie, who was upstairs

having her wedding dress fitted, arguing with her mother over what shade of ribbon would best suit the flowers in the bouquet. She was marrying William Rutherford, Viscount Mears—*Caroline's* William, the man she'd known all her life, the eldest son and heir of the Earl of Halliwell, a neighbor and dear friend of her parents'. It had always been expected that she'd wed one of Halliwell's sons, but Sinjon, the earl's younger son, had left home to join the army and go to war rather than propose to Caroline. And now William, who even Caroline thought would make an offer for her hand, had instead chosen Lottie's hand. Caroline shut her eyes. It was beginning to feel like a curse. Not that it mattered now. William had made his choice. Still, a wedding should be a happy thing, the bride as joyful as Lottie, the future ripe with the possibilities of love and happiness.

Caroline didn't even *like* her suitors—well, they weren't really *her* suitors. They were courting her dowry, and a connection to Somerson. They needed her money, but they didn't need her.

An Excerpt from

HARD TARGET

by Kay Thomas

Kay Thomas' thrilling Elite Ops series kicks off
with an unlikely hero and a mother determined
to save her child. When Anna Mercado's son is
kidnapped, Former DEA agent Leland Hollis
agrees to deliver the ransom into dangerous
territory south of the border. Getting the boy
out of a violent cartel region involves risking
everything. And for that, Leland will have
to convince Anna to do the scariest thing
of all . . . open her heart and trust him.

"Could you hand me my top, please?"

Leland bent down to retrieve Anna's shirt and turned away, staring at the floor in front of him to give her privacy. What the hell was he doing? At least he'd given the room a cursory inspection to rule out cameras or bugs before he'd practically screwed her against the bedroom wall.

What he'd really wanted to tell her, before they'd gotten sidetracked by the birth control issue, was the same thing he'd wanted to tell her last night: She didn't have to do him to get Zach back. Whether or not they had sex had no bearing on whether he'd help find her son.

Not that he didn't want her. He did. So much so that his teeth ached.

He hadn't known her long, but what he knew fascinated him. To have dealt with everything she had in the past year and still be so strong—that inner strength captivated him.

It was important she not think he expected sex in exchange for his help. Sex wasn't some kind of payoff. He needed to clarify that right away.

Besides, neither of them was going to be able to sleep now. He sighed, zipped his cargo shorts, and pulled on his t-shirt and the shoulder holster with the Ruger. He shoved the larger

Glock into his backpack. This was going to be a long evening.

The night breeze had shifted the shabby curtain to the side, leaving an unobscured view into the room. He turned to face her, wondering if anyone on the street had just gotten an eyeful.

A red laser dot reflected off the wide shoulder strap of her tank top. Recognizing the threat, he dove for her, shouting, "Down. Get down!"

Leland tackled Anna around the waist and pulled her to the floor. A bullet hit the wall with a deceptively soft *sphlift*, right where she'd been standing half a second earlier.

He climbed on top of her, his heart rate skyrocketing, and covered her completely with his body. His boot was awkward. His knee came down between her legs, trapping her in the skirt. More shots slapped the stucco, but they were all hitting above his head.

The gunman must be using a silencer. A loud car engine revved in the street. Voices shouted, and bullets flew through the window, no longer silenced.

How many shooters were there?

A flaming bottle whooshed through the window. It broke on impact, and fire spread rapidly across the dry plywood floor. The pop of more bullets against the wall sounded deceptively benign.

"What's happening?" Anna's lips were at his ear.

Her warm breath would have felt seductive if not for the shots flying overhead and the fire licking at his ass. He was crushing her with his body weight, but it was the only way to protect her from the onslaught.

"Why are they shooting at us?" Her voice was thin, like she was having trouble breathing.

He propped himself up on his elbows to take his weight off of her chest but kept his head down next to hers. "They want the money."

"How do they know about the ransom?" she asked.

"Everyone within a hundred miles knows about it." He raised his head cautiously.

They were nose to nose, but he ignored the intimacy of the position. They had to get out of the smoke-filled room. In here, even with just half the money, they were sitting ducks.

He needed his bag. It held all his ammunition and the Glock 17. And they couldn't leave the cash, not now anyway. The money might be the only thing that could keep them alive when they got out of here.

"Come on." He rolled to the side and tugged Anna's hand to pull her along with him. "But don't raise your head."

Another bullet hit the wall where she had been moments before. God, how many men were there? Knowing that could make a difference in getting out of this alive.

An Excerpt from

THE WEDDING DATE
A Christmas Novella
by Cara Connelly

In this sexy holiday novella, rising star and
award-winning author Cara Connelly launches
a new series about the magic of weddings!

"**B**lind dates are for losers." Julie Marone pinched the phone with her shoulder and used both hands to scrape the papers on her desk into a tidy pile. "You really think I'm a loser?"

"Not a *loser*, exactly." Amelia's inflection kept her options open.

Julie snorted a laugh. "Gee, thanks, sis. Tell me how you *really* feel."

"You know what I mean. You've been out of circulation for three years. You have to start *somewhere*."

"Sure, but did it have to be at the bottom of the barrel?"

"Peter's a nice guy!" Amelia protested.

"Absolutely," Julie said agreeably. "So devoted to dear old mom that he *still lives in her basement*."

Amelia let out a here-we-go-again groan. "He's an optometrist, for crying out loud. I assumed he'd have his own place."

Julie started on the old saying about what happens when you *assume*, but Amelia cut her off. "Yeah, yeah. Ass. You. Me. Got it. Anyway, Leo"—tonight's date—"is a definite step up. I checked with his sister"—Amelia's hair stylist—"and she said he's got a house in Natick. His practice is thriving."

"So why's he going on a blind date?"

"His divorce just came through."

Julie groaned. Recently divorced men fell into two categories. "Shopping for a replacement or still simmering with resentment?"

"Come on, Jules, give him a chance."

Julie sighed, slid the stack of papers into a folder marked *Westin/Anderson*, and added it to her briefcase for tomorrow's closing. "Just tell me where to meet him."

"On Hanover Street at seven. He made reservations at a place on Prince."

"Well, in that case." Dinner in Boston's North End almost made it worthwhile. Julie was always up for good Italian. "How will I recognize him? Tall, dark, and handsome?" A girl could hope.

"Dark . . . but . . . not tall. Wearing a red scarf."

"Handsome?"

Amelia cleared her throat. "I caught one of his commercials the other night. He's got a nice smile."

"Whoa, wait. Commercials? What kind of lawyer is he?"

"Personal injury." Amelia dropped it like a turd. Then said, "Oh, look, Ray's here. Gotta go," and hung up.

"How did I get into this?" Julie murmured.

The catalyst, she knew, was Amelia's own upcoming Christmas Eve wedding. She wanted Julie—her maid of honor—to bring a date. A real date, not her gay friend Dan. Amelia loved Dan like a brother, but he was single too, always up for hanging out, and he made it too easy for Julie to duck the dating game.

So Amelia had lined up three eligible men and informed Julie that if she didn't give them a chance, then their mother—a confirmed cougar with not-great taste in men—would bring a wedding date for her.

Recognizing a train wreck when she saw one coming, Julie had given in and agreed to date all three. So far they were shaping up even worse than expected.

Jan appeared in the doorway. "J-Julie?" Her usually pale cheeks were pink. Her tiny bosom heaved. "Oh, Julie. You'll never believe . . . the most . . . I mean . . . ."

"Take a breath, Jan." Julie did that thing where she pointed two fingers at Jan's eyes, then back at her own. "Focus."

Jan sucked air through her nose, let it out with a wheeze. "Okay, we just had a walk-in. From Austin." She wheezed again. "He's *gorgeous*. And that drawl . . . ." Wheeze.

Julie nodded encouragingly. It never helped to rush Jan.

"He said . . ." Jan fanned herself, for real. She was actually perspiring. "He said someone in the ER told him about you."

That sounded ominous.

Julie glanced at her watch. Five forty-five, too late to deal with mysterious strangers. If she left now, she'd just have time to get home and change into something more casual for her date.

"Ask him to come back tomorrow," she said. "I don't have time—"

"He just wants a minute." Jan wiped her palms on her grey, pleated skirt. At twenty-five, she dressed like Julie's Gram, but inside she was stuck at sixteen, helpless in the face of a handsome man. "I-I'm sorry. I couldn't say no."

Julie blew out a sigh, wondering—again—why she'd hired

her silly cousin in the first place. Because family was family, that's why.

"Fine. Send him in."

Ten seconds later, six-foot-two of Texan filled her door. Tawny hair, caramel eyes, tanned cheekbones.

Whoa.

An Excerpt from

TORN
A Billionaire Bachelors Club Novel
by Monica Murphy

The boys of *New York Times* bestselling author
Monica Murphy's sexy Billionaire Bachelors
Club are back, and this time, they're mixing
business with pleasure. Poised to snatch up
Marina Knight's real estate empire, sexy tycoon
Gage Emerson is on the verge of making an enemy
for life—even if he can make her melt with a single
kiss! But when Gage discovers that this alluring
creature is the key to his latest acquisition, he
must get to know the fierce woman willing to face
him down—as she steadily steals his heart.

"This is a huge mistake."

"What is?" He settles those big hands of his on my waist. His long fingers span outward, gripping me tight, and I feel like I've been seized by some uncontrollable force, one I can't fight off no matter how hard I try.

That force would be Gage.

"I already told you." God, he's exasperating. It's like he doesn't even listen to a word I say. "Us. Together. There will never be an 'us' or a 'together,' got it?"

"Got it, boss." He's not really listening, I can tell. He's pulled away slightly so that he can stare down at me, enraptured by the sight of his hands on my body. A shock of brown hair tinged with gold tumbles down across his forehead, and I resist the urge to reach out and push it away from his face.

Just barely.

He slides his hands around me until they settle at the small of my back, his fingertips barely grazing my backside. I'm wearing jeans, yet it's like I can feel his touch directly on my skin. Heat rushes over me, making my head spin, and I let go of a shaky exhalation.

"We shouldn't do this," I whisper, pressing my lips together when I feel his hands slide over my butt. Oh my God, his touch feels so good.

What the hell am I *thinking*, letting him touch me like this? It's wrong. Us together is wrong.

So why does it feel so right?

"Do what?" His question sounds innocent enough, but his touch isn't. He pulls me into him so that I can feel the unmistakable ridge of his erection pressing against my belly, and a gasp escapes me. He's big. Thick. My thighs shake at the thought of him entering me.

I need to put a stop to this, and quick.

"I don't think we sh—"

Gage presses his index finger to my lips, silencing me. I stare up at him, entranced by the glow in his eyes, the way he stares at my mouth. Like he's a starving man dying to devour me.

Anticipation thrums through my veins. I should walk away now. Right now, before we take this any further. We're standing in the doorway of the bakery for God's sake. Anyone could see us, not that many people are roaming the downtown sidewalks at this time of night. He's got one hand sprawled across my ass, and he's tracing my lips with his finger like he wants to memorize the shape of them.

And I'm . . . parting my lips so I can suck on his fingertip.

His eyes darken as he slips his finger deeper into my mouth. I close my lips around him, sucking, tasting his salty skin with a flick of my tongue. A rough, masculine sound rumbles from his chest as his hand falls away from my lips. He drifts his fingers down my chin, then my neck, and my breath catches in my throat.

"Gage." I whisper his name, confused. Is it a plea for him to stop or for him to continue? I don't know. I don't know what I want from him.

"Scared?" he asks, his lids lifting so that he can pin me with his gorgeous green eyes. They're glittering in the semi-darkness, full of so much hunger, and my body responds, pulsating with need.

I try my best to offer a snide response, but the truth comes out instead: "Terrified."

He lowers his head. I can feel his breath feather across my lips, and I part them in anticipation, eager for his kiss. "That makes two of us," he whispers.

Just before he settles his mouth on mine.

An Excerpt from

THE CUPCAKE DIARIES: SPOONFUL OF CHRISTMAS

by Darlene Panzera

For fans of Debbie Macomber comes a special
holiday-themed installment of Darlene Panzera's
popular Cupcake Diaries series.

Andi glanced at the number on the caller ID, picked up the phone, and tried to mimic the deep, sultry voice of a sexy siren. "Hello, Creative Cupcakes."

"What if I told you I'd like to order a Mistletoe Magic cupcake with a dozen delicious kisses on top?"

She smiled at the sound of Jake's voice. "Mistletoe Magic?"

"I was guaranteed that the person who eats it will receive a dozen kisses by midnight."

"What if I told you," Andi said, playing along, "that you don't have to eat a cupcake to get a kiss and the magic will begin the minute you walk through the front door?"

Jake chuckled. "I'm on my way."

Andi's sister Kim and best friend Rachel watched her with amused expressions on their faces.

"I hope Mike and I still flirt with each other after *we're* married," Rachel said, her singsong voice a tease. "But the name Mistletoe Magic isn't half bad. Maybe we *should* make a red velvet cupcake with a Hershey's Kiss and miniature holly leaf sprinkles on top."

Kim finished boxing a dozen Maraschino cherry cupcakes and handed them to the customer at the counter. "As if we don't have enough sales already."

"Sales are great," Andi agreed. "We've booked orders for eighteen holiday parties. Now if I could only figure out what to get Jake for Christmas, life would be perfect."

Rachel rang up the next customer's order. "Mike and I decided our Hollywood honeymoon will be our gift to each other."

"Are you serious?" Kim picked up a pastry bag from the back worktable. "You—the woman who can't walk three feet past a store window without buying anything—are not going to get Mike a Christmas gift? Not even a little something?"

"It *is* hard," Rachel admitted. "But I promised him I wouldn't. I also promised I wouldn't go overboard with spending on the wedding arrangements."

"You could always have a small, simple wedding like Jake and I did," Andi suggested.

Rachel's red curls bounced back and forth as she shook her head. "I already booked the Liberty Theater for the reception. I know it's expensive, but the palace-like antique architecture was so beautiful I couldn't help myself. I've always dreamed of—"

"Being Cinderella?" Kim joked.

"I *do* want a Cinderella wedding," Rachel crooned. "I figure I can bake my own cake and skimp on other wedding details to stay within our budget."

Andi didn't think Rachel knew the first thing about staying within a budget but decided it was best not to argue. Instead she turned toward her younger sister. "Kim, what are you getting Nathaniel for Christmas?"

"I'm not sure." Kim averted her gaze. "Maybe I should just get him a new set of luggage tags."

Rachel frowned. "That's not very romantic."

"No, but it's practical," Andi said, coming to Kim's defense. "Nathaniel's probably getting her the same thing."

"He planned to fly to his family's home in Sweden this Christmas," Kim confessed, her dark brows drawing together. "But I told him I couldn't go, and he didn't want to go without me."

"Of course you can't go!" Rachel exclaimed, bracing her hands against the marble counter. "I need you to be my bridesmaid!"

"It would have been awkward spending Christmas with his family anyway," Kim said, piping vanilla icing over the cupcakes. "It's not like I'm part of his family, or like we're even engaged. In fact, I don't know what we are."

"You two are great together," Andi encouraged. "You both are artistic, enjoy nature, and love to travel."

Kim nodded, then looked up, her expression earnest. "But what *else*? I'm beginning to wonder if I should tell Nathaniel to go to Sweden without me."

"And miss my wedding? But you'll need a dance partner at the reception," Rachel reminded her. "He wouldn't go and leave you stranded without a date on Christmas Eve, would he?"

Kim hesitated. "I don't know."

The bells on the front door jingled as a man in his late forties entered the shop with a briefcase in hand.

"Are you the owners of Creative Cupcakes?" he asked, looking hopeful.

Andi stepped forward and smiled. "Yes, we are."

The man placed his briefcase at the end of the counter and sprung the latch. "Then I have an offer I think you might like."

"What kind of offer?" Rachel asked, anticipation lighting her faintly freckled face.

The man handed them each a set of papers a half-inch thick. "An offer to buy Creative Cupcakes."

An Excerpt from

RODEO QUEEN
by T. J. Kline

Sydney Thomas wants nothing more than to train
rodeo horses and hopes becoming a rodeo queen
will help her make the contacts she seeks. She
is thrilled when Mike Findley hires her for her
dream job as a horse trainer . . . until she meets
Scott Chandler, the other half of Findley Brothers
stock contractors. He's arrogant, judgmental,
and, unfortunately, unbelievably sexy.

Scott gave her a rakish, lopsided grin. "Oh, that's right. You can outride me." His brow arched as he articulated her words back to her. "Any day of the week."

It took everything in her to try to ignore how good looking this infuriating man was. He towered over her—well over six feet tall—and the black cowboy hat that topped a mop of dark brown hair, barely curling at his collar, gave him a devilish appearance. With sensuous lips and a square jaw, his deeply tanned face reflected raw male sexuality. She wasn't sure if he was actually as muscular as his broad shoulders seemed to indicate due to his unruly western shirt, but his jeans left no imagining necessary when it came to his sculpted thighs. And his jet black eyes almost unnerved her. Those eyes were so dark that Sydney felt she would drown if she continued to meet his gaze.

So much for ignoring his good looks, she chided herself. "Give me a chance out there today to prove it."

"I don't see why she can't run them, Scott." Jake must have decided that it was time to break up the showdown with his two cents. "She is certainly experienced enough, more than most of the girls you let run flags."

Scott glared at Jake before turning back to Sydney. She

caught Jake's conspiratorial wink and decided that she liked this old cowboy. Scott would be hard pressed to find a reason to deny her request now that Jake had sold him out.

"Fine, you can do both. But, if anything goes wrong, if a steer so much as takes too long in the arena, you're finished. Got it, Miss Thomas?" The warning note in his voice was unmistakable.

Sydney flashed a dazzling smile. "Call me Sydney, and it's no problem." She clutched her shoulder. "Unless I'm unable to hold the flags because someone ran me into a fencepost."

His look told her he didn't appreciate her sense of humor. "I mean it. Rodeo starts at 10 sharp. Be down here at 9:30, ready to go."

As the sassy cowgirl walked away, Scott shook his head. "What in the world possessed you to open your mouth, Jake?"

"Aw, Scott, she'll do fine. Besides, you did run her down with Wiley at the gate. You kinda owed her one."

Scott watched Sydney head for the gate, taking in her small waist, the spread of her hips in her red pants, and her lean, denim-encased legs. That woman was all curves, moving with the grace of a jungle cat. With her full, pouting lips and those golden eyes, it certainly wouldn't be painful to look at her all day. "I guess."

Scott mounted Wiley and headed to change into his clean shirt and show chaps but couldn't seem to shake the image of Sydney Thomas from his mind. He knew that she'd been attracted to him—he'd seen it in her blush—but he'd had enough run-ins with ostentatious rodeo queens over the years, including his ex-fiancée, to know that they simply wanted to tame a cowboy. It was doubtful that this one was any different, although she did have a much shorter temper than most. He chuckled as he recalled how the gold in her eyes seemed to spark when she was irritated. He wondered if her eyes flamed up whenever she was passionate. Scott shook his head to clear it of visions of the sexy spitfire. No time for that. He had a rodeo to get started.

ALSO BY HEATHER LONG

Lure

Blue Ivy Prep
Problem Child
Mad Boys
Party Crashers
Money Shot

Bravo Team Wolf
When Danger Bites
Bitten Under Fire

Cardinal Sins
Kill Song
First Chorus
High Note
Last Word

Chance Monroe
Earth Witches Aren't Easy
Plan Witch from Out of Town
Bad Witch Rising

Fevered Hearts
Marshal of Hel Dorado
Brave are the Lonely
Micah & Mrs. Miller
A Fistful of Dreams
Raising Kane

Wanted: Fevered or Alive

Wild and Fevered

The Quick & The Fevered

A Man Called Wyatt

Heart of the Nebula

Queenmaker

Deal Breaker

Throne Taker

Lone Star Leathernecks

Semper Fi Cowboy

As You Were, Cowboy

Shackled Souls

Succubus Chained

Succubus Unchained

Succubus Blessed

Shackled Souls (Omnibus)

STANDALONES

Kiss of Fate (w/Blake Blessing)

Taste of Karma (w/Blake Blessing)

I'll Be Home... (w/Tate James)

Overexposed (w/Tate James)

Switchboard Duet

Talk to Me

Don't Let Go

Desert Wolf

Snow Wolf

Wolf on Board

Holly Jolly Wolf

Shadow Wolf

His Moonstruck Wolf

Thunder Wolf

Ghost Wolf

Outlaw Wolves

Wolf Unleashed